ABOUT THE AUTHOR

When Chris Behrsin isn't out exploring the world, he's behind a keyboard writing tales of dragons and magical lands. Born into the genre through a steady diet of Terry Pratchett, his fiction fuses a love for fantasy and whimsical plots with philosophy and voyages into the worlds of dreams.

You can learn more about his fiction and download two free books at his website, chrisbehrsin.com.

facebook.com/chrisbehrsin

x.com/chrisbehrsin

goodreads.com/cbehrsin

bookbub.com/authors/chris-behrsin

DRAGONCAT BOOK 5

A CAT'S GUIDE TO TRAVELLING THROUGH PORTALS

CHRIS BEHRSIN

WORLDWALKERS
PUBLISHING

Copyediting by Tarryn Thomas
(https://tarrynthomas.com)
Proofreading by Carol Brandon
Cover Design Layout by Chris Behrsin

ISBN: 978-1-915886-04-0 (paperback)
ISBN: 978-1-915866-10-1 (hardcover)
ISBN: 978-1-915886-16-3 (e-book)

Published by Worldwalkers Publishing Ltd

To Ola

THE MIGHTY MARCH

The dwarf dragons – one black and one white – didn't fly but walked over the plains east of Dragonsbond Academy, approaching it with slow plodding steps. They passed through humid air and over recently-swept roads, between fields of wheat that swayed in the breeze as if to greet them. Above, a light blanket of clouds allowed the sun to poke through occasionally, bathing all below in its warmth. The air smelled of dried grass and fermenting fruit, and wasps buzzed around the wispy stalks.

It was the time of year when it's never wise to go near such insects, because they are drunk on the fruit and easily angered. It was as if the wasps also knew about the warlocks' imminent attack, which we were all awaiting but which never came. To soothe our anxiety we ended up sitting through silly ceremonies like this one instead.

The dwarf dragons were marching towards a momentous occasion – an unusual event for this time of year. Both were carrying a crystal on their backs, and I had no doubt that this somewhat slowed their pace.

I knew of only two dragons who had colours such as theirs: the mighty Olan, who belonged to the Driar Aleam, an elder of the Academy, and Corralsa, who had once been bonded to the late and pompous Prince Arran. I say 'late' because Arran had recently been killed by the vast, untamed powers of the young Initiate Seramina during our most recent battle against the warlocks.

Today three new dragon riders would bond with their dragons, heralding their initiation into Dragonsbond Academy.

One of the three was Max, the smelly Sussex spaniel with the power to walk between dimensions. The dog stood up ahead, with his tongue lolling out, watching Corralsa, the jet-black dragon. She stood tall, a good hundred feet away from us. Max was to become Corralsa's rider today – a destiny designated by the crystal that slowly spun on its axis, hovering right beside the dragon's shoulder.

The second dragon rider was my companion Ta'ra, who had once been a Cat Sidhe fairy before she'd used up her eight transformations and permanently become a cat.

No one knew who the third dragon rider was to be, but my crystal had told me not long ago, during a brief visit to the Fourth Dimension in the Sahara Desert, that all three dragons would bond with non-human creatures. I guess the Council of Three – the three elders who ran Dragonsbond Academy – knew the secret. Perhaps Aleam, my old mentor, did as well. But I doubt any of the teachers, students, or for that matter anyone else had any idea, as much as some of the more gossipy ones liked to pretend they did.

Oh, and by the way – if you didn't already know, I'm a cat myself. A Bengal, in fact, descended both from the great Asian leopard cat and my father, the mighty George. It was I who defeated the great warlock Astravar, and more recently I encountered a cheetah and a sphinx, and I fought in an epic battle against the other warlocks and whirling sand golems. But I'm sure you knew all of that. After all, my story has been carried across the dimensions.

From the pace the dragons were walking, I could see that they probably couldn't fly while carrying that heavy weight. I mean, I'd seen Salanraja lift up one of the crystals in her claws before, but she was three times the size of these dragons. The dwarf dragons were straining to hold the crystals on their backs, and I couldn't help but feel sorry for them.

I mean, if you're a great cat, as I am – it's fine to walk and to walk proudly. But these were dragons, with wings, quite capable of flying. I didn't understand why they needed to carry the crystals anyway, when a much larger dragon could do it for them.

I guess it was one of those pomp-and-circumstance things typical to this world that just didn't make any sense. Or typical to humans, perhaps, who never made sense, neither in this dimension nor in the Fourth Dimension where I used to reside.

"This is the final task they have to complete before their initiation into the Academy," my dragon, Salanraja, told me in my mind. *"We're all incredibly proud of them."*

She wasn't standing on the plains, as we were, but was soaring up in the air with the other dragons. Together they spun around the sky in fanciful aerobatic formations that elicited much applause from the students. We students sat on the plains in neat lines, our leaders in the Council of Three at the front, and the other teachers of the academy also keeping watch to make sure we behaved. Almost everyone human was here, gathered in front of the castle – including the guards and the Dragonsbond Academy staff. The only person who wasn't present was Aleam, who still lay sick in bed.

"We didn't have to do anything like this," I replied to Salanraja. *"You never had to march with our crystal."*

"That's because I went rogue before I bonded with you. No one at the Academy other than Aleam and Olan thought it was a good idea at the time. Now it seems everyone's minds have changed, after they saw what we could do."

I purred, feeling proud. Then I looked back at the dwarf drag-ons, and I felt a twinge of pity. *"But look at them. This is virtually slave labour. I mean, one of you other dragons could have carried the crystals for them and made things easier all round."*

"It's not meant to be easy," Salanraja continued. *"They will soon complete their march from Bestian Academy in the Crystal Moun-tains, and when they finally arrive here, they will be full-fledged drag-ons, ready to accept a rider."*

"And I guess this was a human idea?" I asked.

The humans, I'd noticed, were great at setting silly challenges for themselves.

"No," Salanraja said. *"This is a dragon thing. Some think that our three-hundred-year-old trainer, Matharon, invented it, although he claims it's been around for a lot longer."*

"And what's the point? Why don't you just fly?"

Even though I couldn't see Salanraja, I could hear the menace in her voice as she replied, *"Every single one of us has completed this ritual, and we're all proud of our achievements."*

"You're not answering my question…"

"That's because you're not giving me time to do so. When we march like this, we behave like humans, and so it will help those two dragons understand what they are sworn to protect."

"But they're bonding with animals," I said, *"not humans."* I was at the front of the crowd, so I could see Ta'ra's matte black fur ahead, though she had her back turned to me so I couldn't see the white bib on her chest. If I were in her situation, I'd be licking my fur right now – that's one of the best things to do while waiting. Instead she sat regally, with her head craned forward, as if this stuff actually mattered.

"Those animals will have to behave just like humans," Salanraja said. *"Just like you have learned to do … and you forget that Ta'ra was*

brought up as a fairy. She's much closer to a human than you and I will ever be."

"*Whatever,*" I said, and I decided that it was a good time to give myself a good grooming.

I was so engrossed in my routine that I didn't see Ta'ra approach. She brushed up next to me. She was the only cat I knew who liked to bathe in lavender water. I mean, as a great and mighty Bengal who doesn't mind water, I also enjoy a good swim, but I saw no need to put so many flowers in it.

"I don't think I've ever been this nervous, Ben," she said, and she let off a soft meow as she said it. She'd finally learned to speak the cat language quite eloquently, admittedly after several days of tuition from yours truly.

I turned to her and brushed my head against hers in greeting. "Why? You've been preparing for this for days."

"I mean, I could fly once and cast magic. But when I became a cat, I didn't think I'd ever cast another spell. Now I have to go through the same journey you did, accepting gifts from the crystal and casting spells which feel nothing like the fairy spells used to feel. Human spells are so brutish. They're so unnatural."

I twitched my whiskers. In all honesty I'd not mastered the whole magic thing by this point. Don't get me wrong – I'd done some pretty awesome things, including summoning a whole school of salmon to do my bidding. These flashes of excellence came at times when I had absolutely no other option. But I still didn't know any magic other than the ability to turn into a chimera, speak the language of every living creature, and shoot dark magic beams that were only useful against other dark magic users – namely warlocks and their creations.

"I'm sure you'll work it out," I said. "You're good at working things out. Say, I wonder which gifts you're going to get."

"I have no idea. You do know that your gifts are an anomaly, right?"

I nodded in a very human way. That's one thing that Rine had told me over and over again: usually a crystal gifts a dragon rider with abilities related to their school of magic, and we all only ever got three.

Rine got his staff as his first gift, and later learned a couple of extra tricks with it. It was the same with Ange, and Bellari, and most of the other students and Driars here. I guess Aleam, Asinda, and Seramina were the exceptions, as they were dark magic users just like me. But they'd never shared their magical history with me and I'd never thought to ask.

"I know," I said. "Except my crystal always wanted to gift me with dark magic for some reason..."

"Because you're about the only creature in all the dimensions who will use it for good. I've heard that dark magic consumes the soul, and you've got to be careful with it. You do know that, right, Ben?"

"I do ... I just wish I could work out how to use it effectively. Whiskers, if I knew how to right now, I'd hunt down the warlocks and get to them before they can kidnap Max and remove the key to the Sixth Dimension from his body."

Ta'ra didn't answer, but she was purring. She liked me to sound like a hero, I guess. Even when she'd just reminded me that I still didn't have as much power as the stories seemed to think.

She nestled up even closer to me and sat down in the long grass. I appreciated her warmth against me. We watched and waited for the dwarf dragons to complete their cumbersome march. It wasn't long until they'd lowered their heads and charged the rest of the way, looking like two bulls with a personal vendetta against the great jet-black dragon.

Corralsa craned her head, turned around to face them, and let out a mighty roar. This was followed by the call of a bugle from the Academy's Keep Tower behind us.

The Council of Three stepped forwards so that they were standing behind Corralsa and the two dwarf dragons, who had now drawn to a halt and taken position on each side of her. Above us, three dragons broke off from the flock. These were the ruby dragon, Farago, the sapphire dragon, Flue, and the emerald dragon, Plishk. They belonged to the members of the Council of Three — Driar Yila, Driar Farago, and Driar Brigel respectively — and their scales were the same colour as the glowing crystals on each of the Great Driars' staffs.

They lowered themselves to hover in front of Corralsa and the two dwarf dragons.

The members of the Council of Three each turned to face the teachers and students thronged before them. In unison, they called out in commanding voices: "It is time for your bonding ... step forwards, noble dragon riders!"

It was at that moment I first realised that Ta'ra, my faithful companion whom I cared about more than anyone in all the worlds, would never be the same again.

THE THIRD DRAGON RIDER

The sun emerged from the clouds at an angle that made it seem to glint off the scales of the three dragons. For a moment a rainbow appeared in the distance; it must have been raining over the Willowed Woods. But this prismatic display didn't last for long, and I'm not sure any of the others saw it. They were too engrossed in the three dragons standing before them.

I nudged Ta'ra with my head because I thought she might have fallen asleep. "It's your moment, Ta'ra."

"What?"

"Just go and meet your dragon. I think it's the white one."

She meowed, as if to tell me she already knew who it was, then strolled forwards towards the white dwarf dragon. The smell of lavender left my vicinity, to be replaced with a freshness that suggested rain. Ta'ra adopted a casual pace, walking in a straight line with her head held high, just as I'd taught her. Really, I'd never been so proud as I watched her back paws touch the point where her front paws had been, with nearly perfect accuracy. One of the first things I'd taught her was how to walk properly, but she'd taken a long time to master it.

The small white dragon – who must have been only a little shorter than the tallest human – lowered his scaly head to Ta'ra. He bawled in a voice that I could swear was even louder than Salanraja's on a bad day.

"I, the great dragon Kada, take this fine specimen of a feline to be my rider. That is if you'll accept my bond…"

He spoke in the dragon tongue, so the dragons and I would be the only ones to understand him, although everyone knew what he was meant to say anyway. At the same time, he would have translated the words in Ta'ra's mind into a language she could understand.

Silence hung in the air for a moment, and the wind whistled through the fields. I caught a whiff of distant pollen. A massive fly buzzed awfully close to me – too close for comfort, in fact – and I swiped it away with a heavy paw.

The rest of the students waited, soft murmurs bouncing around the crowd. I guess some of us were wondering if Ta'ra was going to refuse her bond. A selfish part of me wished she would. After all, I enjoyed her companionship, and I didn't want a dragon to become closer to her than I.

I lifted my head up to the sky, to see Salanraja swooping around in a loop the loop. Ange's emerald dragon, Quarl, was on her tail and Rine's sapphire dragon Ishtkar chased playfully after him. Salanraja dropped down underneath them, as if she wanted to leave them to their games.

"*Now you know how it feels,*" Salanraja said in my mind.

"*How what feels?*" I asked.

"*Having to accept that someone else might threaten our bond. When Ta'ra entered your life, and when you became so enamoured with her, I thought I'd never get you back again. I thought our bond would die and that we'd never be the same again. Our lives would suddenly become meaningless, all because of your feelings..."*

"Do you have to be so melodramatic?" I asked, licking a paw.

"Wait, are you saying that I'm the drama queen?"

"Well it can't be me, because I'm a Tom, and Toms don't do drama..."

"Don't you, now?"

"No, I don't. Now shut up, this is Ta'ra's moment, not yours." Perhaps I was being a bit hard on her. But I didn't want to miss a moment of Ta'ra's special occasion, particularly given I was worried she might later test me on the details and not be too happy if I got anything wrong.

Salanraja stilled, braking to a hover, and turned her head to watch Ta'ra and the dwarf dragon, Kada. The other dragons also came to a halt, and soon they were all facing Ta'ra and her dragon, like wasps lingering in search of a new target.

Perhaps this was all a part of the ritual, but no one had told me about it. Mind you, my experience of bonding with a dragon had been a little unusual, as I'd done so without the prior approval of the Council of Three and the dragons. I hadn't had a choice in the matter either, as Salanraja had tricked me into it. Despite all that, I guess it had turned out for the best.

Eventually, Ta'ra broke the silence. "Yes, Kada, dragon of the white. I accept your bond and I will serve as your rider."

Kada let out a loud roar, followed by whoops and cheers from the students. But I think the loudest of all was the Sussex spaniel Max, who was yipping excitedly. I was the only one who understood what he was saying, of course.

To my chagrin, he wasn't congratulating Ta'ra. Rather, he was barking, "Can't wait! My turn soon! Can't wait!"

I was half tempted to go over and shut him up with a sharp swipe of the paw. I mean, I didn't mind Max as much as I had when

I first met him. But still, I couldn't let a dog try to steal a cat's thunder. If the old Ragamuffin back in my home country of South Wales ever heard about it, he'd give me a good talking to. He'd tell me how I should stand up for my allies of kin, particularly one as close to me as Ta'ra.

I hadn't even taken half a step towards Max, when Corralsa let out the loudest roar I'd ever heard from a dragon – even Aleam's great white dragon Olan, whom I could see hovering above all the other dragons in the sky. Then the jet-black dragon also spoke in the dragon tongue, her voice coming out as quieter, high-pitched croons.

"I, the great dragon Corralsa, take this fine specimen of a canine to be my rider. That is, if you'll accept my bond…"

"I do!" Max barked. "I do, I do, I do-do-do!"

"Fantastic," I grumbled, licking my paw. "I'm happy for you, Max."

At the same time, the students around me started to murmur, probably wondering if Max had said the proper words for the ritual, which of course he hadn't. Corralsa also cocked her head to the side and looked at Max as if she was considering eating him. But she was just acting her part, and she soon let out a roar of approval.

The crowd whooped and cheered, and I swear I even saw the stern Great Driar Yila pump her fist in the air. She'd taken to Max far more than she had me and Ta'ra – I guess she was a dog person.

Corralsa gave Max a few moments of triumph, letting him run around in a circle, as he yipped away chasing his tail.

"There you are, Ben…" It was Rine who was talking, pushing his way through the crowd. "You're getting harder to find."

Ange followed after him, with the desert cheetah who had joined her side in the Fourth Dimension, before they had both saved our skins in the battle against the warlocks in Capitut's Pyramid in the Calimar Desert. Rine and Ange weren't holding hands yet, unfortunately, but I hadn't seen Rine spending any more time with Bellari, his ex-girlfriend, and so I thought the two finally had a chance of getting together.

"We thought you might want to say hello to Pali here before she became a dragon rider," Ange said. The cheetah's real name was Palimali, but Ange called her Pali for short. She reached down to stroke the cheetah under the chin, and Pali let out a soft chirping sound. I growled at the cheetah, and then looked up at Ange with wide, jealous eyes. Ange laughed, then ducked down to stroke me as well.

"How do you know it's going to be the cheetah?" I asked.

Ange shrugged. "Who else would it be?"

"I don't know," I said. "Maybe a mouse, or a rabbit…"

At that, Rine guffawed. "We can't have a dragon rider who doesn't eat meat – they wouldn't have anything to eat when we sat around the campfire and ate our mutton sausages."

Ange put her hands on her hips and gave him a stern look. "Rine, you can be so prejudiced sometimes."

"What?"

"There's no reason we can't have vegetarians in Dragonsbond Academy. I'm sure we've had some here before."

"But what would vegetarians eat at our campfires?"

"I don't know," Ange said. "Maybe they could roast courgettes?"

"That's disgusting," I said. I couldn't think of anything worse than eating courgettes.

"Anyway, shush," Ange said, with her head turned towards the dragons. "Something's happening. This is your moment of triumph, Palimali. Maybe the crystal will give you the gift of all languages so I'll be able to talk to you, too." She crouched down again and put her arms around Palimali's neck as she ruffled the fur on both her sides.

In the distance, the black dwarf dragon let out a heavy and deep roar – though these dragons were small, they really did pack a punch vocally. The noise of the crowd fell to silence, and everyone snapped their heads around to look at the dragons.

"It is my turn," the dwarf dragon said in the dragon tongue. "Rider, you may reveal yourself now—" He craned his head upwards to look at the Dragonsbond Academy's gate tower.

I turned just as the sun came out of the clouds. A shadowy form emerged on the ramparts just below the turret. As it moved, I saw it wasn't a mouse, a rabbit, or a cheetah at all, but another cat, and a female one at that.

ALL POWERFUL SHE-CAT

It wasn't until the cat had leaped off the wall and started to stalk towards us that I recognised her. I'd admired her hunts many times in the night, when the humans let the cats out to chase mice, rats, and crows away.

The cat was slender and moved as if she'd been born into grace. Really, she didn't belong in this castle, but with kings and queens, dining on the finest meat this world had to offer. It made me wonder what she'd done to end up in Dragonsbond Academy as a mouser. But I guess the humans had no respect for that kind of thing.

The humans called her Esme, I believe. She was an Abyssinian, with a pink nose and fur as white as a swan's feathers in the midday sun. She made her way through the students, who parted to make way for her. It was unusual for them to treat a cat this way, but somehow the way she moved seemed to hold even them in awe. Maybe they were just shocked that a third dragon was accepting a cat as a rider. Or maybe they were all just starting to realise what a superior species we cats are.

The Abyssinian passed by me, brushing against me slowly as she went. Somehow, Ta'ra had made my senses believe that it was normal to smell of lavender and other flowers. But Esme smelled exactly the way a cat should.

Her tail raised, she looked back over her shoulder and gave me a demure and flirtatious look, before turning back to the dwarf dragon who awaited her with stooped head.

Ta'ra seemed to notice me gawking at the cat and gave me a cruel look with narrowed eyes that I'd not seen from her since we'd first met. For a moment I pulled my gaze away from the Abyssinian and turned my head to the sky. The sun warmed my neck and the back of my head as I watched the dragons, who were now flying in criss-cross patterns.

Usually I could stare at them while they did their flight training for hours, mesmerised, as I could a flock of swallows. But Esme's fluid motion drew my attention towards her again. The alabaster she-cat turned around and faced the students and Driars as if ready to address us. From her side, Max gave a quick bark at her, though I couldn't tell from his posture if it was meant to be friendly or aggressive. To this, Esme turned her head and gave a sharp hiss without even arching her back. It was so sudden that Max lowered himself onto his front paws and whimpered, then ducked behind Corralsa's wing to hide.

Esme resumed her previous posture, facing us. And then, to everyone's surprise, she spoke in the human language.

"You have called me Esme, all these years," she said. Her voice wasn't just melodic, but also filled the space around her. Her manner of speaking had the same kind of haughtiness as Prince Arran and Captain Alliander had – the only two royals I'd met in this world, apart from Prefect Asinda who didn't speak like them at all.

"You've kept me locked away in your cattery. For years I have studied your language, and long ago one of your crystals gave me the gift of speaking your tongue, as also happened with your Bengal, less colloquially known as Dragoncat. Since then I have stalked the grounds, learning the language of all your crystals. They have spoken to me in ways they cannot use to speak to you. They have told me much of what is to come.

"Now it is time for me to emerge and claim my destiny.... For the world has need of me, just as it has need of the Dragoncat, the dog, and the former Cat Sidhe." She gave Ta'ra a sideways glance. "I shall play a grand role in your battle against the warlocks, and to keep the more dangerous magicians amongst your students in check. For I answer not to the wardens who look after the cattery, but to King Garmin himself."

She paused for a moment, as if to give us time for this to sink in. Her ears perked up to listen to the confused voices that rose amongst the students. Even the Council of Three and the other Driars of Dragonsbond Academy started to talk amongst themselves.

"Well, I never," Rine said. "I thought you were pompous, Ben. Who does this cat think she is?"

"I'm sure she's nothing compared to you, Pali," Ange said as she rubbed the scruff of her cheetah's neck. "Are you?"

Palimali ignored Ange. Or rather she was looking at me with intent, and the fast blinks of confusion that humans might not always read correctly but any cat could.

"Might you tell me what's going on here, Dragoncat?" she asked, and she spoke in the cheetah language which was naturally the only one she knew. "All this commotion is rather ... I don't know ... but I guess these humans, and these flying lizard creatures you all seem to ride ... well, I can't think of a better word for any of them but *odd*."

"I really don't know," I replied. "No one was expecting any of this. This cat – she speaks the human tongue, just like me."

"I noticed," the cheetah said. "But how is she doing it?"

"That's exactly what I'm trying to work out. She says it's to do with the crystals. It's always to do with the crystals, you know."

The black dwarf dragon, all this time, had been turning his head between Esme and Corralsa, as if unsure what he should do. Esme seemed to be running the show, and clearly the dragon hadn't yet been briefed about his new rider.

After a moment, the black dragon roared. Esme must have been communicating with him in his head all this time. Presumably, Esme was telling the dragon what to do – a strange relationship between a dragon and its rider, or in this case, rider-to-be.

The roar was loud enough to quieten everyone down. As in the previous two cases, I waited for the dragon to speak in the dwarf language. Instead, there came a brilliant flash of light from the Abyssinian.

As the light faded, I blinked in disbelief, because hovering beside Esme was what looked like a giant white human hand, just like my own staff bearer. Except her hand didn't carry a purple-gemmed staff like the one I'd retrieved from the Ghost Realm; in fact, her staff didn't have a crystal affixed to the top of it at all – the type that dragon riders used to cast spells of ice, or fire, or lightning, or nature. Rather, it had smaller white crystals dotted all along the length of it, and the staff itself wasn't straight, as if made of birch or pine, but rather looked like a section of a branch of a gnarly oak.

A White Mage – a dragon rider? Whiskers, what was going on?

Esme turned back to her dragon and spoke out in her commanding voice: "You can start the ceremony, Gratis."

Her dragon-to-be, Gratis, tossed back his head and let out another sky-splitting roar. "I, the great dragon Gratis, take this fine specimen of a feline to be my rider. That is, Esme of the White, if you'll accept my bond..."

She replied first in the dragon tongue. "As has been destined, I, Esme, accept your bond as a dragon rider." She repeated this in the human tongue for the benefit of everyone else's ears. But she didn't say anything in the cat language, and I felt partially offended by that.

The crowd whooped and cheered, and a loud round of applause followed this. Great Driar Brigel – the gentle bald giant of the Council of Three – then bellowed, "It is done.... Now it is time to receive your first gifts."

"No," Esme called back, without allowing even a pause. "There is no time."

"What in the Seventh Dimension do you mean?" Driar Brigel said.

"Because, as it is destined, the honour guard of the king has arrived for a much more important mission."

In unison, she and Gratis turned their heads towards a cloud of dust roiling up from the direction of the Willowed Woods to the north. I caught a whiff of horse upon the breeze.

UNICORNS AGAIN

It didn't take me long to see the glint of a unicorn's horn on the horizon. But there wasn't just one, there were many of them, looking like floating stars on a sea of emerging mist. My ears perked up at the sound of whickering, and the pounding of hooves. Dust rose in the distance, and soon enough the unicorns came fully into view, storming towards us at full gallop, sunlight gleaming off their fur.

"*Gracious demons,*" Salanraja said in my head. "*The White Mages never seem to give us any rest nowadays.*"

"*Perhaps it's Captain Alliander of the White Guard, coming to arrest that cat, Esme, for pretending to be one of them.*"

"*Are you telling me that a cat can't be a White Guard? I thought that Ben, the descendant of the great Asian leopard cat, would stick up for his kind.*"

"*I'm not saying that cats can't be White Guards necessarily – I mean, I'm sure I could have bonded with a unicorn and not you, if one had chosen me, though I can't think why I'd want to do that. But*"

White Guards, and all White Mages for that matter, are meant to ride unicorns, aren't they? Not dragons..."

"Well, there is that," Salanraja said, and I heard her distinct screech as she performed a loop the loop above.

In fact, every dragon seemed to be putting extra effort into its aerobatic display, as if each wanted to show the White Mages that dragons were far better than unicorns. I couldn't agree more. Dragons, after all, breathed fire and could fly over mountains, whilst all the unicorns seemed able to do was flash their horns.

We watched and waited for what must have been a good ten minutes. Rine kept spouting rumours that, given the number of unicorns approaching, someone here must be under arrest. He even surmised that they might be coming to arrest Seramina after hearing about her show of power at Capitut's burial chamber. Back then, Seramina had cast an ultra-powerful spell that had destroyed an army of Manipulators and bone dragons, killing the traitorous Prince Arran – whom we'd come to know as the Warlock Prince – in the process.

Ange rebuked Rine's assertion by pointing out that if they were going to arrest Seramina they surely would have done so by now, and she recommended that Rine stop spreading gossip. Honestly, since Rine had broken up with Bellari a second time, I felt that Rine and Ange had been arguing more. When I was younger I would have thought that was a bad thing, but I'd spent a lot of time with Ta'ra since, and we also bickered. Ta'ra and I were close, so I took this as a sign that the two teenagers were also getting closer.

Ange and Rine would be lovers soon, I was sure of it. Then, as I'd planned, we could all retire together with our dragons to a cottage out in the countryside. By then I would have mastered my abilities as a dark mage and learned to summon salmon from the Fourth Dimension whenever I wanted it. Rine could milk the cows out in the front meadow every morning, and I could drink milk and have smoked salmon for breakfast. After plenty of nap time, I'd spend my afternoons flying on Salanraja, and use the nights to hunt moths and mice through the fragrant summer grass. Ta'ra would live with us too, and Seramina if she wanted to. Whiskers, if it came down it, I'd even let them adopt Max.

Still, Rine's gossip had made me a little worried, and I scanned for Seramina in the crowd. She'd been doing what she did so well lately – keeping a low profile. In fact, she'd been doing such a good job that I'd completely forgotten about her until Rine had mentioned her name. I sniffed around for even a whiff of her snow-drop perfume, but she was nowhere to be found.

Maybe she'd glamoured herself and run away already. If so, I'd have to stage a rescue mission. What with Seramina's untamed powers, I couldn't let her go out into the wilderness all alone. Whiskers, if one of the warlocks kidnapped her and corrupted her as her biological father, Astravar, had almost done, then we were all doomed.

"Are you okay, Ben?" Ange asked.

"No—" I said. "I can't find Seramina. Please tell me she's not run off somewhere. That wouldn't be good."

"Of course she hasn't," Rine said. "She wouldn't abandon her dragon, now, would she?" He pointed up at Hallinar, Seramina's charcoal dragon, who was swooping low overhead right alongside Shadorow, Prefect Asinda's dragon of the same colour.

"How do you know that's Hallinar and not a glamour?" I asked. "I've seen her tricks."

"Oh stop it, will you, Ben?" Ange said. "You're just as bad as Rine with all these rumours."

"Well, can you see her?"

Ange glanced over to the right. "She was right there. Though to be honest I wouldn't blame her for hiding behind a glamour right now. She won't run away, and I doubt the White Mages are after her; she hasn't done anything wrong."

"So what are they here for, exactly?" Rine asked, a smirk on his face.

Ange put her hands on her hips. "The White Guard does a lot more than arrest people. Why don't we wait until they arrive? Then we'll surely find out."

The Council of Three had arranged themselves in a row in front of the students, forming a barrier between them and the unicorns. They had their staffs held out in front of them, the crystals on their tips glowing slightly.

With their hoods over their heads, the White Mages galloped towards us. Their cloaks were flapping in the cool breeze coming off the Willowed Woods. It didn't take me long to recognise Captain Alliander at the head of the formation, of what must have been a good twenty unicorns. Her springy red hair pushed her hood outwards, making her hard to miss.

While the Abyssinian stalked over to join the Council of Three, Captain Alliander put up her hand to halt her troops. Their horses reared as she reined in her unicorn, who if I recall correctly was called Tanni. Alliander dismounted and strolled over to the Council of Three.

Fortunately, being a cat, I had directional hearing quite suitable for picking up on their conversation. Esme and Ta'ra, sitting beneath her white dwarf dragon Kada, did the same.

"I see," Alliander said looking down at the Abyssinian. "King Garmin told me that our new agent would be an animal. I might have known it would be another cat."

"Are you implying that there's anything wrong with cats?" Esme asked, and she raised a forepaw to bat at what I guessed was a passing insect.

"Not at all," Alliander replied. "Though I must admit I prefer dogs. They're much more amicable creatures."

Very faintly, I heard Esme growl. "Then I know why the other cats tell me the Dragoncat despises you so much. It sounds like the rumours are true – you're just as unlikeable as your brother."

I bristled as she mentioned my title. I hadn't even once had a conversation with her, and now she was potentially dropping me in trouble. If I was going to be so easily implicated, I couldn't miss a word of this conversation, and the chatter around me might force me to lose my focus. I left my companions behind and stalked a little closer. I stopped next to a small gravelly boulder covered in dry lichen. My fur had picked up some burrs along the way, and I meticulously licked them off as I continued to listen.

Fortunately, Esme's insult had caused Alliander pause. The captain was now trying to stare down the cat. Humans never seemed to learn how pointless this was. We'd either glare back until they got bored, or we'd get bored ourselves, yawn, and close our eyes casually as if we were never playing in the first place. Either way, we won.

"My brother is dead," Alliander said after a long moment. "And the world is much better for it."

"Is he now?" Esme asked casually.

"Of course he is. We have reports from multiple students of Dragonsbond Academy that he died at Capitut's Pyramid. I interviewed them myself."

"And yet no one ever saw the body. How do you explain that?"

Alliander opened her mouth, but before she could say another word, Driar Lonamm let out a loud cough. "If you'll excuse us, Captain Alliander. You came here to discuss something with us, I presume, not to engage in *internal* politics. I'm presuming it's internal, of course, as this cat claims to be one of your own..."

"That's right," Alliander said. Her gaze roved over the students, who were all gawking back at her. Her eyes continued to search until they eventually fell upon me. Then she looked back at Driar Yila, who was tapping her foot on the cobblestone path that led to the castle's drawbridge. "This conversation isn't for ears attached to gossiping tongues," she continued. "Allow me to cast a Privacy Glamour..."

Driar Brigel started to stammer something, but Alliander raised her palm. "I know we're in difficult times, but please understand that no member of the White Guard would ever intentionally harm anyone in allegiance to the king." She lowered her head, drew her staff from her back, raised it, and called out, "Mages! Remember your orders!"

Momentarily, the mages on the unicorns behind Alliander also raised their staffs. Wisps of light floated from the unicorns' horns towards the riders' staffs, and orbs of white light pulsed out from the centres of the staffs, surrounding unicorns and mages alike.

The light around Alliander glowed brightest of all, expanding further and further. It soon washed over the Driars, then all the students, and filled out into the sky to cover the dragons too. It was so bright it was blinding, forcing me to see spots in front of my eyes and close them.

When I opened them again, I wasn't standing amidst the fields to the east of Dragonsbond Academy. Rather, I was on a sandy beach, with soft white waves lapping out of a turquoise sea.

❧ 5 ❧

A BEAUTIFUL GLAMOUR

Fortunately, this wasn't my first encounter with glamour magic; otherwise I surely would have run straight for the smoking volcano that cast a thick shadow over the palm trees walling the beach.

I'd seen Seramina cast glamour magic, and I'd seen the glamour that had surrounded Ta'ra's fairy home of Faerini, masking a whole city.

In all honesty, I wouldn't have lasted very long in the Faerie Realm. In their tiniest forms, fairies dart around so fast that instinct would have me chasing after them, just as I chase dragonflies. Then, as soon as I caught one, they would surely banish me to another dimension for being so violent. There was a reason there were no cats in the Faerie Realm. ... Cats and fairies simply couldn't coexist.

After my brief excursion into Faerini, my nemesis Astravar had teleported me through a portal to the Seventh Dimension, and then my crystal had pulled me out again into another glamour of a desert oasis, where the water had tasted so fresh, I'd thought I could live there forever. Alas, it wasn't meant to be.

Until that moment on the beach, I had no idea that White Mages could teleport a select number of us to a completely different place. It wasn't real of course; I'm sure I was still physically standing outside Dragonsbond Academy, and undoubtedly the topography of the surrounding terrain would match contour by contour to the landscape I was really on. It's just my mind and my senses thought I was in a tranquil seascape that Alliander had no doubt chosen specifically to soothe our nerves, in acknowledgement of the terrible news she was about to deliver.

The sea before me must have been the moat, the pier the drawbridge that led over it, and the huge galley docked there, casting a cool shadow over the undulating sands, would have been Dragonsbond Academy proper. I guessed the palm trees represented the White Mages and unicorns whom Alliander had brought along to help feed the illusion. Clearly one White Mage couldn't have been enough to hold this illusion alone.

I could probably break my way out of the glamour by trying to climb the volcano or going deeper into the silken water, but I had no intention of doing so, despite the fact that I hadn't had a good swim in months. Regardless of popular belief, some of us cats like to swim and I'm one of them, being a Bengal.

I wasn't alone in this illusion. The Council of Three still stood alongside Esme, and in front of Alliander and her unicorn Tanni. Ta'ra was here too, as were Max, Rine, Ange with her cheetah, Asinda, and Seramina.

Our dragons had all been included in the Privacy Glamour – Ta'ra's and Esme's black and white dwarf dragons stood where they had been previously, looking at each other, their leathery eyebrows furrowed. Corralsa had strode away from them. She'd moved close enough to Alliander to attack her, and presumably would if she decided the White Mage captain was a threat.

Ange's sapphire dragon, Quarl, swept down from the sky and

landed behind them, followed by Rine's emerald dragon, Ishtkar, who landed clumsily behind Quarl. Asinda's and Seramina's charcoal dragons, Shadorow and Hallinar, came down next and landed gracefully on either side of Quarl and Ishtkar. Salanraja came down last, and she landed right next to me, sending out gusts of wind so strong she almost blew me down.

The first human to react to Alliander's glamour was Seramina, who strolled forward, her staff clutched in her hand. The glamour was so real that the sea breeze was even stirring her platinum blonde hair.

To my great alarm, she had the flames burning at the back of her eyes which I always saw when she was about to lose control. The hackles rose on my back at the sight. Seramina wasn't even fourteen, yet she held more power within her than any of us could even dream of.

"I was trying to hide from everyone," she said. "I didn't want to draw any attention to myself today – and now you've removed my glamour. What is it that you want with me?"

Driar Yila bestowed a hard stare on the young girl. Her staff glowed bright red as she spoke in a stern voice: "Initiate Seramina, you must treat your superiors with respect. Now calm yourself. This doesn't have to be about you today. Remember everything Aleam has taught you."

For a moment the air became charged with a static that tugged on my fur. The sand, the sea, the sky, and the palms around me all shimmered violently as if the glamour were about to break.

"But the rumours—" Seramina said. "I heard people talking. You're here to arrest me, aren't you?"

Alliander looked upwards. Her gnarled oaken staff was glowing brightly all along its length. Tanni's horn also glowed, and the unicorn had lowered its head as if ready to charge Seramina.

"I am not here to arrest you, Initiate. Though if you continue this display, that might change."

"I don't believe you," Seramina said. "My power ... what I can do ... you can't let me exist anymore. Why can't you all leave me alone?"

Whiskers, I had to do something. After all the work I'd put into looking after Seramina, using my innate cuteness to keep her calm, I couldn't let her explode now. I sauntered forward and rubbed my head against Seramina's calf. It felt cold to the touch, as if all her blood had been pumped somewhere else. She smelled a little less of snowdrop perfume, and more of the rotten vegetable juice miasma that oft accompanied dark magic. Her staff was sheathed upon her back, but it didn't matter because the purple crystal on its tip still emitted a purple, eerie light.

I let out a soft chirp, then I said, "Seramina, remember who you are..."

She looked down at me, that rage burning in her eyes. For a moment, I thought she was going to attack me. But instead, she took a deep breath.

Max had run over to join me, but instead of the wise tactic of trying to show her affection, he started barking at her. "Bad magic! Bad magic! Must do something! What can I do?"

I tried to ignore him. Honestly, Max wasn't the smartest of dogs – not to say that I'd consider any dog intelligent.

"Seramina," I said. "The captain said she's not here to arrest you. Nobody wants to hurt you."

Time seemed to still, much as it had when Astravar had yanked me through the portal to the First Dimension so long ago. Silence enshrouded us, and for moment I thought Seramina would bring lightning down out of the sky to hit Alliander.

Instead, the young teenager took a deep breath, and lowered her head. "I'm sorry. I guess I got a little carried away."

Captain Alliander slowly shook her head, then turned to the Council of Three. "I'm going to have to watch this one closely." She reached into the inner folds of her robe and produced a scroll, which she handed to Driar Yila.

Yila took hold of the document and unrolled it. Her eyes ran quickly over the words and she sighed deeply. "By order of the king." She handed the document to Lonamm, who read it with furrowed eyebrows. In turn, the round woman passed the document to Brigel. After he'd read it, Brigel lowered the scroll to his hip, and puffed a full mouthful of air out through puckered lips.

"What did I tell you?" Esme said. "There will hopefully be time for your new Initiates to accept their gifts, but that time certainly is not now."

No one responded to her. Everyone present waited in anticipation, knowing that either Alliander or the Council of Three would tell us what was in the document soon enough. Rine and Ange in particular were both leaning forward, curiosity expressed on their faces.

"When will the attack come?" Driar Brigel asked.

"We think within half a day," Alliander said. "But if they have nothing to gain from an assault, the warlocks are unlikely to risk their numbers."

The hackles shot up on my back as I heard that. Warlocks were the bane of my existence; now, no doubt, they were going to uproot my life once again.

Max was the first to speak out. "What is it?" he barked loudly. "What is it? Dragoncat, translate for me..."

"I don't know yet," I hissed back at him, and then I watched as Alliander strolled forward to address us all.

The White Guard captain pulled back the hood of her robe before she spoke: "All students and animals present within this privacy glamour are to follow me under the escort of the White

Guard. Your lives are in danger, and you must come with us at once."

"But where are we going?" Asinda asked, her red eyebrows furrowing above her cornflower eyes. "And what about Lars?"

Driar Yila looked back at her. Her eyes this time didn't display her usual sternness, but instead a hint of apology. "We have granted you, Prefect Asinda, an automatic pass on your exams. Unfortunately, High Prefect Lars still has to take his. I'm afraid this is something you must do alone."

"We also have to move, now," Captain Alliander added. "For the risk of a miscalculation on our intelligence reports is high."

Asinda's jaw dropped. Honestly, I'd never seen her away from her boyfriend before. Lars and Asinda belonged together more than Rine and Ange did. It also meant that if anyone attacked us en route, we wouldn't have a shield mage to help protect us.

"You still haven't told them where they are going," Esme said, while examining an impressively sharp-looking claw.

Alliander scowled at the cat. Though I still wasn't sure what to think of Esme, I did feel proud that one of my own species was daring to challenge Alliander's authority.

"We're going to the safest place in the world right now," Alliander affirmed. "We will travel to Bestian Academy, where we will take refuge under the watchful eye of the great Matharon himself."

In unison, the dragons let out deep rumbles and groans. They couldn't understand Alliander, but they could understand what we dragon riders translated in our own minds for their benefit.

Every single dragon present had trained under Matharon at Bestian Academy. Under his iron watch, their training had been so gruelling that each of them, and probably every dragon I knew, had never wanted to go back.

6

FLYING AND FLIRTING

The setting sun cast an amber glow over the white caps of the Crystal Mountains. Admittedly there wasn't as much snow up there as I was used to seeing, but then it was late summer, and I'd not yet lived in the First Dimension for an entire year.

Still, the mountains looked impressive, offset against a low layer of fluffy-looking clouds. I had no doubt that up on the ridge between the Taur and Versta Peaks, on which Bestian Academy stood, it would be freezing.

It was, in fact, getting unpleasantly chilly on Salanraja's back as we climbed higher and higher, flying in a V-formation with the other dragons. As a descendant of the great Asian leopard cat, a beast that was used to much warmer climes, I didn't react well to the cold.

The dragons carrying cats, and the one with a dog, took the rear of our formation. The four humans on their dragons had formed a line at the front. Corralsa stayed slightly below Salanraja and the two dwarf dragons, apparently keeping an eye out for any dangers that might emerge.

The unicorns galloped at the same pace across the mountain range – the terrain not seeming able to trip them up in any way. A good two dozen White Guards that Alliander had brought to Dragonsbond Academy with her had joined the escort.

Before we'd left, Alliander had explained that out of all of us, Max was in the most danger. The warlocks' mission was simple: primarily they wished to retrieve the key to the Sixth Dimension that was currently in Max's belly, or at least somewhere inside his body. During the battle at Capitut's Tomb, Max had swallowed this key, giving him the ability to walk between all the dimensions. None of us had seen him use this ability as yet.

The reason we all specifically had to go with Alliander was that King Garmin had consulted with the Royal Crystal in Cimlean Palace. It had showed him that Max would be killed if each one of us didn't come along for the ride. Max's death would inevitably mean the warlocks would retrieve the key to the Sixth Dimension, which wouldn't be a good thing at all. So each one of us was present, including the strange Abyssinian, Esme, in order to fulfil the prediction.

The threat, according to the Royal Crystal, wasn't merely from the warlocks but also from a great demon snake lord called Apopis. How this snake would leave the Seventh Dimension and enter into our realm, I had no idea.

Ta'ra, sitting on top of the white dwarf dragon Kada, didn't seem to be handling the flight too well. My companion cat in fact looked a little airsick as she nestled herself in the ridges from which Kada's wings extended. Whiskers, if we were attacked by bone dragons right at this moment, I wasn't sure she'd stand a chance.

Ta'ra had been on flights with me on Salanraja, but I'd always instructed my dragon to go easy on her. Also, Salanraja's corridor of spikes, arching out from each side of her back, made it pretty hard to fall off.

Kada only had open space between her back and wings, and one shift in the wrong direction could send Ta'ra tumbling to the mountain peaks. So she kept herself crouched as low as possible, and Kada kept completely rigid, taking minimal risks as she flew.

Esme, on the other hand, seemed to have warmed to flying. She sat on Gratis' back with her head high and her ears flat as the frigid wind brushed back her silken fur. Gratis took riskier turns and dove and banked a little more than was normal. But all the time Esme kept her posture, as if her paws had been glued into place on the dragon's back.

She caught me looking at her, turned, and gave me that demure look again, blinking slowly a few times to express endearment. I looked away, as the last thing I wanted to do was anger Ta'ra. Fortunately, the former Cat Sidhe was so focused on staying on Kada's back that she failed to notice.

I took a peek at Esme again.

"*I think you like that one, Bengie,*" Salanraja said.

"*Not again...*"

"*What?*"

"*It's not Bengie, it's Ben. And yes, I have a lot of respect for that cat – I always have done in fact – but that doesn't change a thing.*"

"*Why? It's not as if you and Ta'ra are married or anything.*"

"*It's not that. It's just...*" I growled deeply. I didn't like being challenged like this.

"*What?*" Salanraja said.

"*I saved Ta'ra's life,*" I said. "*And she needs me. She needs help navigating this world.*"

"*That doesn't mean you can't spend time with other females of your species, though, does it?*"

"*Just shut up, will you, Salanraja? ... I don't want to talk about this right now. Okay?*"

"*Suit yourself, Bengie.*"

"*Ben,*" I said. But Salanraja, completely obedient to my request, didn't reply to correct herself.

I looked once more at Esme, and she turned to me again. The sun glinted off her pink nose as she cocked her head. She held my gaze for just a moment, then turned away as Gratis entered another dive. The dragon's tail flicked up, concealing the Abyssinian from view.

7

CAMP

It was getting colder by the hour, so it seemed like a smart move to camp for the night. The dragons might make it to Bestian Academy safely if we travelled over the mountains after dark, but their riders would become icicles in the process, and we didn't have a fire mage along to warm us up again.

So once the sun had set, Alliander cast a white beam into the sky to signal us down to land. It spread out over the clouds and was so charged with static that it pulled my fur towards it. On the ground, long shadows spread out from the pines, giving the whole scene a disturbing quality.

The dragons obediently began their descent. We could all have flown away, admittedly. But Alliander had told us previously that if any of us strayed from our intended course, she would signal Matharon to send his Guardian Dragons after us.

"Matharon's Guardians are to be feared," Salanraja told me, as she caught me thinking about them. *"More than any dragons that roam the sky."*

"Even more than Corralsa?"

"More so than her, and mightier even than Olan. Alongside Matharon, the Guardians were our tutors during our training at Bestian Academy. Legend has it that they are shaped from the rock of the mountains."

"So, they must look a bit like demon dragons, then?"

"Maybe not that large," Salanraja said with a chuckle. *"But certainly as solid. Anyway, we'd better land."*

Corralsa had already pushed her way to the front of the formation. She would have been difficult to see against the encroaching night had she not kept as close as possible to Alliander's beacon. Max sat like an idol on Corralsa's head. This was the first time that the dragon had let him ride her. The old creature believed in the ancient tradition that a dragon rider should be officially bonded before taking their first flight.

From my position, I could see the outline of Max's tongue lolling out of his mouth. His tail was beating against Corralsa's brow so quickly that she must have been rethinking her decision to bond with the dog.

Salanraja, Kada, and Gratis were the last dragons to reach the ground. The other dragons had created a wide circle in a clearing to demarcate the landing zone. As soon as Salanraja touched down, I leapt off her tail and headed straight towards the campfire that the White Guard had set up, just a little distance away from the landing zone.

They had already retrieved kindling from panniers on the unicorns' flanks. They'd also set up a couple of supports, using some branches from a pine tree, and one of the White Mages – who I recognised as Larmend, with his dark skin and bald head – was hoisting a spit onto the supports. I started to salivate as I looked up at it, imagining the mutton sausages that I'd be eating soon.

That was the best thing about camping: the piles and piles of provisions that always got sent along for the ride. We cats always said that you should never embark on a journey on an empty stomach, and this was something both humans and dragons seemed to agree on.

"We're going to need some more firewood," Alliander said to Rine. "And I'm sure you're not the kind of gentleman who leaves the carrying to the ladies, are you?"

Rine shrugged. "Can't we just use magic to move the firewood? I'm sure Ange could conjure up some powerful leaf magic. Why use muscles when you have vines?" He punched Ange lightly on the arm, and she scoffed playfully at him.

"Most certainly not," Alliander said. "She might need to reserve her magic for later. We're not safe until we get Max to Bestian Academy, and we have no idea where the warlocks might have posted spies."

"What about your White Mages?" Rine pointed to Larmend, and then gestured to another couple of males who were tossing firewood onto the fire. "Can't they help as well?"

"I have already deployed them to their own tasks," Alliander said. "You are now, under the orders of King Garmin, under my employ also. Which means you must do as I say, or suffer the consequences." She raised her hand to Tanni's head and stroked her fingers slowly down his mane.

Rine huffed. "Fine, then," he said as he delivered a half-hearted bow. "I'll be a perfect gentleman. I just hope I don't end up eating last because of this, because I'm starving." He stalked over towards Ishtkar.

I contemplated going to help him, as I could turn into a mighty chimera and carry some over for him. Whiskers, the White Mages had horses with horns, and I didn't know why Alliander hadn't tasked them to carry the firewood. They certainly were strong enough. But it seemed that in this realm, horses with horns had special privileges. They were always treated better than everyone else.

"I'll help too," Ange called, and skipped along after him. I watched her for a minute, my whiskers twitching in excitement. For a change we were going on an adventure without Rine's ex-girlfriend, Bellari, tagging along to ruin their potential relationship. All, it seemed, was going according to plan.

Ange looked at Alliander for approval, but she huffed in response.

"What?" Ange said. "Surely I should be allowed to do some of the work if I wish to. Gender equality and all that."

Alliander nodded, then turned back to her own task of supervising the White Mages in setting up the camp.

As the White Mages, Rine, and Ange worked away, the rest of the humans in our party sat down on tree stumps placed around the fire pit, which was still unlit. Ta'ra had lain down on Seramina's lap and her eyes were closed. Seramina was gazing wistfully into the darkness between the trees in the nearby forest.

I strolled over, passing Esme and Max, who both lay on a blanket underneath Asinda's feet. Esme raised her head to look at me as I passed, and she let out a loud meow that was actually an invitation to go to her and talk.

I ignored her, and instead joined Seramina. She needed me right now. As I approached, Ta'ra opened her eyes sleepily, yawned, and then closed them again. Seramina looked down at me, barely moving her head.

"Hey Ben…"

I brushed up against her calf. I looked for a spot where I could also sit on Seramina's lap, but Ta'ra had taken up all the space – Seramina was only a small girl after all. Instead, I jumped up on the stump, and sidled up to Seramina for some extra warmth.

She reached out to stroke me. It didn't last long, because Ta'ra meowed for attention again, and Seramina shrugged and returned to stroking her.

It didn't matter. I didn't need affection right now, but I could tell Seramina did.

"You looked like you needed some company," I said. I glanced at Ta'ra. "Company that's awake, I mean. Someone to talk to you and draw you out of your thoughts."

Seramina gave me a smile, but it looked forced. "I've got all the company I need right now."

Ta'ra was purring loudly. I was happy to hear that, and so I started purring too. Perhaps my body thought that doing so would lift Seramina's spirits a bit. But she remained silent, breathing very lightly.

"You know, you shouldn't blame yourself for what happened at Capitut's Pyramid."

Seramina lowered her head. She opened her mouth, then closed it again. Finally, after a moment of consideration, she spoke so softly that I doubted anyone could hear her but Ta'ra and me.

"I killed King Garmin's nephew, and everyone here knows that."

"So what?" I asked. "I vanquished Astravar, and it's not as if everyone hates me for it..." I trailed off for a moment, remembering that Astravar was in fact Seramina's father by blood. She didn't seem to care about that, though.

"Astravar was an evil warlock," Seramina said. "But Arran – he was a prince, and he'd garnered a lot of respect before he turned traitor. This is what dark magic does to you, remember? It corrupts your mind. Isn't it better they're taking me to a place where I won't dare to use it at all?"

I growled. She really wasn't listening to me. "They don't want to imprison you, Seramina. Our journey is all about Max; I'm sure about it. He has the key to the Sixth Dimension inside of him, and that's what the warlocks want."

Seramina shook her head. "It might be partly about him. But it isn't *all* about him. Now they're taking me along to Bestian Academy, Ben, and do you know why? Because there's no better place to keep me under guard. If I ever try to escape, I'll have Matharon himself to deal with. We've all heard the stories about him. He's the fiercest of them all."

"So why are they bringing Rine and Ange and Asinda along for the ride?"

Seramina laughed shallowly. "I suppose Asinda is a dark mage too. It would make sense to bring her along, to imprison her alongside me. We're liabilities. Arran proved that, didn't he?"

I ignored the question. "That doesn't explain Rine and Ange's presence."

"They're probably tagging along just to make me comfortable and so I don't suspect anything. This isn't only about protecting Max. It's keeping me in a place where the warlocks can't get to me and corrupt me. I'm a prisoner, Ben. I saved the world, and this is how they repay me. But then I guess, after my what my father did, this is what I deserve."

"You aren't responsible for what your fa—" I stopped myself "—for what Astravar did, Seramina. You need to forge your own path."

She said nothing more. I guess she'd made the points she wanted to make, and I could see I wasn't going to change her mind about the situation so easily. I'd also been so distracted by comforting her that I'd failed to notice that the White Mages had already added food to the fireplace.

I couldn't see what they had put on the spit yet, given how dark it was, nor strangely, could I smell it. Usually, mutton sausages give off quite a scent even before cooking. So I waited to see what would happen.

Soon enough, a jet of flame hit the bundle of wood on the

ground. As the fire flared up, I saw that it had come from Corralsa's mouth. She towered over the fire pit.

That's when my eyes went wide in horror as I saw that there were no mutton sausages on the spit above the fire. Instead, it had been staked through a line of marrows, turning lazily above a pot of what smelled like rice.

I didn't waste a moment in storming over to Captain Alliander to give her a piece of my mind.

8

FOUL FOOD

"What the whiskers do you call this?" I asked Alliander. "Cats can't eat marrows!"

The White Guard captain looked down at me in surprise. She was sitting on a stump next to the young female White Mage, Carmista, who was turning the spit slowly using a wooden crank handle. "I don't know what it is about the new programs in Dragonsbond Academy, but they seemed to have stopped teaching our dragon rider Initiates respect."

"Respect? Respect starts in the stomach, your *excellency*. Cats don't eat vegetables, and cats don't eat rice." Those marrows were starting to absolutely stink the place out, in fact. How humans could eat something that turned so slimy after cooking, I had no idea.

"Who said I was planning to give you vegetables?" the White Mage captain said. "I've already planned your meal perfectly. But please bear in mind that in these troubled times we have to be conservative in our food choices."

"I..." I hesitated. "What happened to the mutton sausages? We always have them when we go camping. It's a tradition." It was also one of the highlights of any journey I embarked upon with the other students of Dragonsbond Academy.

Alliander scowled. "In our current state of affairs, King Garmin can't afford to hand out mutton sausages willy-nilly to his military expeditions. Besides, the scent of meat cooking might attract undue attention. There are ice wargs around here, which are drawn to the smell of roasting meat. Better to cook what inhabitants of these mountains would usually cook, don't you think?"

I had no idea how to respond to that. This wasn't just about the sausages; it was about Alliander's supposition that food needed to be rationed, and because of that this was about the future of my kind. First they'd take the mutton away, then the fish, and the beef, and the chicken. Before we knew it, there'd be no meat left anywhere. We cats would starve.

I glanced around at my companions, hoping for some support.

Max watched me lazily from his sleeping spot on the blanket by Asinda's foot, his head raised as if wondering what the commotion was about. Ta'ra also opened her eyes, and yawned. Her first flight must have made her so sleepy that she didn't seem to care what she ate.

Asinda gave me a smile as if to humour me, and Seramina was still gazing off longingly into space. Meanwhile, Ange and Rine were still with the dragons, busy fetching extra firewood to fuel the fire.

Esme, on the other hand, was stalking slowly towards us. Her head was high, and her footsteps were perfectly aligned. "I'll handle this, Dragoncat," she said in the cat language as she brushed past me.

I stepped aside slightly, and she sat down and looked up at Alliander with wide blue eyes. Her tall ears seemed to pierce the night, and the firelight danced over her fur and sent pretty patterns across it.

Alliander looked down at her and chortled. Her unicorn tossed her head upwards and gave a whickering snort.

"You know," Esme said to Alliander. "Rumour has it that you don't respect any animals other than unicorns. Now I know these rumours to be true."

"This isn't about who I respect," Alliander said. "The Dragoncat here was complaining about our choice of a menu tonight, without even knowing what we were going to feed you animals."

"So what were you going to feed us?" Esme asked.

Alliander sighed. "I was going to wait for the marrow to cook a bit better before I dealt with that, but if you're going to be pushy ... Larmend, dish out the meals for the animals, will you?"

Larmend looked up from his spot beside his unicorn. He was currently in what looked like a deep conversation with another female White Mage.

"At once, Ma'am," he said, and he rummaged around in his unicorn's panniers. From these, he produced a few small sandy-coloured clay pots, wrapped in hemp string to keep their lids on. He cut the strings, and, gathering the four pots together in a bundle, brought them over. These he placed down in a neat line just in front of us, and he took the lids off each one and carried them away.

I didn't like what I smelled inside, but just to be sure I edged in for a closer sniff. It caused me to immediately turn up my nose in revulsion. It stank of meat that had been preserved in jelly for so long that it had lost all its flavour.

"What do you call this?" I asked. "This isn't food. ... It's even worse than those vegetables that you're cooking above the fire."

Ta'ra had already dashed over from her place on Seramina's lap, apparently drawn by the scent of this swill. She scooped up a lump of it on her tongue without even stopping to sniff it first.

"You know, it's not that bad..." she said in the cat language. "I've eaten much worse."

Max strolled over happily too. He was panting and wagging his tail as his took up a mouthful from the bone. "Good food! Good food!"

Alliander had a smirk on her face. I wanted to climb right up her cloak and bat it off with a sharp claw. "This is the kind of food that cats and dogs around the country eat. It's perfectly nutritious and it will keep you going until the next meal."

"No," Esme said after taking a second sniff at it. "We know the tricks you humans pull. This stuff is full of the minced stuff of animals that you don't want to eat yourself. Half of it is probably ground up bone."

"I'm afraid that's all we have," Alliander said, her arms crossed. "You can eat it or sleep hungry tonight. Though I don't recommend trying to get through a night this cold on an empty stomach."

"Oh no, we won't, will we Dragoncat?" Esme said, and she turned away from the bowl.

"What are you going to eat then?" Alliander asked.

"We will hunt for our own food." Esme followed that by asking me in the cat tongue, "Are you coming, Dragoncat?"

"You will do no such thing..." But Alliander's words were lost on the Abyssinian, who was already sprinting off into the woods.

I glanced back at Ta'ra, whose nose was buried in her bowl. From behind her, Max was continuing to pant between mouthfuls. "It's good! It's good! Tell them to save some marrow for me, Dragoncat!"

I growled in response. Esme was right; I didn't want to deal with this nonsense. Without further ado, I sprinted off into the forest, following Esme's scent as best I could.

9

COLD TREES, WARM HEARTS

It didn't take me long to regret my snap decision to follow Esme. By the fire it had been comfortably warm, and I'd started to take it for granted.

The forest on the other hand was as chilly as an open freezer. There wasn't any snow, fortunately, but still the twigs on the ground were frozen solid, and they snapped loudly whenever I stepped on them. It made it impossible to traverse the forest silently, and I had no idea how we were going to catch any prey.

Esme was easy to follow. The cold made her scent stronger, and her fur almost seemed to glow as it reflected slivers of moonlight. The sky above us was clear, and it stretched out in all directions, clothed in a canopy of stars that seemed to whirl around the moon.

Esme was a fast sprinter, though I had a hunch she had slowed her pace a little to allow me to catch up. Soon I was sprinting right beside her, and she turned her head towards me and let out a friendly meow.

"I knew you hadn't fully forgotten who you were, Dragoncat," she said, not needing to stop to catch her breath between words. "You have that true cat smell about you. I like that."

"Can we just stop and rest a moment?" I asked. "I don't go out hunting every night like you do."

"Of course. But let's get off the ground first."

She turned towards a sturdy-looking alder tree and clambered quickly up the rough bark of its trunk. Her movements were so spry – a bit like my Asian leopard cat ancestors that I'd encountered in the Ghost Realm. I couldn't help but feel that I was in good hands.

I glanced through the leaves that wavered in the howling wind, shivering. I had lost sight of Esme and squinted to try and find her in the canopy. She emerged on a thin wiry branch, stalking so unnervingly close to the end of it that I thought it might snap. But it seemed to be holding her weight well.

"Are you coming, Dragoncat?" she asked. "Because the dangers are down there, and it's always better to survey our prey from up high."

I examined the tree. It didn't seem as easy to climb as I'd first thought. Once, in South Wales, I'd ended up stuck in a tree as a kitten. Back then, the two Savannah cats had dared me to climb an oak to test my worth. I had, and I couldn't find my way back down again until a red truck had come, making a racket and with flashing blue lights, and a man in a helmet had climbed up a ladder and carried me back down again.

"Come on," Esme called from above. "I'd never have thought the mighty Dragoncat to be such a coward. You can ride dragons, but you're too scared to climb trees."

Her challenge set the hackles up on the back of my neck; I could feel the chill pricking my skin there. I swallowed bile, then took a mighty leap at a sturdy-looking piece of bark. The skin around my claws felt raw when I exposed them to the cold air, but still I used my strength to pull myself up, growling as I did so.

I reached Esme's branch, all my muscles aching and also slightly out of breath. She was right – I had become weak as a dragon rider. I really had forgotten how to be a cat.

Still, Esme seemed to admire, or at least respect, my bravery. She touched her wet pink nose against my cheek, then sidled up next to me. The feel of her warm body against mine felt good. It was comforting, in fact.

"My hero," she said. "Vanquisher of the warlock Astravar. Oh, how I've dreamed of the day I would join you in battle."

My whiskers twitched. I knew that my tales of bravado had spread amongst the humans and the dragons, but I had no idea they'd also carried across to the cats. "How long have you known about me?"

"Since you came to our castle. Every night when I was set free to roam the grounds, I was drawn towards the crystals, fascinated by their pretty displays. Every time I passed one, it would light up to show me something. When you arrived, they started showing me visions of your future, and mine as well. It didn't take me long to realise that our destinies were intertwined..."

Esme was purring, and I was purring too. But I was also worried. I felt that I shouldn't be here; I should be back with Ta'ra, eating my meal like a grateful cat, despite the dire quality of the food. I edged away from Esme, and she turned her head towards me, a questioning gaze in her brilliant blue eyes.

"I don't belong with you. I'm sorry – but I have another. Ta'ra. You know her."

Esme turned her head towards the fireplace. "You mean the former fairy. She isn't even a cat, you know. Or at least, she wasn't born one."

"She is now. I taught her how to be a feline. I taught her how to walk straight, and how to eat properly."

"Caring for someone isn't enough, Dragoncat. There must be

genuine animal attraction. Besides, you're meant for greater things. I've seen the visions, and I've seen how we're destined to combine our magic and work together in battle. I can help you become who you were meant to be."

"I've not seen these visions," I said.

"Have you ever looked for them? Because I fear that your sense of companionship with the humans, not to mention the fairies, has made you blind."

My heart was pounding so hard inside my chest that I thought it might leap out of my rib cage. Though something did feel different about this moment, I also felt I had to get away. I didn't belong here—

I looked down at the ground, considering leaving my perch. But there was nothing to invite me onto the forest floor, only pitch black and cold darkness that seemed to inch outwards as the night progressed.

I turned back to Esme. She was gazing at me ruefully, and I found myself drawn towards her gaze. For a moment, I was lost in those alluring blue eyes of hers. I wasn't sure if I was imagining it, but the inky blackness at their centre seemed to swirl. As if from deep inside them, I could see the reflection of the stars and moon.

I knew she was right, though I was loath to admit it. There was something about her: a sense of belonging, as if I had truly discovered my own kin.

I pushed forward to touch my nose against hers, but before I could make contact, my ears perked up, hearing a shrill howling sound. I backed off, remembering myself, then I focused on the sounds.

More howls – a loud snarling – the gnashing of teeth.

"Do you hear that?" I asked.

"I do," Esme said, now standing alert. "Ice wargs – they must have latched onto our scent."

She looked down at the ground, then edged around me and made her way down the tree trunk. The next movements were a whirr as the white hand – her staff bearer – appeared beside her. It swooped over to her, and in one deft motion Esme's oaken staff was between her jaws.

"We should call our dragons," I called out. "It could be dangerous."

"Don't," Esme said, looking back up at me, and her staff glowed almost as brightly as the moon. "Come down, Dragoncat. It's time for us to finally fight together, for it is I who is destined to finally show you the way to true power. Tonight is the night, Dragoncat, that you will discover your true potential."

10

LIGHT AND DARK

For what I hoped was only a very short while, I stood frozen in the tree, listening to the approaching gnashing of teeth and disparate howls. I felt just as I had in the oak tree that day. The ground was dangerous, and the only safe place for me in the world was this tree, despite the bitter and deathly wind.

I was considering summoning my staff bearer and trying my hand at some dark magic. But really, the staff would only have hampered me on my way down.

"Come on, Dragoncat," Esme called. "I don't want to have to fight them alone."

I felt incredibly embarrassed. "I-I-I'm," I stuttered. It was so cold. "I don't know how to get down, Esme."

"Just put your claws in the bark and pull yourself down. It's soft enough."

I growled, then saw a white shape darting around the trees. It wasn't Esme this time, but something larger, and it was moving fast. Another shape shifted across my vision to the right. Then I heard a howling sound from somewhere below me, but it stopped so suddenly that I couldn't identify its source.

Whiskers, Esme was going to get us both killed, but I couldn't let her die alone. I tested the trunk beneath me with my claws, then I took a deep breath. I'd like to say I slinked down naturally; in fact, I think I tumbled, and though I landed on my feet, the forest floor responded with a loud crunch.

A barking sound came from close by. Then something darted out at me. But it was only a leaf picked up by the wind.

"Your staff bearer, Dragoncat," Esme said. "We haven't much time."

My back arched, I willed my mind to stop panicking, and I called the white hand out of the darkness. It glowed as it appeared, and it reached forward to thrust my staff between my jaws. My mouth warmed, and the power surging into the staff burned the back of my tongue.

The purple crystal glowed, and my muscles burned with fury and destruction. I smelled a whiff of rotten vegetable juice, and a sense of power started to swim in my head. Then there was fire, but it wasn't outside of me. Rather, I saw two raging flames in my mind's eye. They were there, I knew, burning somewhere at the back of my mind.

"That's it," Esme said. "This who you are, Dragoncat. This is your true destiny."

I felt empowered, but this feeling ebbed as I remembered the fires burning at the back of Seramina's eyes. Memories flashed through my mind of all the times I'd seen her lose control. I remembered the vision we'd seen in the Ghost Realm, of Seramina in battle against the warlocks. She had plunged her staff into the ground, rending the world to pieces with her magic. Whiskers, I didn't want to become like her.

I stopped summoning magic to my staff. The power started to leave me for a moment.

"I can turn into a chimera," I offered, my words coming out clipped owing to the staff in my mouth. "I can fight them three on one."

"No, you shall not," Esme snapped. "It's time for you to start to use your magic. For years I've been studying the crystals, training for this day. Now concentrate."

Before I even had a chance to do so, a white shape charged out of the undergrowth. It leaped at me, and I just managed to tumble out of the way before it clawed me to pieces. The ice warg seemed to be twice the size of a regular warg, and faster too.

I turned to face it as it charged back into the darkness and disappeared from view. I willed power to my muscles, visualised them tearing into the mighty chimera form. But before I could take the transformation any further, Esme whipped her staff underneath my feet, knocking me over.

I picked myself up, growling. "I thought we were on the same side. We're meant to be fighting together."

"Transforming into a beast so you can fight them alone isn't working *with* me," Esme said. Her voice was calm, despite the loud and violent snarls that were emerging from the underbrush.

I listened closely, trying to work out when the next charge would come. But I couldn't work out their position. Or rather, the beasts always seemed to be moving. All of a sudden, I heard the bounding of heavy feet from behind me. This time, the warg didn't charge at me but at Esme.

She looked at it, her eyes glowing with the same brilliance as her staff. "Now, Dragoncat," she said, and a white light shot out of her staff. She hadn't aimed at the ice warg, however, but at me. My fur glowed, and my muscles burned with raw energy. Time slowed, and

I could see the warg with such clarity that I imagined I was looking through the snake-tail of my chimera.

Except I wasn't. I was still a regular Bengal cat, the vanquisher of warlocks, descendant of the great Asian leopard cat and the mighty George.... My father would have been proud to see me today, because under Esme's spell – whatever she'd done to me – I was surging with power.

I focused on the warg, still bounding in slow motion. Its jaws were wide open, and its sharp teeth seemed ready to snap Esme in two. My staff rumbled in my mouth, and a mighty purr resonated through it that perhaps even turned into a deep growl. I closed my eyes, and I imagined a wave of purple energy pulsing outwards from the crystal on my staff.

I opened them again just in time to see the effect. I had sent a line of red energy across the ground. It charred the leaves as it went, running its course like a spark through wire. Time sped up, and the magic collided with the ice warg, sending up a brilliant explosion and a loud boom. I smelled charred fur, and the warg yowled in pain.

In an instant its entire body crumbled to ash, not leaving even a skeleton. The air had the scent of dark magic in it. A faint purple mist surrounded me, tendrils of it dissipating into the void. Two howls sounded in the underbrush, but these soon were reduced to whimpers and the ice wargs scampered away in retreat.

"That was marvellous, Dragoncat," Esme said. She blinked gently as the glow left my fur. "Our power ... just think what we can achieve."

My legs were shaking, and my head was spinning. My body felt strangely warm and part of me wanted to lie down and go to sleep. But I knew at the same time that we hadn't eaten. "About that hunt?" I asked Esme.

"Good idea," she replied. "I have a hunch as to exactly where we shall find prey."

She slinked off into the darkness. I watched her for a moment, but this time I had no reservations about following her. I knew I could learn a lot more from her than from any other creature here, and it felt good.

Working together, perhaps, we could even discover how to bring salmon into this realm.

SLEEPY

By the end of the night, Esme and I had recovered two rabbits from their burrows. We didn't use magic to hunt them, since Esme had agreed with me that doing so would spoil the honour of the hunt. But we combined a couple of spells to roast them to crispness. Under the fading moonlight, and off a brittle carpet of leaves, we ate them side by side, happily purring away.

It was the first moment in my life, admittedly, that I'd truly felt that we cats could fend for ourselves.

We both returned to the camp with full stomachs. Our party did not seem to have missed us, and probably in full confidence that we'd return, they'd set up tents for the night. Shadows from the surrounding trees played patterns on the white canvas, lit to amber by a fire that continued to burn brightly. They must have used an awful lot of firewood, and perhaps even a dose of magic.

Larmend and Carmista sat as guards on two of the tree stumps, situated next to a massive bundle of firewood. They both turned and watched us stalk towards the firelight. The dragons were all sleeping in a circle, their snores rumbling the ground around them. I could smell the sulphurous fumes coming from their nostrils.

I looked around for Ta'ra, and soon caught her lavender scent coming from the same tent as Seramina's. Both cat and teenager were fast asleep, as were all the remaining White Mages and dragon riders, in their own designated tents. Sadly, I noticed that Rine had paired up with another male of the White Guard and Ange with Max.

Surely they knew each other well enough to sleep in the same tent? I'd have to quiz Rine on what had happened there later. Just when I'd thought they'd been getting on so well.

"Looks like all our pet food has been eaten," Esme said, gesturing to the bowls that lay empty on the floor.

"My guess is Max had triple portions," I said. "Anyway, where shall we sleep?"

"By the fire pit in the open air, of course. Where else would a cat sleep?"

I wanted to suggest that we cuddle up for warmth with one of the humans, until I realised that Esme's way was much more logical. Indeed, the body giving off the most warmth here was the fire itself.

I slept well, and I finally I awoke to two bright green eyes framed by dark fur. Ta'ra was there staring down at me, her look sorrowful. I turned to see that I had nestled up next to Esme in my sleep, or perhaps she had nestled up to me.

"Well I never," Rine called out, and I snapped my head around to see him poking his head out of his tent. The White Mage who had shared with him had already left. "I'd never thought you the type, Ben. But I've always told you that's the way to play it. Way to go, you old dog."

"I'm not a dog, I'm a cat," I said, but Rine didn't seem to hear me.

Ta'ra took a deep breath, and then she lowered her head and

stalked away. She joined Seramina, who was back on her tree stump, gazing into the distance as if she had nothing left in the world.

Max came over to chide me next. He pushed his nose right up to me, sniffed me, then recoiled and started barking. "Bad Ben!" he screamed in the dog language. "Bad Ben! Ben hurt his friend!"

Esme shot up, then hissed at Max, which sent him scampering away. "That's better," she said, and licked her fur. "Dogs will never understand the importance of sleep."

Though the air was still cold, the sky was clear, and the sun was sending down a pleasant warmth. Captain Alliander emerged from the largest tent of them all, and she bawled out at the top of her voice.

"Okay, everyone. Move out! Move out!"

"But we've not even had breakfast," Asinda objected.

"That's why I instructed you all to fill up your bellies last night," Alliander snapped back. "We'll eat when we get to Bestian Academy. Now pack up the tents and move fast. Our scouts have reported ice wargs in the vicinity and we don't want to be on the ground when they come looking for us."

"It's not as if we don't have dragons to protect us," Esme commented in the cat language.

"And some powerful magic," I replied.

"Yes ... let's just keep that one secret for now. I've heard rumours that Captain Alliander doesn't appreciate the use of unsanctioned magic – both white and dark."

The White Mages and the Initiates of Dragonsbond Academy made short work of getting everything packed up. As they moved, I listened to the swishing of the wind, and the sounds of distant howling. Alliander wasn't wrong about the nearby ice wargs, but after our adventure the previous night I didn't fear them as much as I had before.

Without turning into a chimera or using 'unsanctioned' magic, there wasn't much I could do to help. So, I clambered up onto Salanraja's back and surveyed the scene from her corridor of spikes.

"*Well, you seem mighty proud of yourself,*" my dragon said to me in my head. "*You're not going to tell me there's still nothing going on with you and the Abyssinian, are you?*"

I growled. "*That's none of your business.*"

"*What do you mean none of your business? I'm your dragon, which means everything concerning you is my business.*"

"*Not this. This is a private matter, Salanraja, and you will not do anything to interfere.*"

"*Fine,*" Salanraja said. "*Maybe I'll see if I can get some more information out of Gratis instead. I hear that Esme is much more willing to share.*"

"*What do you mean she's willing to share?*" I glared over at Esme, who was sitting on Gratis' head, grooming herself. She gave me an innocent look, pouted, then returned to her routine.

I heard a growl from behind me and looked down to see Ta'ra crouched low on the ground staring up at me. I hissed back at her and hid myself behind Salanraja's back.

Soon enough, Alliander had her White Mages mounted on their unicorns, and all the dragon riders had returned to their dragons. Corralsa took off first, with Max sitting casually behind the spike that rose from the tip of the dragon's head.

Captain Alliander galloped after Corralsa, her unicorns in tow. Presently, Salanraja lifted off, and we were soon high in the sky.

We weren't flying for long before we could see Bestian Academy, a great stone fortress offset between the peaks. It wasn't the architecture I spotted first, but the black smoke rising from the base of it. This was soon accompanied by a whiff of sulphur on the breeze.

"*Gracious demons,*" Salanraja said. "*Surely not. Not with Matharon and his Guardians there...*"

"*What?*" I asked. "*Salanraja, what's the matter?*"

She didn't respond, but I guess she didn't have to. I knew instinctively what had happened; I could see it in the astonished gazes of the dragon riders staring dead ahead at our destination, and the slow, mournful beating of the dragons' wings.

Bestian Academy had been attacked and Matharon and his Guardians were nowhere to be seen.

ABANDONED

Fortunately for us, whatever had attacked the fortress had already left. They'd not been gone long, though. Bundles of wood were still burning around the low obsidian walls, flames ringing the inner and outer baileys. The walls themselves, being made of stone, couldn't burn.

The dragons wouldn't have been the ones to place the wood. Given they could breathe fire, and constantly had it burning in their bellies, they had no need for flammable materials. Instead the wood must have been placed by the attackers. They must have known we were coming, and they had wanted us to see the full extent of their power. They had wanted us to be afraid.

Fortunately, there were no signs of any dead dragons. Either they had escaped, or they had been kidnapped. Given what Salanraja had told me about Matharon and his Guardians, they would have been able to deal with the normal conjurations of the warlocks, the worst of them being forest, stone, and sand golems.

Which meant something mightily powerful must have visited

this land, like a demon dragon, and potentially not only one. I shuddered at the thought.

The unicorns fanned through the open gate at the front of the fortress and set up a perimeter. The White Mages had their staffs clutched in their hands, and in brilliant cascades of magic involving glowing unicorn horns, they soon extinguished the flames, leaving smouldering piles of ash.

Ahead of the unicorns, a second smaller gate led to a precipitous looking path into the mountains beyond. I had no idea, of course, why dragons needed paths. Maybe this one signalled the start of the dragons' march after they left Bestian Academy to travel to Dragonsbond Academy. Salanraja had spoken so fondly about such pilgrimages before.

As the White Mages worked on securing the ground, we dragon riders circled in the air, looking out for any sign of danger on the distant peaks. A heavy grey mist had started to sweep over from the north, crowding the path and making it difficult to see anything at all.

Soon the unicorns had clustered together underneath us, forming three rows, with Alliander and Tanni standing separately at the front. The captain sent up the beam that pulsed in a specific pattern that we'd learned was to signal us downwards.

This time, Ishtkar and Quarl led the way, with the two charcoals, Hallinar and Shadorow, following close behind. I swept down on Salanraja with Kada on one side of me and Gratis on the other.

Esme gazed at me alluringly from her spot on Gratis' back. Honestly, I wasn't sure I'd be so unsettled if Ta'ra wasn't on the other side of me, trying hard to look at anything but me.

"Gratis says to tell you that Esme told him that you need to stop looking out for the Cat Sidhe all the time," Salanraja said to me.

"I thought we said that we weren't going to talk about this," I snapped back.

"I'm just passing on the message."

"Well, you should be more worried about what happened to your former tutor."

"Of course I'm worried. As I said, I'm just the messenger."

"Let's just focus on landing, shall we?"

Salanraja said no more, but she let out a loud rumbling growl from her belly. I looked again at Esme, who was now completely focused on the cobblestones that were hurtling towards us. Presently Salanraja landed with a violent thud, almost sending me tumbling off her back.

"Salanraja!"

"What? I thought we needed to get down onto the ground fast."

"Not at the expense of my life," I said, and I scrambled quickly down her tail before she could do any more damage.

The grounds inside the fortress were strangely warm. I guessed the fires must have generated an awful amount of heat, and the low pressure from what looked like an approaching storm was keeping it tamped down here. It was quite pleasant, in fact, and a part of me wanted to lie here for a while and have a good groom.

But I knew I should join Esme, Ta'ra, and Max in searching the area for any clues. So I put my nose to the ground and engaged in a little feline detective work. The ground had a familiar sulphurous odour to it. Perhaps I was the only one familiar with it, as I doubted anyone else present had yet been to the Seventh Dimension. Admittedly, Max might have decided to visit there for a spell; the dog could, after all, shift between the dimensions whenever he pleased. He'd have to be mad to want to, though. The whole place was a pit of obsidian and lava.

It didn't take me long to realise that the stench of sulphur was everywhere, as if something had slithered across the ground, oozing the stuff as it went. The more I followed the scent, the more I mapped out an image of something ginormous traversing the terrain in sinuous motions.

Apopis.... I thought. *No, it couldn't be....*

Yet I knew of no other massive beast which could move that way, and whatever had left this trail was indeed massive. I'd never seen Apopis myself, but I could all but imagine him. The Overlord of Overlords, ruler of the Seventh Dimension. The demon of chaos, to be feared above them all.

Lasinta, the leader of the warlocks, had threatened to summon him into this realm. Now she must have acted on her threat, which I guessed meant the warlocks were nearby too.

I perked up my ears and listened for the grunt of a condor, or the caw of a seagull, the shriek of a hawk, or one of the other signature cries of the carrion eaters that the warlocks transformed into. All I could hear was the swishing of cold wind in the distance.

A chill gust came from the encroaching cloud. It was dark and menacing and looking at it sent me growling. This wasn't a normal cloud, but a storm cloud. Given the cold, it could even be a blizzard coming this way.

Whiskers, the last thing I wanted was to get trapped in a blizzard, eventually to be buried under a mound of snow. Fearing the worst, I hurried over to Captain Alliander to deliver my report.

ROTTEN EGGS

"Stinks of rotten eggs! Stinks of rotten eggs!" Max had beaten me in rushing up to Captain Alliander to report his findings. What he hadn't considered was that Alliander didn't speak the dog language and so had no chance of understanding him.

Alliander turned up her nose, probably not appreciating the smell of the dog. She looked at me. "Care to translate what this dog is telling me? Is it of any importance whatsoever?"

I looked at Max. Really, there was something endearing about him, even to cats. Perhaps it was due to him being the goofiest animal I've ever met. He was even sillier than a rooster, to be honest, and that's saying something.

"He's saying he smells sulphur. Maybe it's from those marrows you all ate. Don't say I didn't try to warn you they were bad for the tummy."

Alliander scowled, then strapped on a white glove from her hip and bent down. She scraped some dust off the ground and examined it. The residue on her finger gave off a faint red glow. She blew it away and shook her hand vigorously through the air.

"Demons," she said and cast an alarmed glance at Carmista who was standing a little behind her. "What have the warlocks been up to?"

"Not just demons, I might add," I offered. "What you smell there is part of the trail of a great demon snake."

Alliander turned back to me and narrowed her eyes. "What did you just say?"

"Have you heard of Apopis?"

"Of course I've heard of Apopis." Alliander blinked a few times. "But you must be mistaken – Apopis is the ruler of the Seventh Dimension. There's absolutely no reason that he'd come here."

"Unless he wanted to scare away a whole host of dragons. Maybe he even tried to kidnap them."

"And why would he do that?" Alliander asked, with her hand on her chin.

"I don't know," I said. "Fewer problems to deal with when we arrived, I guess."

Alliander nodded and her gaze grew distant. She looked up at the storm cloud with a sigh. She didn't seem to want to get caught in it either. "Something doesn't feel right in this place. Wait right here. I need to check something."

She walked over to Tanni and wrapped her hand around her horn, which began to glow steadily. Alliander closed her eyes, taking deep breaths. She looked as if she were meditating – another of those human activities that had absolutely no point to it.

Her eyelids flickered fast, and all of a sudden her body spasmed. Her eyes shot open and I recoiled in shock when I saw she was displaying only the white of her eyes, her pupils and irises absent. Her body shuddered even more as her feet lifted off the ground a few inches. She hovered there and a glow surrounded her.

From somewhere behind me Esme hissed, and Max let out a gruff bark. Alliander, or whatever had possessed Alliander, paid them no heed. She spoke in a voice that wasn't her own; as soon as I recognised it, I knew that it would sound different to everyone here. To me, it had a soft lilting accent that was almost Welsh. The voice of the crystals.

"You are still not safe here," Captain Alliander said. The rest of the White Mages behind her crowded in slightly, their heads turned towards her. "For you rested for too long, and destiny has moved too fast. Hurry up the path into the mountains, and there you will find temporary refuge. You cannot let the dog perish."

Max had stopped barking by this point. Instead, he sat with his head bowed, his eyelids sealed tight. Once Alliander had finished speaking, his eyes shot open, and he looked at me. "A crystal has given me another mission! Another mission! This is great, Dragoncat!"

I groaned, not liking the sound of that one bit. The last 'mission' that the crystals had 'given' him had ended with him swallowing the key to the Sixth Dimension, which was the whole reason we were in this mess in the first place.

Alliander's feet had returned to the ground, her skin no longer aglow. She opened her eyes, her hand held to her temple as if she were recovering from a sudden headache.

"What did you do?" Esme asked, stalking towards her. "What was that?"

Alliander shook her head. "Because of my bond with a Greater Unicorn, I have the ability to consult the King's Crystal from afar. You are new to our ranks, young Esme. But when you finally have time to study at the School of the White, you will understand how our power structure works."

Greater Unicorn my back paw. Tanni looked no different from the other unicorns, and she still smelled like horse – the most untrustworthy animal of all.

It didn't matter what Alliander could do, because the crystal had warned us to get out of here fast. I looked back to see a nervous expression on Ange's face. Her feet and shoulders were turned towards her dragon, Quarl.

"We need to get out of here," Alliander said. "The crystal told us to take that path." The same path, I might add, that ascended towards a cloud that was now sucking the warmth out of this place. To add insult to injury, it had also started to flare with occasional lightning.

Before anyone else could speak, a roar split the air. It didn't belong to any natural creature; rather, it had a gravelly essence to it, and it was so loud I could imagine it splitting boulders in two. Another similar roar followed, and then a third.

"Demon dragons," Asinda said, her eyes wide. "Captain Alliander, with much respect, we have to move now!"

Alliander didn't waste another moment. She removed her hand from Tanni's horn, leapt onto her unicorn's back, and clutched her thighs tightly around its flanks. "To the path! Dragon riders, follow my magic, and White Mages, stay close…"

I heard a heavy sigh from the White Guard's ranks. "We're heading into a blizzard, Ma'am," Carmista pointed out.

"I know that," Alliander said. She tried to say something else, but another roar drowned her out, accompanied by a devilish shriek. Alliander swallowed hard and a massive lump travelled down her throat. "But there's a lot more than demon dragons out there. Move out!"

She let her troop of mounted White Mages trot in front of her towards the exit that led onto the winding path. After they had gathered a short distance away, she lifted her staff in the air, and from out of it shone a beam of white light.

"I won't be able to see you within the storm," she said, now addressing only the dragon riders. "Whatever you do, don't lose sight of my beacon."

Of course, losing her was the last thing any of us wanted to do.

14

DEMONS AHOY!

I clambered up Salanraja's tail as fast as I could, and she didn't waste a moment in lifting off the ground and flying towards that horrible-looking cloud. I stood on her head this time, as I wanted to look out for potential trouble.

Once we were high enough, I peered over my shoulder and indeed saw demon dragons approaching. The air shimmered around them, as if their very act of flying could distort time and space.

I'd been right on top of a demon dragon once, and I'd never forget its craggy obsidian skin and the wide cracks in it through which I'd peered into its molten, fiery core. They were famously impervious to any magic or weapons, and the only way to be rid of it had been to command it back into the Seventh Dimension using my gift of language.

They also had great gaping maws that never seemed to open and close. Rather, they sucked the air in front of them into great spinning vortexes. In other words, if they got anywhere near us, we were doomed.

Beneath them, a massive beast slithered across the ground. It must have been as long as the height of fifty men, with glowing red streaks crisscrossing its body in rough diamond patterns. As soon as I caught sight of it, it disappeared from my view, as if it had an innate ability to camouflage itself. Moments later, I saw it again in another place. It seemed able to easily keep up with the demon dragons, moving smoothly along the ground without exerting any effort at all.

I turned my attention to the path ahead, glad that we didn't have to climb its meandering course. It appeared the unicorns didn't need to either, galloping instead up the steep slope as if they were mountain goats. Alliander had fallen behind the rest of her troop with her staff held high above her head. Out of it still shone the beacon that I hoped would guide us through the storm.

The wind had already picked up around us and was howling with ample volume to fuel my pounding heart. Snow drifted, then swirled around us, and squalls of it dove towards the ground.

We flew in a V-formation to allow for the greatest speed. Corralsa was at the front, being the strongest flyer. The two dwarf dragons took the outermost wings of the formation, Salanraja and I flying almost beside Kada and Ta'ra. When Ta'ra saw me looking at her she scowled back at me. Somehow, her expression looked almost human.

I looked back at the demons again. They were gaining ground mighty fast. The snake was down there, too, visible only when I wasn't looking for it. It wasn't alone on the ground, either; other smaller, craggy bodies bounded along beside it. There must have been hundreds of them – glowing red as they moved.

At first, I wondered if it had brought along a load of demon Maine Coons, like the one that had called itself Hellcat – Astravar's demon cat that I'd defeated so long ago. They didn't move like cats, though, but more like dogs. As I observed them, I saw their long noses and skinny legs. These weren't dogs at all but foxes; they were even worse than dogs and almost as bad as wolves.

Demon dragons, a demon snake, and demon foxes. What the whiskers was going on?

It wasn't meant to be easy for demons to come to the First Dimension, and apparently they didn't come willingly. Someone powerful must have summoned them. But still, I'd heard no call of any warlock birds of prey.

"Can't we go faster?" I asked Salanraja.

Salanraja growled back at me. *"If you want to complain to Corralsa, then go ahead. But we're going as fast as we possibly can as a group. If we need to fight, we'll be much stronger if we're not scattered."*

"But they're gaining on us."

"And how long do you gather we've got until they catch up?"

"I don't know – maybe around five minutes."

"Which should be enough time to lose them in the clouds. Gracious demons, if it weren't for this storm, we wouldn't stand a chance."

There came a bright flash from up ahead, and I heard a crashing sound. I almost fell off Salanraja's head, I was so startled. It was only thunder, followed by another few flashes of lightning from the charged cloud. A couple of more distant crashes of thunder followed. I glanced over my shoulder again, to see the demon dragons toss back their heads and respond with their own cacophonous rumbling roars. They seemed to want to challenge the storm.

"Brace yourself, Bengie," Salanraja said in my mind.

"Ben—" I didn't manage to get another word in before we hit a sheet of icy cold. We had entered the cloud, and all I could see through the fog was Kada's alabaster toothy snout behind me and Quarl's emerald tail beating from side to side up ahead.

The wind strengthened, and I almost slid off Salanraja's head into whatever abyss lurked below. I shrieked and scampered down

Salanraja's spine, hiding myself in her corridor of spikes. I peered around her neck, keeping my body wedged inside the two right-most spikes nearest her shoulder to stop myself from getting swept away.

I squinted, trying to make out the beacon of light shining up through the murk. It was ever so faint. But I guessed as long as Corralsa could see the light and we didn't lose her, we'd stay on course.

We carried on this way, listening to our fates. My heart wouldn't stop hammering against my chest, the wind wouldn't stop howling, and the demon dragons wouldn't stop roaring at the storm. I said nothing to Salanraja, knowing it best that she concentrated. Instead I kept my focus on that white light, not letting myself lose sight of it.

That was when the wind seemed to change direction, and I caught a flash of light from my left. A second beacon found its way through the murk, dissipating only when it hit the roof of swirling fog. Other beacons popped up in front of us, and there must have been a good two-dozen in total.

"What in the Seventh Dimension?" Salanraja said.

"What? Why would the other White Mages activate beacons? Are they trying to tell us something?"

"No," Salanraja growled, sucking in a breath and making a high-pitched whistling sound. *"That's not white magic, but Manipulators. It's an ambush, Ben. Brace yourself!"*

Through the murk, almost lost in the howling of the wind, my ears homed in on a terrifying shrieking sound. I would recognise that noise anywhere; it was the cry of a bone dragon latching onto its target, and it sounded awfully hungry for blood.

15

FOGGY AMBUSH

The first bone dragon – a tangle of bones and claws – attacked from the left. It spewed forth a jet of purple acidic flame, threatening to singe my fur and burn me to a crisp. But Salanraja ducked underneath it just in time. She swooped down so fast that she sent me tumbling backwards, only to be caught by a convenient nook in her corridor of spikes. I looked back up to see two sharp bony talons swoop by overhead.

I scrambled up to my vantage point on Salanraja's back, and scanned the faint outlines of the terrain below, trying to make out the beacon. The lights searing through the clouds all looked the same. One of them was Alliander's beacon, but the rest were the energy that the Manipulators were feeding into the bone dragons above them, making the skeletal creatures invulnerable.

Usually, in battles such as these, dragon riders would dismount to take the Manipulators on the ground first, so that the dragons could reduce their bone nemeses to ash. The problem was that we didn't want to lose our guide, and we also had a whole host of demons on our tail. What we really needed was to escape this ambush, and then take cover from the demons in the storm.

"*Do you know which beam is the beacon?*" I asked Salanraja. My hackles were raised so high that the skin underneath them itched slightly.

"*It's the one Corralsa is still heading towards. Now quiet, Bengie, I need to concentrate.*"

"*Ben, and don't you forget it.*"

"*Will you shut up?*"

I growled, but I knew it wasn't a good idea to aggravate my dragon any more.

Squinting, I could very faintly make out Corralsa's lumbering form through the grey. She was still following a beam of light which seemed to shine a little brighter than the energy coming upwards from the concealed Manipulators.

More shrieks came from the murk, and I turned my head every which way, trying to work out from where the next attack would come. Not wishing for my staff to get tangled up in Salanraja's corridor of spikes, I rushed up to her head and crouched there as I dug my claws into her leathery skin for purchase.

I summoned my staff bearer. The gigantic white hand hovered beside me in the air, tracing Salanraja's path. Suddenly, it charged forward and plunged my staff into my mouth. I willed energy into it as a bitter warmth rushed to the back of my tongue.

I was now ready to defend myself if another bone dragon attacked. My muscles thrummed, and I found myself wishing Esme was nearby so that she could augment me with her white magic again. In truth, I had no idea how she was faring on the other side of the formation. For all I knew, she could be plummeting on Gratis toward the mountain floor.

There came another shriek, and I turned around to see a bone dragon charging at Ta'ra and Kada from behind. It let out its horrible purple flame, which got so close to my allies that it looked like it would melt them to pieces. I didn't hesitate to react.

Without thinking, I summoned energy to my staff. A red beam shot out, of the same type that I'd used to defeat Astravar. It hit the bone dragon right in the centre of its mouth. The skeletal creature roared and dove away, giving Kada time to veer to the side.

Ta'ra looked down at the bone dragon, then she edged closer to Kada's neck. But the dwarf dragon didn't have a saddle for her to hide behind. She was exposed, without even a spell to protect her. Perhaps if she were still a Cat Sidhe she could have transformed into a fairy, flown off Kada's back, and defended herself using her innate magic. But she could do so no longer.

A rumble came from below me. A jet of flame from Salanraja's mouth cut through the fog, lighting the path ahead. Other flames lit up the sky in front and behind me, all the dragons breathing fire in unison.

"*What the whiskers are you all doing?*" I asked Salanraja.

"*The flame will help us guide each other. We cannot be separated right now.*"

She was right, I guess. I could now clearly make out Corralsa. But it would also make us more vulnerable. Everything had a cost.

I traced the beams of light moving through the fog like searchlights. Now that we were visible, they converged towards us. One was getting awfully close, and so I turned my staff towards it, ready to see a bone dragon emerge.

It came in from the front this time, at an angle. It spewed forth a purple flame directed right at me on top of my dragon's head. I met the flame with a purple beam of dark magic. It didn't damage the bone dragon, but it cut through the acidic flame, making it pass to either side of Salanraja and me. Ahead of me now, and to the other side of our formation, I could see the glowing crystals on my comrades' staffs, and the spells flaring out from them.

Shards of ice shot out from what I knew to be Rine's staff, and just ahead of him Ange cast out vines in an attempt to entangle the bone dragons, to slow them down. Purple beams shot out from the opposite wing of the formation. Right behind it, I saw a swirling pattern of white light.

I let out a breath that I hadn't realised I'd been holding. Seeing the white magic told me that Esme was still alive. The whole display looked quite impressive, and would have rivalled any of the firework shows back home. But we still weren't attacking the Manipulators, and so we had no way of defeating the bone dragons.

Suddenly I noticed two beams of light, more distant than the others, both converging towards the front of the formation.

"*Salanraja,*" I said. "*Corralsa – she's in danger.*"

"*I see it,*" Salanraja said.

There came two ear splitting shrieks from up ahead. A huge, bellowing roar followed that could only be Corralsa's. The fog seemed to clear, to make way for the jet-black dragon's massive form as she fell. Her flames cut a path through the murk in front of her. I squinted to try and make out where Max was crouched on her back, but the dragon was falling far too fast. The mist swirled behind them, swallowing them completely from view.

"*She's hit,*" Salanraja said. "*She needs to land.*"

"*Whiskers.... What do we do?*"

"*We need to protect the dog, remember?*" Salanraja said. "*We cannot let the warlocks get the Key to the Sixth Dimension.*"

And just like that, the decision was made.

16

DOWN IN THE VALLEY

Corralsa led us down towards a high valley, and she landed right in the centre of a snow-filled plateau. Her right wing looked charred, a large section of it having lost its shine. Max was sitting on her head, gazing through the fog ahead. His tail thumped angrily against Corralsa's scales, and I could only imagine his fierce snarl.

As we descended, I tried to follow the light that I knew was Alliander's beacon, but that soon became lost in the fog. I guessed the White Mages knew nothing about the ambush. I tuned my ears to the galloping of hooves; the sound gradually grew more distant and then I lost it entirely, only for it to be replaced by the whistle of the bitter wind that was buffeting my ears. I flattened them against my head, growling.

Salanraja brought us down to land a short distance away from Corralsa. The rest of the dragons came down around the same time, and we soon formed a protective ring around Max's shiny jet-black mount. Together, we riders climbed down from our dragons, and formed a wider perimeter, keeping our staffs drawn.

Strangely, the storm didn't seem to be so strong down here. Perhaps the surrounding peaks – which I couldn't see through the grey – were blocking the wind. The dragons had stopped using their flames as beacons, and we ceased pumping magic to our staffs, meaning their crystals no longer glowed. The last thing we wanted was to alert our enemies to our position.

I could still hear the shrieks above, and see the pillars of light floating towards us, converging inwards. Soon enough we were surrounded by a good two dozen Manipulators, their bone dragons hovering obediently above the streams of white energy that fed them from their hosts' spectral staffs.

They didn't seem to want to attack, and so we held still as well. It was freezing; my paws stung against the snow, and I could swear that if we didn't get moving soon, I was going to get frostbite.

I heard a rustle from my right, and I turned to see a shadowy form marching through the fog, his cloak whipping behind him. As he came closer, I noticed his cloak and much of his attire was a bright scarlet. I was sure I wasn't the only one who shuddered when I heard his pompous voice.

It was Arran – the Warlock Prince – but he was dead. Seramina had killed him; I'd seen it with my own eyes.

His voice carried over the wind, almost as if he could control the weather.

"The thing about being able to walk between the dimensions, is that you can see across all of them. A storm in one is a sunny day in another, and you can stay in one and glance across the rest. I could see all of you clearly from the Faerie Realm, and the funny thing is you didn't have a clue I was watching."

It took a short while for anyone to say anything. I think we were all in shock.

Seramina was the first to speak: "Arran." Her jaw was low, and her voice had a hint of relief in it. But this soon turned more venomous as her eyes narrowed, and she turned towards him. "I thought I'd killed you."

Before her face had spun out of view, I could swear I'd seen fire burning at the back of her eyes.

Arran opened his arms, a wide, toothy grin on his face. "So take another shot. As soon as your magic leaves your staff, I'll move to another dimension, and you won't hit anything. This ability to move between dimensions makes me invincible. I can do whatever I want."

Whiskers, it made perfect sense when I thought about it. We'd all been so blind. Back during the battle at Capitut's Tomb, Arran had grabbed hold of the key to the Sixth Dimension for a very brief moment. It had glowed in his palm before a blow to his hand caused him to drop it. He must have activated it, giving him Capitut's Brand – a marking that was also on Max's flank and allowed anyone who wore it to walk between the dimensions.

The knuckles clutching Seramina's staff were white. She didn't cast any magic at him. But her jaw remained tight.

Don't do anything, Seramina, I willed her in my mind. *We need to see how this plays out.* I didn't say anything out loud, not wanting Arran to hear it, but I hoped Salanraja would relay this to Seramina's dragon Hallinar, who would in turn relay it to her.

Meanwhile, Max was barking from his safe position up on Corralsa's head. "Old master bad! Old master bad!"

Arran chuckled, and he clucked at the dog and clicked his fingers. "Here doggy, doggy. Why don't you come back to your master? It can be just like old times? Wait—" he let out a loud guffaw "—how incredibly ironic. My old pet has bonded with my old dragon."

Esme stepped forward slightly. "I think the dog would like to kill you right now."

Arran turned his smarmy smile towards the white cat. "Ah, and more legends come to pass. The dragon rider cat who's also a white mage. I might have known that King Garmin would select more cats to aid him. Particularly after the Dragoncat over there defeated Astravar in such a momentous battle."

"It is none of your business why he selected me."

"No, I guess it's not. But as legend dictates, you are the creature who is meant to try to fell me in mortal combat, much as the Dragoncat was meant to fight Astravar. Why is it we warlocks always end up fighting cats? Who designed it?" He cocked his head. "Before you say it, don't give me that 'fate' nonsense. All of you rely too much on your crystals and their premonitions. It's a wonder anyone gets anything done."

Esme had her glowing staff clutched in her mouth, but white magic couldn't kill directly. If the Abyssinian was powerful enough, and I didn't doubt she was, she could summon a phoenix, or a wind-dragon, or even a spirit-chimera, and send them after Arran. But Arran was powerful himself, and we were surrounded by a good army of his creations.

Whiskers, Arran must have also been the one who summoned the demons here, which meant that he had control over them, since nothing could leave the Seventh Dimension without being shackled to a master. If we killed him, that bond would be broken, leaving the demons free to unleash chaos upon the land. They would start, I was sure, by eating all of us.

Besides, I'm sure everyone here actually wanted to know what the whiskers was going on.

"*You've grown wiser, Ben,*" Salanraja said in my head. "*I thought I was going to have to explain all of this to you.*"

"*Is there anything we can do, exactly?*" I asked Salanraja.

"*Keep it quiet. Corralsa is working this one out. She wanted us to check that no one was going to do anything rash.*"

"Is she talking to Arran at all? Because those two used to be bonded."

"No.... We were all tricked over that. All this time, Arran kept Corralsa under a dark spell, and because of that she never officially bonded with him at all."

I sat, waiting. Ta'ra, I noticed, had crept around Kada's legs and come closer to me. She wasn't close enough to feel my warmth, but she probably still felt safe at least knowing I was in her vicinity. Even if the look on her face was telling me she never wanted to speak to me again.

It was Asinda who eventually stepped forwards to represent us all. I guessed being a Prefect made her the most senior amongst us. "You'll never get away with this, Arran. Captain Alliander of the White Guard was among our escort. She'll be on her way back to us, and she will bring you to justice."

At that, Prince Arran let out a loud cackle. The weather responded with a thundering roar. "My stepsister, yes – well, let me tell you about that."

Arran looked upwards, then clicked the fingers on his free hand. His staff glowed, and several tight purple beams shot out of his crystal in various directions. They hit some points in thin air, which glowed bright blue. From these, several crystals tumbled to the ground.

It was as if the air had suddenly freshened. The storm in the immediate vicinity faded, as if we'd entered the eye of it. The wind was calm, but still we could see a wall of grey cloud surrounding us, bellowing out its might from all directions.

"This is an invention of mine, you see. I call them wind golems, and they control the weather in the vicinity. There's much you can learn when you can visit whichever dimension you will on a whim. As for your friend Captain Alliander of the White Guard, I'm afraid she shall remain lost in the storm."

Asinda clenched her jaw. "Tell us what you want, Arran," she said. "Because it sounds like you came to negotiate."

I hadn't thought it possible, but Arran's grin stretched even wider. He turned his head upwards and pointed his staff at Max. "Give me the dog. That's all I ask – then I shall let you leave alive."

"And what happens if we don't?" Asinda asked.

"Why, as soon as my demons arrive here – and they are admittedly a little late – then I shall order them to dispose of you. Demons, they say, enjoy the taste of living flesh, and I'm sure they will leave quite satisfied. Dragons are quite a delicacy to them."

"And if we give you the dog, what's to say they won't do so anyway?"

Arran smirked. "Dear ... Prefect Asinda, is it? You surely have known about me for a long time. After all, we are family. Pray tell me, have you ever known me to break my word?"

Asinda hesitated, and she wasn't the only one who seemed to suck in a breath. For a long, silent moment, it was as if everyone around me didn't breathe at all. Eventually, Asinda swallowed hard. I tracked the lump as it travelled down her throat.

"Very well. You shall have him."

Arran raised an eyebrow. "Really? It was that easy? You're not going to put up a fight?"

"As you've already made perfectly clear, *Prince* Arran. We cannot win this." She looked up at Corralsa and she gave the dragon a brief nod.

With a grumble, Corralsa lowered her head. On it, Max stood on all fours, his tail wagging and his long, wet tongue hanging low. He looked ready – eager in fact – to return to his master.

My whiskers twitched nervously. Something was wrong. We couldn't be giving up this easily.

"*What's going on, Salanraja?*" I asked.

"Be quiet, Bengie. This is the moment. It's going to take precise timing, and you must not interfere."

"What do you—" My thoughts were interrupted by a high-pitched scream that came right from Seramina's mouth.

"No!" she cried. "You cannot have him!" She had turned slightly so I could see her face. The fires were burning at the back of her eyes, and terror lurched in my chest as I watched her thrust her staff forwards, the crystal on its tip glowing white.

An intense beam shot out of it and hit Max right on the flank. An explosion of white intensified, filling out until I couldn't see anything but spots before my eyes. When it had all faded, everything was as it had been before, except Max was no longer sitting on Corralsa's head.

In fact, he was nowhere to be seen....

17

WHO'S THE BOSS?

"You foolish, imbecilic child!" Arran screamed. "What did you do?"

"I killed him," Seramina said, her voice dry and remorseless. As the fires raged at the back of her eyes, her hair seemed to flare out around her. An amber glow suffused her face where shadows would normally hide.

Her voice no longer had its usual meekness, but commanded enough power to topple kingdoms. "I destroyed the dog and the key to the Sixth Dimension with it. I cannot let you take it, whatever the cost."

The wide grin had left Arran's face. His features tightened, and he pointed his staff at Seramina.

The teenager also had her staff pointed forwards, and her pose was taut. She glared at Arran, the wind whipping around her face, the fire continuing to rage at the back of those once-grey eyes. In a battle between the two, I'd place my bets on the teenager. But if she destroyed the former prince, we'd still have to face the demons, who were impervious even to dark magic. Arran, at least, would be able to call them off.

My heart pounded in my chest, my stomach was in knots, and the same question kept whirling around in my head. I'd warmed to Max, and though he was often annoying, he'd become like family. Had Seramina really killed him? I guess she'd had to make a difficult choice, because the cost of handing over the key to the Sixth Dimension would have been much greater than the value of Max's humble life.

Meanwhile, somewhere in that storm that whirled and thundered in the distance, the unicorns would still be galloping, their beacon shining up into the sky, believing that they were directing us towards relative safety.

Everything was silent as Arran and Seramina continued their staring competition. Meanwhile I watched the demons approaching from behind us, my breathing getting shallower and my tail lashing in the snow. The wind seemed to roar even louder. Each grumble of thunder and flash of lightning made me want to scarper for the hills. But if I ran anywhere, I'd be struck down by one of Arran's magical creations.

The clouds had shifted further to the north. Or rather, they had parted to make way for a new convoy, headed by the slithering demon snake, Apopis.

Everyone but Seramina and Arran's magical creations turned their head towards the snake, who lifted himself on his tail as if held up by magic and raised his head high. The legends were true – Apopis was massive – as long as fifty men stacked one on top of the other, if not longer. He let out a hiss, sounding like an orchestra of a thousand blenders. The demon foxes fanned out, and the demon dragons circled around his head, all of them dwarfed by the Overlord of Overlords.

When Apopis spoke, his voice boomed like a foghorn.

"WARLOCK! WHERE IS THE KEY TO THE SIXTH DIMENSION?"

Arran craned his head upwards as he tapped his foot against the ground. "She killed the dog," he said, and he thrust his staff at Seramina. "She destroyed Capitut's Key in the process!"

"IMPOSSIBLE! THE KEY CANNOT BE DESTROYED."

"But I saw it. She cast her magic right at him. This one is powerful, you know. Have you seen what she can do?"

I'd never heard a snake growl before, but that was exactly what Apopis did. I guessed a beast as tall as a skyscraper would make completely unexpected noises. "YOU'RE TELLING ME THAT YOU WERE BEATEN BY A TEENAGE GIRL?"

Arran frowned. "She destroyed the dog, I'm telling you!"

The gigantic snake cocked his head. Lava dripped from one side of its lips, and sizzled when it hit the ground. "HOW DO YOU KNOW?"

"Because I saw it with my own eyes!"

"THEN YOU MUST BE MISTAKEN. THE KEY CANNOT BE DESTROYED!" Apopis repeated. "I'VE HAD ENOUGH OF THIS NONSENSE, WARLOCK. YOU KNOW THE DEAL: IF YOU FAIL TO RETRIEVE IT, THEN YOU WILL DIE YOURSELF."

Arran's face displayed a snarl. He turned his staff up towards Apopis' head. "I summoned you into this dimension, and so you are unable to do me harm. You want to see my power? I command you to lower your head to the ground, Apopis. O Overlord of Overlords, bring yourself down to my level."

Apopis let out a screech that was so high-pitched, I swear it could have split atoms. The ground trembled violently enough to cause an avalanche. Still, the beast's resistance was futile. Under Arran's command, Apopis still brought his head downwards. It crashed onto the ground inches below the rise on which we stood. A tuft of snow landed on my back, and I tossed it off with a shiver.

"Perhaps you were a fool to let me summon you here, Apopis, because you know you are now bound to serve your summoner." Arran cackled, then tossed his head, his oily hair whipping backwards. "Demon dragons – land on the ground just in front of Apopis in a nice, neat row."

From the sky, the demon dragons let out another of those boulder-splitting roars, and then plummeted down. Their landing was so violent that the snow underneath them exploded upwards, as if they had just crashed into a puddle of water.

"That's the spirit," Arran said, clapping his hands. "Now what about the foxes? What can they do? Oh, I know. There's a tune in the Fourth Dimension that I'm quite partial to. Demon foxes, I want you to yip the melody to Ride of the Valkyries. You know how it goes: dum de dum dee dum, dum de dum dee dum, dum de dum dee dum, dum de dum dum."

I knew the tune as well. My master back in South Wales used to play it on his fancy speaker system at an incredibly loud volume whenever the mistress went out to visit her friends. There was something so menacing in those notes that it always sent shudders down my spine. But the way the foxes yipped and howled out the notes just made it sound ridiculous.

"ENOUGH!" Apopis screamed.

Arran slowly turned his head back down to him. "And what will you do to stop me?"

"YOU FORGET WHO I AM. I HAVE AGENTS FROM THE SECOND DIMENSION SCATTERED THROUGH THE WORLDS, AND IF THEY SAW WHAT YOU WERE DOING RIGHT NOW, THEY WOULD SEND AMMIT TO ENACT HER REVENGE."

Ammit ... I remembered that name. During my brief excursion to the Seventh Dimension, I'd been attacked by a demon hippopotamus, of all creatures. It had threatened to take me back to his mistress, Ammit, for supper. Fortunately, instead of doing so, he'd missed his charge at me and tumbled right off a ledge into a sea of lava. Since that terrifying experience, I had no intention of meeting Ammit, whoever she was, and I'm sure Arran didn't either.

"Ammit..." Arran said, and he cocked his head as if considering.

"Imagine the largest crocodile you'd ever seen," Apopis said. "Then remove its body and replace it with that of a gigantic lion, and add the hindquarters of a hippopotamus for a powerful charge. You haven't met fear until you've met Ammit, I tell you."

Arran put one hand on his hip, then scanned around a little, still keeping an eye on Seramina. "So what will you have me do?" he asked. I could smell his sweat, despite the cold.

"Go and get the dog back, and this time do not mess it up. Because Ammit will not let you survive to tell the tale of your failure."

Arran sighed and gave a mocking bow. I only needed to blink, and he had vanished into another dimension. In pursuit, no doubt, of Max.

At the same time, he released his hold on all the magical beings that surrounded us. Crystals fell from the Manipulators to the ground, and the bone dragons hovering high above them crumbled to meal. The cloud to the north suddenly dissipated, and I caught the glint of sunlight off a distant crystal as it tumbled to the mountain slope.

The snow-capped peaks of the mountains once again towered over us, reflecting their magnificent whiteness into the pale sky. Apopis stared at the spot where Arran had vanished for a moment, then spoke in a voice that sounded as if a troll had decided to use two granite boulders as cymbals in an orchestra.

"So," the giant demon snake said, "what are we going to

DO WITH THE REST OF YOU?" A flaming forked tongue lashed out of his mouth and then retreated again.

Presently, the five demon dragons lifted into the sky. At the same time, the demon foxes yipped out another lament of the Ride of the Valkyries, this time seeming to both enjoy it and hit the right notes.

Then, like pools of magma flowing over the snow, they charged.

18

A FAIRLY FAIRY RETREAT

"*B en. Orders from Corralsa. Get on my back now.*"

"*Are we retreating?*"

"*We most certainly are. Better this than our remains being left smouldering in the snow.*"

I didn't waste a moment. I scrambled up Salanraja's back, taking a quick look around to check that everyone else had done the same. Ta'ra was a little clumsy getting up onto Kada, and she slid down the white dwarf dragon's tail. From beneath us, the yipping of Ride of the Valkyries cut through the wind. The foxes were getting quite good at it. I shuddered as I imagined Ta'ra getting swarmed by a hungry pack of the creatures. I couldn't let that happen.

"*Don't go yet, Salanraja,*" I said.

"*What? Are you mad?*" She tossed her head back to get a view of our approaching enemies.

"*Ta'ra – she needs help.*" The other dragons had lifted off at this point. Ta'ra was closer to the demons than we were, so she would be eaten first. Of course that was unacceptable, especially after everything we'd been through together.

I almost leapt off Salanraja to push her up. Whiskers, I would have even carried her by the scruff of her neck up onto Salanraja's back to make sure she escaped okay. Fortunately, on the second try, she clambered up to the spike at the top of Kada's neck successfully and held on with her claws and all her might as Kada lifted off.

The dwarf dragon got ahead of us. Meanwhile, one of the demon dragons was getting too close for comfort.

"Go…" I screamed to Salanraja, and I did so out loud.

Salanraja roared, kicked back her hind legs, tucked in her front legs, and took off into the sky. A demon dragon was already upon us. It let out its own terrifying roar, causing Salanraja to shake violently. Out of its mouth came that high-powered vortex, designed for sucking in anything that got in its path. I felt my hackles getting tugged towards it.

Last time I'd encountered one of these demon dragons, I'd climbed upon its back and used my gift of all languages to confuse it, by commanding it to return to the Seventh Dimension. It had worked, for a while, but now there were five of these demon dragons. Meaning our only option was to flee.

"*Go faster,*" I screamed in my mind at Salanraja. I probably said it at the top of my voice in my own native language at the same time.

"*I can't…*" she said. "*Ben – we're doomed!*"

"*No!*" I said, and I glanced back at the demon dragon's massive red glowing eyes. I swallowed hard. "*You're right! We're doomed.*"

We were caught within the vortex's embrace. Even the mouth of the creature itself was large enough to wrap around Salanraja. I swear that as we got pulled towards it, the gap became bigger. Rumour had it that the larger of the demons could distort space time, among other things.

I saw stars before my eyes. I still had my staff clutched within my mouth, and I considered shooting out some dark magic at our assailant. But my mind was in such a panic, I'd forgotten even how to perform the most basic of spells.

My muscles went slack, and I was ready to accept my fate. But a beam came right past the left side of Salanraja's corridor of spikes, a bright white one that hit the demon dragon right on the bridge of its nose. It had come from Seramina's staff. She flew past us broadside on Hallinar, her eyes aglow in furious concentration.

I don't know what spell she'd cast; I'd had no idea that any magic could affect a demon. Driar Lonamm had told us in our lesson, *A History of the Seven Realms*, that demons were immune to magic, much as Max apparently was. But the visions in the Ghost Realm had shown us an image of Seramina displaying power more vast than any magician I'd ever met.

The demon let out a terrible shrieking sound, not too dissimilar from the sirens on police cars that I used to hear whizzing down the main road in South Wales. Time seemed to slow for a long second, and the demon dragon's head glitched and split in two. This also split the vortex into two halves, side by side, creating an eddy that Salanraja instinctively dived into. She pulled herself to a halt beneath the demon dragon, which barrelled past us.

Salanraja corrected herself, and then adjusted her course to follow Corralsa as before.

I moved back up onto my dragon's head, my breathing heavy. I glanced back at the demon dragons who were in pursuit of my comrades. Somehow we'd managed to evade them.

Meanwhile, in the midst of the battle, Seramina seemed to be the one who was running the show. On Hallinar, she was weaving around in elaborate patterns, casting all kinds of spells that I'd never seen before. Every time a demon dragon got too close, she would swivel around and shoot out a new kind of magic. She never killed them, but she kept disrupting their flight paths. She really did have raw, unbridled power. Maybe I'd been wrong; maybe she wouldn't end up destroying the world, but one day saving us all.

"*What do we do now?*" I asked Salanraja.

"*Corralsa says we have allies here to help us. Gracious demons, get yourself somewhere safe, Bengie. I don't want to end up throwing you off.*"

"*Ben!*"

"*Just shut up and do it!*"

I growled and clambered back down to a safe spot behind Salanraja's neck, feeling powerless. "*So who are our allies?*" I asked, once I had a vantage point with much lower visibility.

"*Look out for the golden glows...*"

My ears perked up. "*Fairies?*"

"*Yes, Bengie ... fairies.*"

A glance over my shoulder, and I saw that the demon dragon that had attacked us had resumed its flight path and was heading straight towards us. This time, it was coming in slightly from the left, and within thirty seconds or so it looked like it would ram right into us.

I looked out for the tell-tale golden glow of fairies nearby, praying for some sign of their assistance. We were moving so fast, though, that we hadn't a chance of seeing their golden, wispy forms. But when I squinted my eyes, I caught sight of something big developing in the distance. A portal opening.

"*I see it, Ben,*" Salanraja said.

I looked back at the demon dragon again. Seramina had sent another bolt of purple energy at it, knocking it off course. But it hadn't budged much, and we really didn't have much time.

In front of us, the fairies were a little easier to see, now I could see them summoning the portal. They had sped ahead of us, and were spinning around to create a disc shape in the air, up and down and around and around. A light emerged at the centre of the shape they had formed. A white glow, that faded to green, and seemed to split time and space in front of us.

Every single dragon adjusted its course, heading for the emerging portal.

But behind us the demon dragon was so close, and I felt the pull of the vortex again. Corralsa passed through the portal, then Ishtkar and Quarl, then Kada, with Ta'ra looking like she was about to fall off her back. Seramina and Hallinar passed through next, leaving only Gratis and Salanraja approaching the portal. It seemed Esme was holding her dragon back to ensure that I got through.

But the pull of the vortex coming out of the demon dragon's maw was too strong.

"*We can't make it,*" I said.

"*Maybe some magic, Ben … just try something.*"

I still had the staff in my mouth. "*I don't know how.*"

"*Don't overthink it.*"

Whiskers, she was right. I spun around with my staff, imagining that I was as powerful as Astravar, as Lasinta, as Seramina. A glow came from behind me. A beam of white light hit me on the side, filling me with strength.

"*Esme … is she helping me?*" I felt weak.

"*Just focus, Ben.*"

"*Yes.*" All of a sudden I surged with power, my muscles coursing with strength. I cast a spell out of my staff. It hit right in the centre of the demon dragon's mouth. Then I don't know what happened, but the sky behind me filled with red.

Intense heat washed over me. Something was burning: the smell of charred fur; a ferric taste at the back of my tongue; it was impossible to breathe. I was going dic.

I was wrong, though, because as soon as I passed through the portal, I breathed fresh air. The way to the First Dimension quickly closed behind us, and Salanraja tumbled down towards the ground.

In the corner of my eye, I saw Gratis coming in to land too, and a white cat like an angel sitting on top of him.

Salanraja landed, sending me rolling over long, fresh grass. The aroma of flowers surrounded me. I tumbled right into the claw of the largest non-demon dragon I'd ever seen, his scales shiny and the colour of bronze. He also was the fiercest dragon I'd ever seen, smoke rising from his nostrils and a permanent expression of anger stretched across his brow.

Matharon, I thought, and it was the last thought I had before I blacked out.

19

CAT HEALING

I awoke to the rough sensation of a cat's tongue licking the fur on my face. My body felt warm, as if I were back in my litter, nestled up against the warmth of my mother once again. A second lick came, and I found myself purring deeply.

Whiskers, I could do this all day.

"Esme?" I asked, as I opened my eyes.

My vision was blurred at first, but it didn't take me long to notice the eyes I was looking at weren't sky blue, but bright green. My heart sank, and I know it shouldn't have, to see Ta'ra looking down at me.

She took a step backwards. "I'd hoped that the first name you'd mention when arising from a coma was mine. You used to say my name often upon awakening, once. But I don't suppose you remember."

I tried to stand up, but my legs felt like lead, and I collapsed once again.

"Take it easy, Ben," Esme called from somewhere to my side. I turned and saw a beam of white light trickling out towards me from the gnarled oaken staff in her mouth. She was sitting on the branch of a cherry blossom tree, almost camouflaged behind the pink fluffy flowers. Captain Alliander stood to her side, supervising.

"Focus on the spell, Esme," she said. "Healing is the most delicate of all the magics. You must give it your utmost concentration, otherwise you may find that what you've intended to heal has ended up atrophying instead."

"I know what I'm doing," Esme snapped back. I really don't know how she managed to talk so easily with that staff in her mouth. Whenever I tried, it came out as a sequence of ms, ps and bs. "I've learned all of this on my own through years of studying the crystals."

"And what makes you think you're so powerful?" Alliander asked. "You seem to think you're of a higher station than the members of my White Guard, whom I have been training for years."

"Because I'm the only White Mage in your entire kingdom who can perform such magic without the help of a unicorn."

"Yes – someday in the future we'll have to study why that is."

As if to snap my attention back towards her, Ta'ra gave me another lick on the brow. This time she pressed so hard it felt like she wanted to shear my fur off. "My tongue can work better than any of that magic. If only I still had my fairy magic, I would have healed you a lot quicker than any of those White Mages can. Particularly that cat."

The thought didn't occur to me until later as to why, if that was the case, the fairies hadn't healed me already. I mean, we were in the Faerie Realm after all.

"Ta'ra..." I said. "I didn't mean to hurt you. But now you're behaving like a kitten who has just been stung for the first time by a nettle."

"What? Are you saying you don't need me anymore?" She leaned in for another lick, but I ducked my head underneath her.

She ended up butting with her forehead, and I yowled out because my head was tender there. "Stay still, Ben. You need be healed."

"Will you leave our patient alone, Initiate Ta'ra?" Alliander called out. "You're not doing him any favours."

Ta'ra arched her back and showed a sharp set of yellow teeth as she hissed at Alliander, then she stormed away. Admittedly, I'd not seen Ta'ra behave like this for a long time. She'd reverted back to being that angry cat I had met when I'd first entered Dragonsbond Academy.

I lifted myself up onto my legs again. This time I managed it, though my paws felt like they were being pricked by a thousand needles. The fur on my sides had gone slightly grey. I scanned the immediate vicinity for Salanraja, amidst the verdant trees, many of them full of pink, and purple, and yellow flowers. Pollen hung fragrantly in the air.

Though we were in the Faerie Realm, there were no fairies to be seen. Maybe they'd all flown away in fear of the dragons. Salanraja had told me many times that fairies and dragons often didn't see eye to eye.

If they were afraid of any dragon, it had to be the giant beasts – namely Matharon and his Guardians – that towered over us all. The sun glinted off Matharon's shiny bronze scales. The other dragons also had a metallic look to them, except I noticed they all had dull grey patches in places, as if they'd been charred hundreds of times. They'd probably seen many battles. After all, they were rumoured to be hundreds of years old.

The unicorns stood a little distance away from the dragon guardians, their heads lowered to a clear lake from which they were drinking water. With the exception of Tanni, who stood near Alliander, each unicorn had a White Mage positioned next to it, grooming their coats or manes with a soft brush. I wasn't sure when the fairies had saved the unicorns and White Mages, but I guessed they hadn't become lost to the storm as Arran had surmised.

A good hundred spans away from them lay the rest of the dragons – that is, the ones who weren't part of Matharon's entourage. They had all clustered together on the long grass, quite a distance away from their former dragon teachers. Together, they sunned themselves like lazy dogs on the sward, their croons letting out a rhythmic rumble that seemed to harmonize with the birdsong and the soft swish of the wind through the trees. I don't know why I'd never considered settling in the Faerie Realm, because it really was the most beautiful of them all.

The Dragonsbond Academy students were also here, much to my relief. They were sitting on some giant, wide-brimmed mushrooms with sturdy stalks. There were no sign of any fairies, and I knew that because fairies had a distinct smell to them. This was undetectable to humans, of course, but any species with superior noses couldn't miss the faint mix of lavender and thyme with a faint pinch of jasmine.

"*Salanraja...*" I said in my mind, elation washing over me as the white magic coming from Esme worked the knots out of my muscles.

Salanraja turned her head. "*Ben.... I didn't hear you awaken.*"

I was thirsty and the grass was fresh with drops of dew. I licked off enough to at least wet my tongue, then I raised my head again. "*What happened?*" I asked my dragon. "*I don't know why I passed out.*"

"*It wasn't the demon dragon. When you were sprayed by that bone dragon before, some of its magic got onto your skin. I'm sorry, Ben.*" Now Salanraja apparently wanted to get into my good books again, because she'd resumed calling me by my proper name.

"*It's not your fault.*"

"*But I flew too close to it.*"

"I think it's more like it got too close to us. We couldn't see it through that storm, remember?"

"I guess..." Salanraja said, and she looked up at Matharon and trembled. It made me wonder if she'd had a telling off from her former mentor for what had happened to me. I could just imagine Matharon lecturing her on how a dragon should always protect its rider.

While Salanraja had been speaking in my mind, Captain Alliander was continuing to patronise Esme. Part of me wanted to go and stick up for her. But another part didn't want to make Ta'ra even more angry. Whiskers, I'd never engaged in any of those human marriage ceremonies, or the like. Why was she being so difficult, anyway?

I turned my ears back to the conversation between Alliander and Esme, having nothing more to say to Salanraja.

"I think you can stop now, Esme," Alliander said to the cat. I rolled my gaze towards them.

"Why? He seems to be enjoying it."

"Because if you use too much magic, you'll tire yourself. Preserve your own spirit first, then the animals that augment you, then finally focus on who you can help. That's one of the first things you'll learn in the School of the White. It's one of our central foundations, which you must internalise before you become one of the White Guard."

"But I won't ever study there," Esme said.

"Why ever not? I've seen your talent. You'd be an asset to King Garmin and the Kingdom of Illumine."

"Because I've seen my destiny, and the School of the White isn't part of it."

Captain Alliander sighed heavily and looked away. "Whatever you say." She turned her attention back to the warm beam coming from Esme's staff. "But really, that's enough. He has enough energy to recover."

"Just a little more ... I like helping the Dragoncat."

"No. You will stop, and that's an order."

I heard Esme growl. "Fine!"

The warmth in my side cut off, and Esme disappeared behind the flowers on the tree. Shortly afterwards, she slinked off the trunk and slid towards me. She touched her nose to my cheek.

"Thank you, Esme," I told her in the human language, because we didn't have any words to express the same in the cat language.

"You know such expressions make no sense in our tongue."

"But I just—"

"Be a cat, Ben, remember. Because that's what and who you are." Esme touched her nose once more to my cheek, then she slid past me and stalked over to a spot in the grass that was covered in sunlight. I looked back at Ta'ra, who narrowed her eyes and gave me a hateful look.

I turned my head away, feeling tremendously guilty about how I'd made her feel. But then, I wondered why the guilt had hit me at all. It wasn't a feline emotion – it was a human one.

Besides, I didn't have time for all this drama. I needed to work out how to save Max, whom Arran was currently chasing across the dimensions. So I went over to talk to the one here who exuded the most authority, and that wasn't Captain Alliander.

20

THE GREAT AND MIGHTY
MATHARON

Matharon's breath was even more odorous than Salanraja's. He towered high above me, not willing to lower his head to my level. Rather he rolled his eyes downwards, his pupils seeming to lead into a cavernous darkness.

Behind and around him, the trees and bushes waved gently in the breeze. It almost looked as if they were worshipping these massive dragons. Butterflies alighted on the rims of pollen-filled flowers and stopped a moment as though to watch; bees buzzed lazily through the sticky air, but even they seemed to keep their distance from this beast whom all the dragons had learned to fear.

The gigantic Matharon spoke in the dragon tongue, and so he must have already known about my ability to speak the languages of all creatures. His voice was so deep and rumbling that it sent shudders down my spine.

"Yes, cat," he rumbled. "Is there anything I can do to help you?"

I took a deep breath. Surely, I'd come this far, and I wasn't about to get eaten by this gigantic dragon now. I replied in his own language. "I've heard tales of your might. I thought you might be able to help in a certain matter."

Behind me I heard Salanraja groan. She clearly didn't like me talking to her old dragon tutor, as if I were breaking an unwritten code.

"Is that right?" Matharon cocked his head proudly. Already the menace had left his brow, and his nostrils seemed to be emitting a little less steam. "So tell me, young one. What have you heard?"

It took a moment for me to realise that perhaps this dragon wasn't as scary as he'd first seemed. I let out a friendly chirp. "I've heard that you strike fear into everyone who meets you, that every dragon trembles when they hear your name, and no creature born of this land would dare go up against the mighty Matharon."

"Well of course." If dragons knew at all how to smile, then the curved line stretching from one of Matharon's cheeks to the other might be the closest they could get to one. "Dragons need to first encounter ferocity before they learn to become fierce themselves. Don't you think?"

It was strange. Despite Matharon's reputation, his size, and the sheer strength evident in his muscles, he actually seemed quite friendly, or at least he did to me. Maybe the mighty dragon also had a soft spot for cats.

"I do—" I said and hesitated, thinking how to phrase my question. Matharon automatically filled the space with idle small talk – if rampant boasting could be called that.

"Did your dragon ever tell you the tale of how I defeated a pride of chimeras with my wings completely paralysed by their venom, and one of my forelegs maimed? That's quite a tale, that one."

"She didn't..."

Matharon looked at Salanraja and shook his head slowly. "What about the time that I used my dragon flame to divert a forest fire and save an entire town, five villages, and seven hamlets from burning to the ground?"

"Nothing about that, either."

"Really, I've been telling that one to my students for years. Tales get better with each retelling, don't you think?"

"They certainly do," I replied, as I imagined all the stories that the cats across the Illumine Kingdom must be telling about me right now. As if to compliment me, a cooling breeze brushed over my ears and a blackbird chirped out a song from a nearby oak.

"So, what tales has your dragon told you about me exactly?" Matharon asked.

"Well..." I took a moment to think exactly how to phrase it. "My dragon told me that you're rather scary."

Matharon looked up at the branches behind him and dished out a grunt. A slight jet of errant flame came out of his nostrils with it. He turned back to me. "It's good to know that my act still works in my old age. Every teacher needs to take on a certain persona. Students can't learn who you really are in the flesh, or you'd never have a private life."

"Perhaps," I said, not knowing how else to respond.

I guessed the rattling sound that came out from between Matharon's teeth was meant to be a laugh. "While we're dishing out compliments, young one, I've heard all about your exploits from the other dragons. You know, you're quite the hero amongst dragonkind. They're always talking amongst themselves about the cat who could defeat warlocks."

"Is that, right?" I raised my head high. I glanced back at Salanraja, who had her head buried in her front claws. Clearly this conversation was embarrassing to her, but I had no idea why.

"*I didn't tell you about that because I didn't want to bloat your ego,*" Salanraja explained, her voice sounding rather meek.

"*Not now,*" I said. "*I'm enjoying this conversation.*"

"You would be. Unfortunately, I'm not."

"Yes..." Matharon continued, and he scratched one of his front claws through the ground, leaving a long mark in the soil. He must have found some rock underneath because his claws made an irritating screeching sound. "We teachers are always looking for fine role models to use as teaching material, if you get what I'm saying? That's why I've even started telling my students some tales of your heroism – putting my own spin on them, of course. It's amazing how a creature so small can achieve so much...."

"Really? What stories do you tell?" I decided selectively not to register the part about being small. Size is relative, anyway, and being big often makes you clumsy. I'd know – I'd transformed into a chimera often enough.

"Well, there's that one where you ripped a crystal from where it was wedged between two plates of chitin on the back of a terrifying creature, hence removing the life force of the giant magical spider that wanted to eat you. Then, there's the time you clambered right onto a demon dragon's back and singlehandedly commanded it to return to the Seventh Dimension. Oh, not to mention your fight against the demon cat as you rammed it, while in the form of a chimera, into a shield wall conjured by none other than the student protégé High Prefect Lars. It's very rare for a mortal to defeat a demon, you know. I think, perhaps, you and I are amongst the few in this realm to have done so."

"Well, when you put it that way ... I guess I am a mighty hero."

Salanraja groaned even more deeply, and I could feel the embarrassment at the pit of her stomach as if it were in my own.

Perhaps my words had come out meekly, because the old dragon didn't seem to hear me. Instead, he wanted to continue his diatribe around heroism. I began to wonder if he were partially deaf.

"Of course, the bigger the demon, the harder they are to kill. That's why those demon dragons are virtually invulnerable, and rumour has it that the demon overlords can only be overthrown by another immortal. But just now, I heard you got close to killing one of those demon dragons, didn't you?"

Whiskers, I'd almost forgotten about that, and it had only just happened.

"What happened to it in the end?" I asked.

"It survived," Matharon said after a moment. "But perhaps another blow into its mouth from your dark magic might have sent it back to the soil where it belongs. I've heard you hold raw power in that staff of yours. A remarkable power, indeed."

For some reason, that caused a cold shiver to run through me. I mean, I should have been proud of my progress as a mage. But then I still didn't know what I was doing. I kept saying that Seramina had no control, but the spells I was able to cast seemed to have no direction. None of us could be relied on if we had no consistency. Still, as Matharon pointed out, it was good to put on a persona.

"It's nice to know that other species appreciate what a mighty cat I am," I said. "Because I am a Bengal, descendant of the great Asian leopard cat and the mighty George."

"Oh, I wouldn't call you mighty," Matharon said, as he lowered his massive head towards me. "But you are certainly *plucky*. Anyway, what can I do for you, little one? You said you came over to ask a question."

"Plucky?" I asked, a little offended.

"It's a great compliment. To persevere against all odds – that's the impression I've had about you from your stories."

Ah well, I couldn't have everything. I also realised that Matharon and I had spent so long comparing our courageous exploits that I'd completely forgotten why I'd gone to talk to him in the first place.

"Matharon," I said, "tell me something. We need to rescue a Sussex spaniel with the key to the Sixth Dimension from a dangerous warlock who is chasing after him. You're in charge around here, right? Do you know where we might find him?"

Matharon turned his head towards Alliander, who strolled over to us with her unicorn, Tanni, in tow. "If you're asking Matharon what we do next," she said. "We're currently waiting for a delegation from the fairies."

"I was asking that, in fact," I said.

"Once again, you're not trusting authority to handle things the right way. No respect for the chain of command. You students at the Academy are all the same."

I decided to selectively ignore her complaints. After all, I'd heard it all before. "What delegation?" I asked instead.

Alliander raised her eyebrows. It took a moment for me to realise that I'd asked the question in the rumbling dragon language, and so I asked it again in the human one.

Captain Alliander put her hand to her chin. "The fairies know something we don't, apparently, but it's top secret amongst them. The ones who rescued us from the mountains near Bestian Academy don't know much. So they scooted off to retrieve someone who does."

I let out a soft chirping sound, which if performed by a human might have equated to a sigh. A large fly got awfully close to my nose, and I took a swing at it with my right paw. Alas, I missed.

I turned back to Alliander, who was watching me with a smirk on her face.

"We're always waiting," I complained. "I don't like waiting."

Her smile widened until it became unnaturally lopsided. "Well, you won't have to do so for long at all, this time. Because it looks like they're already here."

She cocked her head towards a shimmer coming from a clearing in the forest. At first I couldn't make them out, but when I squinted my eyes, I noticed several glowing wisps floating towards us.

21

FAIRY DELEGATION

Alliander left Matharon and me and strode with Tanni over towards the fairies. She beckoned a couple of White Guards over to join her – namely Carmista and Larmend. I'd never really thought about it before, but I guessed those two must be her lieutenants.

The fairies drifted down to the ground and hovered just a couple of feet off it. One of the tiny golden wisps was further forward than the rest of them, and a golden mist started to seep out beneath it. It spread downwards, until it covered a space the height and span of a human.

A man with handsome features and dark, oiled hair stepped out of the cloud. Prince Ta'lon, the fairy I liked the least out of all who dwelt in the Second Dimension.

Every fairy could take two forms – one of a tiny glowing human with wings, and the other of a regular-sized human. The second one, naturally, they used when they wanted to converse with real humans.

Ta'lon had been Ta'ra's former betrothed while she was a fairy, long before Astravar had turned her into a Cat Sidhe. Then once she'd spent most of her life as a cat, he'd hardly visited her, and I'd heard Ta'ra moan about him a lot. It wasn't until I'd convinced her that I was a much better companion that she'd stopped talking about him every day.

Since then, I'd long imagined that Ta'ra and I would spend the rest of our lives together. I'd probably even told her so a few times.

But then Esme had entered the scene, and right now I wasn't sure what I thought at all. Perhaps a tomcat like me could have two companions. After all, I was a Bengal, descendant of both the great Asian leopard cat and the mighty George, as well as a vanquisher of warlocks. Surely I didn't deserve to have my life be so complicated. Cats' lives were never meant to be this way.

As soon as Ta'lon's human feet touched the ground, Ta'ra's ears twitched, and she gave him a slow blink. She sniffed the air, then with a soft mewl she picked herself up and sauntered over to him. Just before she reached him, she turned her head to look back at me with her green eyes for a moment, but she didn't hold my gaze for long.

I directed my ears forwards so I could listen in on their conversation.

"Ta'lon, it's been too long," she said. "For weeks I thought I'd never see you again. Now we meet again in the Faerie Realm. Our home."

Ta'lon, when he looked down at the black cat, didn't seem to recognise Ta'ra at first. Then he took a deep breath, and closed his eyes as if remembering. "Ta'ra ... I'm sorry. You know how it is. Royal life leaves you so busy."

"I can imagine, and really, I forgive you. Just tell me you're happy to see me again, Ta'lon. I can't tell you how much I've pined for you."

Whiskers, her words were getting under my skin, and I didn't know why. She was doing it on purpose as well. She wanted to aggravate me, and I'm sure she knew I was listening.

I felt a warm body brush up next to me. Esme stood there, staring at me, her pale blue eyes blinking softly. "Ben…"

"Not now," I said. "This is important."

Esme growled, but she didn't move away. Instead, her long ears pricked up, and she also turned them towards the conversation. She cocked her head as she listened.

Ta'lon, meanwhile, was studying Ta'ra with his mouth open.

"So," Ta'ra said. "Are you pleased to see me or not?"

Ta'lon looked nervously to Alliander. I half expected Alliander to tell Ta'ra to shut up. But instead she had a sly grin across her face. Ta'lon turned back to Ta'ra.

"Ta'ra, we've been discussing you in the palace recently. But one thing you must remember is you're still a—"

"Don't say it," Ta'ra interrupted. "I know I look different to the creature you remember. But I'm still the same fairy underneath it all." She raised her gaze towards a shimmer of light coming from the distance – presumably from a lake that was familiar to her. "This is still my home, despite everything. I still miss you, my prince."

Ta'lon looked to the side a little, but he didn't break eye contact with Ta'ra. "For a long time, I've wanted to talk to you about that, actually. When we get a chance in private, will. But I must address my duty first."

Ta'lon turned to Alliander. "I have travelled here from Faerini city, on orders of King So'ta of Faerini. We have heard of your plight, Captain Alliander, and have come to provide aid."

Alliander nodded. She stepped forward and shook Ta'lon's hand. "I know that your realm already knows about the dog who carries the Key to the Sixth Dimension. The warlock Arran is alive, it seems, and he carries Capitut's Brand. Arran is currently walking the dimensions to find the dog, and we fear it is only a matter of time before he seizes the key for himself."

Ta'lon lowered his head. "I have heard all this, and more."

"Is there anything you can do? I've heard there is magic in the Faerie Realm that can traverse the dimensions, and we all know it's much easier for fairies to open portals than humans."

"Do not worry," Ta'lon said. "For I have already discussed this with So'ta, and plans are currently underway."

"What plans, exactly?" Alliander asked with a slight bow of her head.

"We have sent a second representative to discuss matters with our Oracle Fairy, and she already wants to speak with you."

"An Oracle Fairy? I've heard of no such role."

"It is not the business of humans to know the workings of our society. But the Oracle Fairy is a very special one of our kind, and there is none like her in this realm. She can see across time and space. Legend states that she lives across the dimensions, and she has knowledge of the past, the present, and the future. We must go to her at once."

Alliander turned to survey us all. "It would take an awful long time and much organisation to get us moving."

Ta'lon smiled. "Not all of you. The Oracle Fairy only wants to see you, Captain Alliander of the White Guard." He glanced up at Matharon and shuddered. "Because she won't warm well to a dragon, particularly that beast ... destroyer of worlds."

It sounded like there was a story in there that Matharon probably didn't want to boast about. I made a mental note never to ask.

"Very well, I shall go," Alliander said. "You will be my escort, I presume."

As they spoke, Ta'ra was turning her gaze between Ta'lon and Alliander, almost as if she were studying to see if anything was between them. Which was stupid, of course. I mean, Ta'lon was a fairy and Alliander a human. Then, as soon as Alliander mentioned the word escort, she leapt in like a panther to stand between them.

She had forgotten, again, that she'd lost her ability to grow to ten times her size, and she ended up looking up at Talon, mewling. "You're not going to leave me after all this time apart, are you, Ta'lon? We've got so much to catch up on."

Ta'lon looked down at her and a smile stretched across his lips. He called over to one of the wisps gathered close beside him. The wisp floated over and turned into a human beneath a golden plume of smoke. She was female, with flowing golden locks, red cheeks, and high cheekbones.

"This is Countess Fa'ite, and she will be your escort, Captain Alliander. Now, with all due respect, I have some business with our fairy princess here."

Alliander raised an eyebrow at him, then nodded. "Lieutenant Carmista, you are in charge in my absence," she said. As she mounted her unicorn, the fairy, Fa'ite, turned back into her golden wisp form. She led the way, with Alliander riding Tanni in tow.

I couldn't help but wonder what 'business' Ta'lon had with Ta'ra. It seemed that Ta'ra was also awfully curious, and I could hear her purring so loudly that she could rouse a rabbit burrow.

"So, what is it you have planned, my prince?" she asked.

Ta'lon had a knowing look in his eyes as he knelt down and stretched his palm towards her, a long fingernail touching her fur. "A taste of what is to come," he said, and he blew some golden fairy dust onto her.

Golden light flooded the forest for a moment. Then Ta'ra suddenly took on a wisp-like form, becoming tiny as she once had been. Together, both fairy and former fairy dashed off into the woods.

I growled to myself as I watched them go. Ta'lon had glamoured Ta'ra to make her look like a fairy human. But she was kidding herself; anyone who knew anything about alteration magic knew that once you became a creature like a cat, there was absolutely no turning back.

No matter how strong the glamour, Ta'ra would always be a cat.

22

TO TRUST OR NOT TO TRUST

I couldn't believe my eyes. Ta'lon had turned Ta'ra into a fairy. Of course she wasn't a real fairy – he'd just made her look like one. What was he up to? The thought of those two together made my whiskers twitch.

"Why are you so troubled?" Esme asked from her place by my side.

I looked down at her wide blue eyes, and for just a moment I forgot about Ta'ra. But it only lasted a moment, until the guilt of how I'd treated her came back to me. I'd betrayed her trust by running off with Esme.

Yet Esme was so slender ... such a fine specimen of a cat ... compared to her, Ta'ra was...

"Dragoncat?" Esme asked. "Are you jealous? You know well that such emotions don't belong amongst our kind."

I groaned deeply. "Those two don't belong together. Ta'ra still loves that fairy prince, and he doesn't love her. He just wants to relive some memory from his past. But he's leading Ta'ra on. He won't want this forever."

"What does it matter?" Esme cocked her head.

"Because that fairy—that Ta'lon will just hurt her. He always does."

"And didn't you just hurt her before?"

"I—" I took a deep breath. "You made me do that."

Esme displayed no reaction to my accusation; her face remained blank. "Did I really?" she asked. "I merely offered help when you needed it."

"I don't know ... but she won't want to come back, now. This could be the last I ever see of her."

Esme studied me, blinking slowly. "You know, I wasn't sure that I believed it at first, but what I've heard about you from the other cats at Dragonsbond Academy is true."

"And what's that?"

"The more time you spend with humans and dragons, the more anxious you become. But don't worry; I can help you defeat this anxiety."

Esme spoke the last word with a lot of breath in it. I suddenly caught a whiff of our last meal, and I remembered our excursion, fighting wargs then hunting rabbits. That filled me with a little confidence. Perhaps if I stayed near Esme I wouldn't need Ta'ra after all.

"I think we should take advantage of Alliander's absence," Esme said, and she turned to look into the forest. "It's time for some more training, I think. I want to show you what you're truly capable of."

I raised my head slightly. "I would like that."

"I'm sure you would. But this time you shall have company. There are three dark mages here, and I need to teach each of you how to bridle your power."

I studied her for a moment. She was different from most cats I knew; she never seemed to flinch at sudden noises, she was never scared, and everything she did was as if she'd planned it all out before. I hadn't believed it completely before, but maybe she was able to foretell the future.

That thought caused doubts to creep into my mind, and a shiver ran down my spine as I wondered if I could trust her at all. Maybe she was like one of those evil siren creatures Salanraja had told me about so many times, that lulled you to sleep with their song, and never let you wake up again.

Yet there was a certain brilliance in her eyes, and behind them I imagined I could see worlds. For some reason I did trust her, and my instinct was usually right.

"Well, what are you waiting for, Dragoncat? Do you want to train or not?"

She turned away, and I gave her a soft chirp. I started to follow her towards Seramina and Asinda. To make sure I was ready, I stopped on the way to sharpen my claws on the bark of a stray birch.

✤ 23 ✤

TRAINING

Esme led Seramina, Asinda, and me into a glade ringed by beech trees. Catkins had recently fallen from the canopy, forming a soft carpet. A cooling breeze came off a lake that shimmered on the far side of the glade, water lilies bobbing up and down lazily on the surface. A couple of swans watched from the centre, but they soon seemed to think us no trouble and returned to ducking their heads under the water for food.

Behind the swans, a waterfall greeted us with a roar. When I had visited the Faerie Realm with Ta'ra – when she was still a Cat Sidhe and had the limited ability to turn into a fairy – she had explained how a waterfall like this could hide a city. It was possible that this was all a glamour.

I'd learned a lot about how different types of magic worked since then, and somehow I knew this scene was genuine. There were no fairies watching us from hidden dwellings, in other words.

"Once again we put our trust completely in a cat," Asinda commented to Seramina as we walked towards the lake.

"She's more than that," Seramina said, glancing down at Esme.

"What do you mean?"

"She knows things that normal folk wouldn't know. It's as if … I don't know, I think that the crystals have chosen her for a mission."

Asinda raised her eyebrows. "Like they did with Max?"

"Yes … but it's more than that. They've selected her for something, and trained her for a long time. She knows more about destiny even than I. It's as if she's studied every single possible thread of the future, and she knows exactly what's going to happen next."

"Then perhaps Captain Alliander doesn't need to go and see the Oracle Fairy after all," Asinda said with a chuckle.

Seramina sighed. "It doesn't matter. Things will unfold as they're meant to unfold."

They walked a little ahead of Esme and me, and they spoke quietly as if they thought we wouldn't be able to hear them. The humans around me often forgot that cats like me, Esme, and Ta'ra had superior hearing. Or perhaps they just chose to selectively ignore it, so they could at least pretend to have a little privacy.

"That will be far enough, humans!" Esme called out, just before we reached the coarse sand leading into the water. Asinda and Seramina turned around. I continued to step towards them. "You too, Dragoncat."

Her voice was laced with such command that it instantly halted me. Esme strode to the centre of our circle, and she called upon her staff bearer. It lunged forward to place her gnarled staff in her mouth.

Asinda and Seramina also drew their staffs. But while Seramina seemed to hold hers quite lightly, Asinda's muscles were taut, and she focused intently on the Abyssinian.

"What makes you think you have the authority to bring us out here like this, anyway?" Asinda asked.

"Did you see anyone trying to stop us?" Esme replied.

"No," Asinda said, "but you're acting as if you are in charge here, and you're only an Initiate of Dragonsbond Academy, while I'm a Prefect…"

Esme raised her head to look up at Asinda. Her pale blue gaze met the mistrusting look in Asinda's cornflower eyes. I'd seen that same expression on Asinda's face many times when she'd first met me. For a while, I'd thought she'd wanted to kill me, but she'd later told me that this was just how she was. In other words she had trust issues, and from what I'd learned of her past I didn't blame her.

"Did you want to come, or not?" Esme asked.

Asinda's eyes narrowed. "I wanted to—"

"Of course, there's no need to answer that question," Esme said, studying her paw. "I know what you want, Prefect Asinda. But for now, you're curious enough to want to expand your powers, and someone is presenting you with that opportunity now. Am I wrong?"

Asinda lowered her staff. "No, I guess…"

"Good. Now, Seramina, perhaps you would like to dispel the glamour."

Seramina's eyes widened in alarm. "You want me to reveal the portal?"

"Yes, that's exactly what I want. For too long, the fairies here have lived under an illusion of safety. But if one of the aeriosaurs on the other side of this portal were to discover the gateway by chance, the fairies would have no defence against them. Soon they'll need worry about this no more."

I remembered aeriosaurs, and the memory of them made my hackles shoot straight up. We'd fought an army of them on the enemy's side in the same battle where I'd cast the final beam of dark magic to bring down Astravar.

"Esme, what are you talking about?" I asked. She showed no sign of answering, so I turned to the blonde-haired teenager. "Seramina?"

"There's a portal to the Fifth Dimension right here," Seramina said. "The fairies must have known about it and glamoured it on both sides."

"And though they can't see it physically," Esme added, "all it would take is for one beast to accidently fly through the portal, and others would follow. Fairy magic can't destroy aeriosaurs, and so this realm would soon perish."

"So how did it get here in the first place?" Seramina asked.

"I don't know," Esme said. "We need to remove the glamour and then do what we can to close it. Unfortunately, that will also mean we'll have a battle on our hands."

"But revealing it will immediately draw the aeriosaurs into this realm," Asinda argued.

Esme chirped in delight. "So isn't it fitting that fate should bring three dark magic users here, and a mentor to show them the way? We shall defeat the aeriosaurs and close the portal. But first, we need to dispel the glamour. Initiate Seramina, could you do the honours?"

Seramina's eyes remained grey, and she shook her head slowly. "I shall not do such a thing." She sounded confused. "I cannot be responsible for unleashing destruction."

Esme let out a growl. "Very well. I guess it's also fortunate that glamours are part of the School of the White." Before any of us could react, she tightened her jaw around her staff. It glowed a bright white and shot forth an orb of white magic.

It travelled slowly yet surely towards a target between the two girls and I. Seramina watched it, the fires now burning at the back of her eyes. I'm guessing she could have dispelled that orb and stopped Esme. But another part of her seemed to want to let things be.

Asinda, on the other hand, had her jaw clenched tight. Her staff was once again pointed at Esme, the crystal on its tip glowing faintly.

Her eyes tracked the orb, but she also didn't make a move to block it. Probably she didn't know how.

The orb hit its target, resulting in a burst of light as bright as an exploding sun. A shockwave washed over me, sending me tumbling backwards with a yowl. I stood up and braced myself against what felt like a torrent of water coming off the flare. It had a cooling, calming effect, but this was white magic after all, and it wasn't meant to hurt.

The spell soon subsided to reveal a man-sized oval ring surrounding a shimmering purple landscape. It was a portal into another realm – the Fifth Dimension.

There came a terrifying shriek, and then out of it swarmed two dozen creatures of nightmare: their beaks as sharp as buzzards', their wings like bats', their size as large as dragons.

If we didn't act fast, they would rain terror upon this land.

24

THE LURE

The Fifth Dimension was a complete enigma.

The only person who seemed to have known anything about it had been Astravar. Apparently no one but he had ever managed to open a portal to this mysterious realm, and the only creatures we knew to come from it were these aeriosaurs which we were now preparing to fight. The only way to defeat them was through dark magic, and very few of us in any of the realms knew how to wield such power.

Astravar had taken control of my mind when I'd first acquired my staff from the Ghost Realm. He'd used it to open a portal and release the aeriosaurs. With them under his control, he'd planned to conquer the Illumine Kingdom. That plan had ultimately led to his demise.

Now Esme had revealed a portal to the Fifth Dimension that had existed since whiskers knows when. The two dozen or so aeriosaurs now swooped around the opening, letting their ear-piercing shrieks fill the sky. The portal's very existence hinted that someone must have come here to open it, which made me wonder even more whether Esme was actually on our side.

Given Asinda's reaction to the whole situation, I clearly wasn't alone in my suspicions.

"What do you think you're doing?" Asinda yelled, sending a purple beam after one aeriosaur that hit it on its flank. The flying beast disintegrated into ashes as the rest of the creatures scattered.

"Now is not the time for questions," Esme said. Her staff was already aglow, her eyes closed as she directed her attention towards another spell. "Focus on our enemies."

"If you don't close the portal, more will come out," Asinda objected.

"I know! Now let me focus." As light flooded through her staff, Esme's fur also lit up, sending a soft sheen over her body.

Another orb came out of the head of the Abyssinian's staff, this one with a slightly greenish tint to it. It travelled upwards before reaching an apex, where it bobbed for a moment then floated gently downwards, like a balloon. As it found a resting position over our heads, a fountain of green light washed down from it.

The aeriosaurs, who had now started to fly away from us, screeched a second time. They turned around in the sky, drawn towards this ball of energy – whatever it was.

"*Bengie,*" Salanraja's voice echoed in my head. "*What's happening out there? Where are you?*"

"*Aeriosaurs,*" I said. "*Esme released them from the Fifth Dimension.*"

"*She did what? Why? And how did she open a portal?*"

"*The portal was already there. Esme just removed the glamour that the fairies had cast to hide it.*"

"*Now that's a secret that the fairies have kept well hidden ... I wonder how long it's been here. It doesn't matter, I guess. We should bring aid at once,*" Salanraja said.

"*No!*" I snapped back. "*You know that you'll only get yourselves into more danger. You can't harm these aeriosaurs, remember? Only dark magic can.*"

Salanraja paused, and for a long moment I waited for her to say something, wondering if she'd finish her thought before the aeriosaurs attacked. "*I guess you're right,*" she said eventually. "*Just stay safe, Ben, will you?*"

"*I will.*"

I turned my attention back to the glowing ball that had gained in strength.

"It's a lure," Seramina said, her eyes now two bright burning embers. Her hair whipped up about her as she cast energy into her staff.

"This is stupid," Asinda said. "A lure will just draw more aeriosaurs out of the portal. Close it, Initiate Esme, and that's an order."

"An order?" Esme snapped her head towards the Prefect. "You are unused to giving those, aren't you?"

"What do mean?" Asinda asked through clenched teeth. "Explain yourself."

"I know well how you've always stood in your boyfriend's shadow, letting him make the decisions for you. After all, he is High Prefect Lars – the man whom everyone admires. But meanwhile your brilliance has been crying out inside you, waiting for you to open yourself up and let it in. You must let yourself shine, Prefect Asinda, and that's the lesson you need to learn."

"How do you know all this?" Asinda asked. "How can you presume to know anything about what I feel – about who I am inside?"

Esme ignored the question. "You are your own person, and you and that boy Lars won't last forever. I have seen the future, and your destinies lie upon different paths."

"You have seen one of many different possible futures," Asinda corrected.

"Not this time," Esme said. "Sometimes, prophecies converge to a singular point, which is how you know you're dealing with true destiny. Somehow those who use dark magic walk much narrower paths than normal folk. Take this moment, for example, and what is about to unfold. There was no other way for it to happen."

Whiskers, I liked Esme, but I didn't like her being mysterious in this way. Particularly when we were staring danger right in the face. "So, are you going to tell us what's going to happen?" I asked.

"No, Dragoncat... You shall have to find that out for yourself, and unfortunately you are not going to like it. But it will all work out for the best in the end."

I wanted to ask more questions, but the aeriosaurs – which had flocked to Esme's orb of light like flies to a naked lightbulb, had now worked out that Esme had only placed it there to trick them. They tried to pull away, attempting to spread far out into the Faerie Realm. But once they reached a certain distance, which wasn't very far at all, the light pulled them back again.

Once they realised their plight, they started to call out into the open sky, clearly communicating amongst themselves. They formed a much narrower swarm and swooped down towards us, approaching fast. I clenched my mouth around my staff, and as the warm energy flooded into it, I braced myself for battle.

25

AERIOSAUR FIGHT

Seramina let off the first shot, the fires now raging at the back of her eyes. She took down two aeriosaurs at once, then rolled out of the way of a third aeriosaur diving towards her. She turned just in time to send out another beam after that one. It disintegrated upon impact with her spell.

I traced a fourth aeriosaur swooping down from the sky. It was approaching Asinda, and about to attack her unawares from behind.

"Asinda!" I screamed. "Duck!"

Her legs buckled, and she crouched. But she wasn't fast enough, because the screeching bat-buzzard creature rammed into her with its beak, sending her tumbling along the ground. Asinda plunged her staff into the earth to stop her roll. The aeriosaur landed and tossed its tapered head backwards. Asinda lifted her weapon upwards and pointed it at her target. Just as the creature was bringing its sharp beak downwards to devour the Prefect, Asinda's beam hit the creature on the bridge of its nose. It vanished in a whiff of acrid smoke.

"Thanks, Ben," she said, and she sent off a second beam that for a split second I thought was aimed at me. It passed right between my ears and hit an aeriosaur that I hadn't clocked coming down behind me. Had Asinda not saved me, the beast would have landed right on top of me, crushing me to the ground.

"Thank you," I replied.

"Let's call this one even. Now focus!"

I growled, then turned my attention to the aeriosaurs above. I kept my staff clenched in my mouth, the magic from it burning the back of my tongue. My body felt alive, and I thirsted for power. It was said that if I overused this dark magic then it could consume me … I would become like Astravar, or worse, if worse were at all possible.

I turned my head as I traced the aeriosaurs above, searching for a target. More of the beasts had emerged from the portal, and they were gathering into a massive flock. It was so thick that I had no idea how many were in it. It cast a shadow over all of us, almost completely blotting out the sun.

"They're going to attack en masse," Seramina said, her voice calm.

Asinda on the other hand, didn't sound calm at all. "We can't defeat that many with our magic alone…"

"I can," Seramina said. "But I don't know if I can do it without also eliminating my friends."

"I will show you how to defeat them without any casualties," Esme said. "That's what I'm here for. The crystals have sent me to keep you three young dark mages under control. But you must work together and limit the amount of power you draw so it doesn't consume you."

"So do what you have to do," Asinda said, her voice still laced with panic. She was panting heavily, sweat matting her red hair against her brow. "You need to do it now!"

Asinda screamed as the aeriosaurs gathered in an attack formation. The flock swooped downwards, looking as if a giant had thrown a massive black javelin through the sky.

Esme turned her head towards it casually. She spoke softly and slowly, as if we had all the time in the world. "Okay, Dragoncat. First cast a spell like I showed you. Demonstrate to the other two how it's done."

She turned her staff towards me, and out shot that beam of white light. My staff felt even hotter in my mouth, and the energy raged through me. I shut my eyes and imagined the beam flowing out towards the flock. Power surged outwards, and I could taste death upon the air. The aeriosaurs shrieked as they perished in numbers, and I continued the beam, putting everything I had into it.

But I couldn't hold it forever. Soon my legs felt like jelly and the power dissipated from my staff. I collapsed to the ground, dropping my weapon from my mouth. I looked upwards to see that I'd defeated the head of the formation, but the rest of the aeriosaurs were still coming in fast.

"Your turn, Initiate Asinda," Esme said, and she turned her white magic away from me and directed it at the Prefect. It hit Asinda in the chest, where her heart was, and I could faintly make out the outline of it beating – heavy and fast. But as the light filled her with white magic, her heart seemed to slow. It beat now, not with panic, but with raw and controlled power.

Asinda's lips curled into a snarl, the light from the beam that was coming out of Esme's staff reflecting off her teeth. Fire ignited at the back of her eyes as her gaze snapped onto the approaching swarm. Then came a brilliant and wide purple beam of magic from her staff. It hit the aeriosaurs dead centre, casting a wide disc of energy that seemed to swallow our enemies whole. The air was filled with the acrid stench of decay, and the chorus of angry screeches grew even louder. Asinda's snarl transformed into a wide grin, as if relishing the surge of power. But at the same time, her breaths quickened, and her legs started to shake.

"She can't hold it much longer," Seramina, who already had her staff braced and ready, called out. She looked down at Esme, her eyes wide with greed. "Give me the power." The fire at the back of her eyes burned even more brightly than it did in Asinda's.

"A little longer," Esme said. "She still needs to learn the extent of her power."

"Then I shall claim it for myself," Seramina said, and she drew her staff to her chest and clutched both her hands around it. Her legs braced, she drove the butt of the staff into the ground, and the glow of the crystal on its tip grew so quickly that I knew what was about to happen.

Seramina's skin glowed also, and with so great a brilliance that she no longer seemed human. Rather, she looked as if she belonged to an ethereal realm, a spirit that had come to judge us all. Her hair whipped around her shoulders and her eyes expressed such serenity that it seemed dangerous. Faint cracks developed in her skin.

She'd cast a spell like this in Capitut's Tomb, when we'd fought Arran and Lasinta. It had wiped out an entire army of magical creatures and had saved us all. But if it weren't for Lars' shield protecting us, it would have destroyed us too.

"She's losing control," I cried out to Esme. "You need to stop her."

It happened so fast: Asinda's knees buckled and she collapsed to the ground. She dropped her staff, and it rolled away from her. At the same time, the energy coming out of Seramina's staff exploded, sending out a shockwave that felt like it was searing off my fur.

And it would have done so, had Esme not spun her staff around and cast her beam of white magic right at the crystal on Seramina's staff. White light met white light, casting jets of energy underneath the emerging shockwave, which cooled like water to the touch. They washed down over us, healing any damage that Seramina's spell had caused.

The light faded, and behind the blur in my vision, I could make out only clouds and the sun wheeling around the sky. The aeriosaurs had been defeated – together, we had wiped them all out.

Seramina stared upwards, an expression of shock upon her face.

I turned back to Esme, who was looking up at Seramina as if concerned. "How are you so powerful?" I asked. "Who exactly are you?"

But she didn't have time to say anything, because I heard a voice from inside the portal to the Fifth Dimension that was still standing there, leading into the purple realm. It was gruff and familiar, and it barked.

"You beat the wargs!" Max said. "You beat the flying smelly wargs!"

Whiskers, Max and his wargs. One day I vouched to myself that I would show him what a warg looked like. Given the number of powerful creatures he'd named 'warg', I doubted he'd be particularly impressed.

26

DIFFICULT DECISIONS

Admittedly, Max had been the last character I'd expected to see standing on the other side of that portal. In fact, I hadn't expected to see anyone at all. I thought that one of us would close the thing, Alliander would return from the Oracle Fairy, and we'd work out what we had to do next.

But the Sussex spaniel sat there, framed by a soft purple light. He was panting happily, his tongue lolling low, and his nose lifted high. "Come on! Come on!" he called in the dog language. "Bastet wants to see you. She wants to see you now."

"Max, what are you talking about?" I barked back at him in his own language.

But he had already turned around and was disappearing into the purple night that seemed to lie behind that portal.

"Was that Max?" Asinda asked.

"None other," I replied.

"What's he doing there?"

"I don't know," I cast a glance at Esme, who showed no sign she meant to reveal anything new. "He said that Bastet wanted to meet us."

"Who?" Asinda asked.

"In my world, in an ancient civilisation known as Egypt, there was a goddess who was half human, half cat. Her name was Bastet." When I had gained the ability to speak the languages of all sentient creatures, I had learned random trivia like this. I was a walking encyclopaedia….

"You mean like that sphinx creature we met outside Capitut's Tomb?" Seramina asked.

"More powerful than the sphinx," I replied. "And hopefully she won't have an affinity for asking stupid riddles that don't have any proper or logical answers."

"And what would this Bastet want?" Asinda asked.

"I haven't a clue. I didn't even know she existed."

"So I guess we follow him, right?" Seramina asked with a shrug.

"Are you mad?" Asinda said. "The Fifth Dimension is teeming with aeriosaurs. They'll skin us alive."

"Max seemed to have survived it," I pointed out. "Maybe all the aeriosaurs have gone."

"Meanwhile, we have no clue what's on the other side. We need to close the portal now!"

Really, I wasn't sure what to think. We had, after all, come on this mission to protect Max. We needed more information. "Esme, would you care to tell us what's going on? You seem to have all the answers around here."

Instead of eliciting a reply, my words seemed to spur Esme into action. She leapt through the portal to the Fifth Dimension. She paused there for a moment, sniffing the air on the other side of the portal with her pink nose. Then she turned back.

"Pounce first, ask questions later," she said. "Are you coming?"

I growled. Most times that I'd jumped through an unfamiliar portal, I'd landed in danger.

Seramina didn't seem to be so cautious. She shrugged, and with her staff held out in front of her she stepped through the portal. "No sign of aeriosaurs in here," she hollered back over her shoulder.

I looked up at Asinda, who was turning her head between the portal and the path we'd taken to arrive here. I took a step forward.

"*Ben, you're doing it again,*" Salanraja said. "*Heading off into another world without telling me.*"

"*I'm sorry, Salanraja, but we need to save Max here. He could be in a lot of trouble.*"

"*But it's the Fifth Dimension, Ben. No one knows anything about it.*"

"*I guess I'm about to find out. I'll let you know when we return, Salanraja.*"

"*Ben, don't you—*" I leaped through the portal. My heart suddenly lurched and I felt an emptiness in my stomach. Usually the bond between me and my dragon was cut off when the portal closed, but there seemed to be some kind of plane that separated the two worlds that didn't allow for telepathy.

Asinda now had her shoulders turned towards the path from which we'd come. She was about to walk away.

"Prefect Asinda, I will close this portal soon," Esme shouted after her. "You must come with us. You are destined to be a part of this quest."

"And what if I don't ... what if I don't believe you, Initiate Esme, if indeed you are an Initiate?"

"Look, I know your heart is still stuck with your boyfriend back home, but you have to let go in order to grow. You must thrive alone, Prefect Asinda."

Asinda took a deep breath, and then she sauntered forwards

towards the portal. She stepped through it with even more grace than Esme had shown. "Can we close it now? Do you know how?"

"It's already done," Esme said, and she didn't have to cast any magic, because the portal had closed on its own accord, sealing us into the Fifth Dimension. "The crystals themselves decide when to open a door to the Fifth Dimension and when to close one. That's why it's remained such a secret for so long."

"That can't be true," I said. "What about that time when Astravar made me release the aeriosaurs from the Fifth Dimension? The crystals can't possibly have wanted them to be released then."

"But if you think about it, your releasing of the aeriosaurs ultimately precipitated the events that were necessary to defeat Astravar."

Trying to wrap my head around all this destiny nonsense was almost as difficult as trying to understand the links between the dimensions. "So why did the crystals want to bring us here?" I asked. "What exactly is here that's so important?"

"I believe that Bastet wants to show that to you herself," Esme said. "So let's all go after the dog, shall we?"

The sky and the outlines of the land glowed purple, everything else seeming a dark silhouette. In the distance, Max stood on a hill, waiting. Esme strode towards him, leaving Seramina, Asinda and me with no choice but to follow.

27

ESME'S IDENTITY

The Fifth Dimension was purple, but not the purple of dark magic, and it didn't stink of it. Rather, the sky had an indigo hue, and a lilac glow painted the edges of the ground and the outline of every object upon it. The air was fragrant with the softness of nature. There were no intrusive smells to deal with, but rather the natural scent of grass and the distant taste of honey.

All around us the landscape rolled, as I remember it used to in South Wales. It was clearly night here, and so the ground was full of darkness. But the dark didn't threaten as darkness often does. Rather, it seemed to wrap around us like a shroud, and it had a latent and comforting warmth to it.

It was so unlike the Ghost Realm, where we'd been surrounded by a darkness that lacked sensation. There was something about this place that made me feel like I belonged.

Max led us up and down gentle hills, all the while keeping his distance from us. The sound of him panting seemed to trail behind him, and occasionally he would stop, turn his head, and bark to remind us of where he was. But he never let us catch up to him, as if he were worried that Arran was also with us, ready to steal him away to another dimension. Esme also pushed on a little ahead of us, while Seramina, Asinda and I followed cautiously behind.

Strangely, though we had just battled a whole host of aeriosaurs, there were none of the bat-buzzard creatures to be seen in the sky. In my imagined impression of this place, I'd anticipated a whole host of them. I'd expected them to be on my tail wherever we stepped, swooping down from the sky ready to wreak havoc. But the air was devoid of their terrible cries and shrieks. All I could hear was a soft buzzing sound, from no determinate direction.

We soon came to a valley that glowed in soft shades of pink. On closer inspection, I saw that this glow belonged to mushroom stalks that towered up, towards even brighter bulbs at the top that I guessed were their heads. Unlike the mushrooms and toadstools I had known, these heads didn't bloom into the night like umbrellas, but rather tapered out as if they were naturally a part of the stalk.

As we continued across this unfamiliar realm, it wasn't long before I noticed the shadows of creatures following us. They moved just like cats, and it didn't take me long to realise that they actually were cats of all shapes and sizes.

Thin cats, fat cats, giant cats, tiny cats. Cats with long sleek bodies, and cats with short squat necks. Cats that were all puffed up, and cats that didn't have any fur at all. All the breeds seemed to be here, slinking their way around the mushroom stalks, occasionally stopping to roll in the dark shades of grass, mewling and meowing and chirping and making happy sounds that told me that they knew of no better place.

Whiskers, this couldn't be Cat Heaven, could it? But that didn't make sense, because if it were, Asinda and Seramina wouldn't be with us.

I sprinted to catch up with Esme, because I had too many questions, and I couldn't wait any longer to get answers. "We're surrounded by cats," I told her. "I thought this place was only meant to be full of aeriosaurs, but I don't see any of those beasts at all."

Esme stopped a moment and looked up. "The aeriosaurs are still above us, soaring through the darkness. Silently seeking those who might threaten this realm."

I shuddered. "You mean they could still swoop down at any moment and eat us." They'd be perfectly camouflaged against the night, and I doubted we'd even see them coming.

"No," Esme said. "You're of no threat to them now that you've passed through the portal."

"What do you mean?"

"They will hunt down anything that tries to cross into this dimension. But now you are here, you are safe as long as you hold Bastet's approval."

"And what do we have to do exactly, to lose Bastet's approval?"

"Not doing as I say," Esme said with a slight growl.

I looked back at Seramina and Asinda, who were talking softly between themselves. If I wanted I could have picked up on their conversation, but they seemed to just be taking turns reassuring each other that everything was okay.

"So what exactly is the Fifth Dimension?" I asked Esme.

She turned her head to me, purring. "It's my home. I grew up here. Do you like it?"

"You're..." I stopped to think how to phrase it. "I thought you were from the First Dimension. I thought that you'd been bred in the cattery and had grown up in Dragonsbond Academy."

"You thought wrong," Esme said. "I went to the First Dimension from here as soon as you arrived there. My quest, given to me by Bastet, was always to keep track of your journey. Now hurry, Dragoncat; we don't want to fall too far behind."

Ahead of us, I noticed we'd lost Max. All I could see was the shadows of cats, stalking over the rolling silhouette of the hills.

"This way," Esme said, and she turned into an opening – a wide cave mouth, invisible until you were right in front of it. It had stalactites on the roof and stalagmites on the floor, rimmed with a pinkish-purple glow. This made the whole structure look like the mouth of a giant beast, and again I couldn't help but wonder if I'd been a fool all along. Esme could be leading us into a trap.

Perhaps I shouldn't have abandoned Ta'ra – and shown her more respect. I shook my body in an attempt to also shake off these foolish thoughts. Esme had no reason to harm us, surely, particularly given Max was also playing such an eager part in this.

Asinda, too, seemed to be slightly unnerved by all of this. She was walking a little behind me, using her staff as a cane to aid her movement forward. Seramina trailed just behind her, but her staff was strapped onto her back. Esme had again pushed on a little ahead, leading us slowly but surely onwards.

"Are you sure this is safe?" Asinda asked me. She was a little out of breath after she'd caught up to me.

I looked up at Asinda's cornflower eyes. "From what Esme had told us, I think we're probably safer following than getting left behind."

"That's reassuring ... I think." In all honesty, Asinda didn't look so sure.

I let out a friendly chirp, and then I leapt onwards to catch up with Esme. Pounce first, ask questions later, she'd said. I guess it was the best possible philosophy when venturing into the unknown.

As we pressed onwards, I noticed that the other cats were following us. They were slinking down outcroppings in the cave walls and trailing after us as if part of a procession. I'd caught up again with Esme because the questions just wouldn't stop rolling into my head.

"What about all those cats?" I asked. "What are they doing here?"

Esme meowed, as if she was happy to play the part of guide. "They're here to protect. That's what we've always been, protectors. Didn't you know?"

"What do you mean?"

The Abyssinian stopped to study me. "Now I understand what the problem is. I understand why you've lost your catness."

"What are you talking about?"

"You've forgotten the pact between cats and humans. The unwritten rule that is as old as time."

"What pact? You're talking in riddles like a sphinx, Esme."

Esme let off a breathy sigh, closing her eyes as she did so. "What do you think brought cats and humans together in the first place? All that food that they used to give you when you were younger – did you think that was a free lunch?"

"Well, yes," I said proudly. "Cats are so intelligent that we learned to get food from humans for free."

"While in return we hunt the mice, rats, and cockroaches that might damage their crops and spread disease. Historically we hunted the snakes, spiders, and scorpions that might poison them. We brought them comfort in hard times, and in exchange they gave us food."

I meowed in laughter. "I never had to do any of that stuff. Not when I was in my home with the master and mistress in South Wales."

"This explains why the cats in the Fourth Dimension have lost their grace, why Bastet never recruits from there.... You've become so selfish that you've forgotten who you are."

I felt suddenly accused. I growled deeply from the pit of my stomach. "So maybe I used to be a bad cat. Maybe I was selfish. But I've changed: I helped the humans, and I helped Ta'ra, and I defeated Astravar, didn't I?"

"And yet you still expect favours from the humans, without

offering much in return. You feel you deserve to settle down and retire because of your one act of heroism. You think because of your one act of heroism that you are entitled, Dragoncat – am I wrong?"

I lowered my head. "No..." I said. "But surely after all the work I've done, I deserve such things. Don't you think?"

"Why do you feel you deserve anything? Why can't you just live? Why can't you just be the creature that you're meant to be?"

"Because I'm a Bengal—"

"Descendant of the great Asian leopard cat and the mighty George," Esme interrupted. She said it in such a mocking tone that she made it sound ridiculous. "I've seen your future and your past and learned all your lines from the crystals. My mother sent me into the First Dimension to find you and bring you back to her. On the way, she requested that I help you become who you were meant to be."

"Your mother..."

"Bastet," Esme said. "You asked who I am, and where my power comes from. Now you know. Now, follow me down to the river, where we will complete the journey into Bastet's Lair."

The path led off to the right, following a cliff that sloped down to the cave bottom. Esme skulked down it, and out of sight. I moved to the edge, inhaling the cool air coming off the river that ran into the distance. It tasted rich with life, which probably meant that down there it would be buzzing with mosquitoes, and I didn't like mosquitoes.

A canoe sat moored up against the riverbed, a lantern at the stern casting a warm pink light into the dark and gently-lapping water. Max sat on the canoe, barking for us to come on board. Esme had already reached the bottom, and she jumped on next to him with such grace that the boat didn't even seem to rock.

"So we go on the boat, I guess?" Seramina asked, as she peered down from a spot awfully close to the edge.

"It leads into Bastet's Lair, apparently."

"Then what are we waiting for?" Seramina skipped down the path towards the boat.

I looked up at Asinda, who was looking down at the boat and saying nothing. Without further pause, I stalked on ahead, knowing that Asinda had no option but to follow.

28

BOAT TRIP

The canoe drifted down the river. It hadn't even needed a push; as soon as we had boarded, Asinda taking her seat beside Seramina at the back, it had started moving on its own accord.

A faint swishing sound and the way that the boat rocked made it seem as if as if it were being rowed by invisible oarsmen. But there was no sign of any oars hitting the water. As I explored, neither my nose nor my whiskers detected anything out of the ordinary.

The cave wall continued to rise to our left, getting darker and steeper as we went. The wall on the right contained a row of alcoves. Each of these contained large triangular glass bottles, with pink flames at their centres. Light shone out from them, each lantern seeming to strengthen its neighbour, and the whole effect illuminated the rimy red rock and the tiny whitecaps on the water beneath us.

"Those are the souls of all creatures, across the four dimensions," Esme said as she noticed me studying the wall. She spoke in the human language so that Seramina and Asinda could understand her. "Each vessel contains the soul of one individual."

"Souls?" I asked.

"Yes, that is the purpose of the Fifth Dimension. It's the Realm of Souls, and the purpose of everything that exists here is to ensure their safety. Bastet has kept this realm a closely guarded secret because of the value of what it holds within it. But Bastet has read the threads of the future, and she feels safe in letting the four of you come here."

I took a deep breath. The coolness coming off the water was truly refreshing, and I'd been wrong – there were no signs here of any mosquitoes. "Are you telling me a part of me is here?"

"Yes ... you and me, and your friends. But I won't tell you where any of them are. We haven't got time for excursions."

Seramina's brow furrowed, then she shook her head and returned to looking at the wall of souls. Both she and Asinda were mesmerised by the lights inside the jars, which flickered like stars in the sky.

"So which dimensions contain creatures that have souls?" I asked. "And why don't all of them?"

"The First, the Fourth, the Faerie Realm, and this one," Esme said. "Those are the realms of the living."

I stopped to think for a moment. "But what about the Ghost Realm? The Third Dimension?"

"On death, a soul will blink out of existence here and find its way to the Ghost Realm. It is the soul's duty to find its body there and connect it with their entire living past."

"So, what about demons in the Seventh Dimension? Don't they have souls?"

"Demons have never had souls, and they never will. They are born to serve an Overlord like Apopis or Ammit, fashioned from obsidian and brimstone – the fabric of the Seventh Dimension."

"Then what about the Overlords? Do they have souls?"

Esme's gaze trailed into the distance. "They used to. Yet, like the warlocks, their souls were corrupted by *Cana Dei* – the source of dark magic and the plague that roams the Ghost Realm – and they were eventually destroyed. You know about the Pharaoh Warlocks? Some of them became so powerful that they let the stuff consume them. They would have destroyed the First Dimension had Amun-Ra not banished them to the Seventh Dimension, which was a barren world before they went there."

I thought about that for a moment, as I licked some dust off my shoulder. Esme had already mentioned six of the seven dimensions, and it was obvious to me why the remaining dimension didn't have souls. The Sixth Dimension wasn't a physical place, after all, but a gateway between them. The first apparition of the Sphinx had told me that the crystals resided there, which was why you could find a version of them in some form in every dimension.

"This is awfully confusing stuff," I said.

"You can say that again," Asinda said. "It's worse than Driar Yila's lectures on *Manifestations of the Mind*. Probably the reason why no one wrote about this place is that they couldn't come to understand it."

"It's more than that," Esme said. "I've already warned of the danger of encountering your own soul, but if the wrong person were to enter this place, they could steal the soul of any living being. With the right tools, they could murder anyone without them even knowing. It would be as if they'd never existed."

I realised that I was a little thirsty, so I dipped my paw in the water and tasted it. It had absolutely no flavour to it, and yet it was fresher than any water I'd ever known. On our left-hand side, the cliff dropped a little, and I could see the pink glowing outline on the top of it once again. A row of cats sat at the top of the ledge, watching us with their ears pricked up into the darkness.

"What about those cats?" I asked. "Do they have souls?"

"The cats are my brothers and sisters, and they also serve Bastet. Our job is to protect the souls of the living. To make sure nothing ever threatens this place."

"Are you alive?" I asked, my whiskers twitching. In a way I felt like I was playing a game of twenty questions, but there was so much to ask.

"Yes," Esme said. "But any creatures who live here age incredibly slowly. The air in this place is filled with a rich ether that preserves life, just as it keeps the souls safe until they are ready to return to the Ghost Realm."

I was starting to understand it all: protectors of souls, the reason that Esme had brought us here... "Arran," I said, thinking out loud. "All this is about Arran, isn't it? He's after Max's soul."

Just as the realisation washed over me, there came a grating sound from beneath the boat. The hull shuddered, and we banked upon a glistening shore. I peered over the edge to see a carpet of coarse grains of sand, each speck glowing in such a way that I could make out the spaces between them.

Max jumped off as soon as the boat ground to a halt, and he rushed up the beach a little. "This way! This way!" he barked. "Bastet has a lot to tell."

29

THE MAGNIFICENT BASTET

The beach rose into a dense forest of thick tree trunks, except the trees were nothing like those I knew in the First and Fourth dimensions. Though the bark of the trees had a texture to them, and I could touch them and feel their roughness, they didn't seem to have much colour. There was only pink light and darkness.

The trunks led upwards to a canopy of crisscrossing, glowing branches, and very faintly I saw movement. The branches shook, and there came the rustle of needles hitting the ground. A giant panther-like creature leapt down from the treetops, her dark and lithe form camouflaged so well against the night that she was almost invisible.

When she halted, pink glowing lines traced across her outline, giving her definition. The tips of her hairs glimmered spectacularly, and I felt as if I was looking at a creature as old as time. She had ears even taller than Esme's, perhaps as tall as the height of her head. The tips of them were so sharp that they looked as if they could be used as weapons.

She wore a circlet that glistened as if made of rose gold. A medallion hung down from this and rattled softly, sending a faint chiming sound through the air. Hearing it was like listening to a pleasant melody – not the kind of loud crashing stuff that the master used to like to play in South Wales, and which always used to send me scampering for the back of the sofa, but the kind that never got too loud or too quiet. The sort of music, in other words, that could both send you to sleep at night and lull you out of sleep in the morning. Beauty in its purest form.

Bastet spoke in a voice so familiar that a shudder went down my spine. It had a Welsh accent, with a lilt to it ... the voice of my crystal.

"Dragoncat," she said, "so you came. And you have brought your friends. Three users of the dangerous dark magic. Yet your souls are so pure ... almost." She sniffed the air and turned to Seramina. "You must watch this one. Her recent past may be dark, but she will see the light in the end, just as Esme and I did."

I was lost for words for a moment.

"You're surprised by my voice, aren't you?" Bastet said, turning her head towards me. "To answer the question you are too afraid to ask, Dragoncat, yes – I have spoken to all of you in the past through your crystal. Every voice must have a medium, must it not? Sound cannot exist in a vacuum."

My mouth had dropped open in shock in a very human way. Seramina's and Asinda's faces didn't look much different.

"All of you have had so much to say in the past," Bastet continued. "But now, when you hear my voice coming from a creature in the flesh, you are lost for words. Just know that it is still your crystals that you communicate with. It always has been. They call on me to translate when they need to. Yet it is not actually my voice you are hearing, nor the voice of the crystal at all. You hear the voice you want to hear. The one that brings you the most comfort. The voice of your soul..."

Sitting on her haunches, Bastet was probably about five times the height of Seramina. Esme sat down next to her and started grooming herself meticulously. Max took the other side, and he gazed up at the giant cat, his tail wagging happily.

Still, no one other than Bastet spoke. We didn't have words, it seemed, to address a creature so great, so powerful. It didn't matter anyway, because Bastet had plenty to say. She seemed to be answering all the questions my brain wanted to ask, despite my lips being too numb to utter the words.

"Alas," Bastet continued, "it's just me and the cats now, here in the Realm of Souls. And the aeriosaurs – they were Horus' last gift before his passing. He and my other brothers and sisters – like the good Anubis, Isis, Osiris, Thoth, not to mention Amun-Ra, the greatest of us all – they were hunted down during the War of the Warlocks thousands of years ago.

"It wasn't dark magic that was their weapon, but that force from the Ghost Realm, the one you know as *Cana Dei*. If it hadn't been for the hero, Capitut, it would have taken a lot more than my beloved companions."

Bastet gave a deep sigh. "When you have lived as long as I have, history will seem short. Dark magic corrupts minds, and it has always caused humans to meddle with issues far greater than they. That man, Arran, is currently driven by greed. His access to the Ghost Realm allows him to draw as much power off of *Cana Dei* as he likes – more than any mere user of dark magic. He thinks he controls Apopis, but the Overlords now serve nothing but the dark force. Once it consumes Arran, he will become just like them. *Cana Dei*'s sole purpose is to destroy everything it touches, like a swarm of locusts, feeding on whatever souls it can find."

Bastet paused and lowered her head to look at me. Her eyes were golden, just like her jewellery. Her gaze pierced into the very depths of my soul. "You wanted to ask a question, Dragoncat?" she asked. "And I know that it's a prudent one."

While I had previously been lost for words, as if by magic my mouth found the courage to speak. "Arran's after Max's soul," I said. "This is what it's about, isn't it? If he can destroy the soul, then the dog will no longer exist, leaving room for Arran to swoop in and claim the key for himself."

Bastet lowered her head towards me, her purr rumbling the ground and sending soft vibrations through it. As she opened her mouth, she breathed on me, and it was like no other breath I'd ever experienced. It felt like the desert wind that blew at the threshold of night and day, bringing comfort between the extremes of hot and cold.

"You have grown wiser in your years, Dragoncat. Well done." For a moment I felt like Ange, who always answered the teachers' questions in class and got their highest commendations. "But you are wrong about one thing. Arran isn't after Max's soul.... He has already retrieved it from this realm, and stolen it away. He is on his way to destroy it as I speak, and the only way to destroy a soul is to feed it to *Cana Dei* through a dark and ancient ritual."

Her voice faded for a moment, and other than the chiming sounds coming from Bastet's pendant, silence hung in the air. Not even Max dared break it, even though it was his life that was in jeopardy.

Eventually Seramina ventured forward. She knelt before Bastet, and lowered her head into a reverent bow. "Can we not claim the key for ourselves?" she asked. "Perhaps if Max could give it up? Could we somehow force it out by magic?"

"No," Bastet said. "Only the darkest of magic can remove Capitut's Key from its current owner, and for each of you such magic would burn out your soul. You would become husks, like that man Astravar became. The other warlocks too will soon be like him. You must protect, and not force. That is your duty upon the worlds."

"But I can do it," Seramina said, and I stepped forward and saw to my terror the fire burning at the back of her eyes. She drew her staff from her back and pointed it at Max, and to my surprise no one moved to stop her. "I can claim Capitut's key as my own and make sure that the Warlock Prince never gets it."

That was when I heard the voice in my mind: it was the voice of my crystal. Bastet's voice. "*You too have a duty, Dragoncat. You and Esme are to be Seramina's protectors, and you must protect her from both the evil without and within.*"

I growled, not liking this. But Bastet was right ... Esme was right ... we cats did have a purpose. I had to stop Seramina losing control, and only I could do it. I was the one that would stop her from destroying the worlds.

"You don't want to do this, Seramina," I said.

"Oh yeah?" she said, looking down at me with that fiery gaze. "I suppose you're going to try and stop me."

I summoned my staff bearer, and I willed the staff into my mouth. It thrummed with warm power. I watched as Seramina also drew power to her staff. As soon as I saw that her crystal was brimming, ready to unleash its spell, I cast a spell of my own, a single red beam like the one I'd used to vanquish Astravar. I directed it right at Seramina's crystal...

But it wasn't enough.

"You cannot stop me," Seramina said. "You aren't as strong as I."

"Not alone he isn't," Esme said, stepping forward. She had her staff in her mouth – I could see it from the corner of my eye. "But with the aid of his *companion*..."

Warmth filled me as the white beam from Esme's staff hit me on the side of my chest. Power brimmed through me, and I let it fill my muscles, drawing it into me. But Esme's magic stopped it overpowering me, and it gave me enough strength to sap the magic out of Seramina's staff, as well as her will to do harm.

She dropped her staff on the floor. The long shadows of the grass wrapped around it. Her shoulders sank, and the fire went out from her eyes.

"I'm sorry, Ben," she said. "I don't know what came over me. I'm not cut out for this; I should abandon my staff and renounce my powers. Someone needs to lock me up."

Bastet had sat watching the exchange placidly all the while, as if nothing had happened. She hadn't needed to move; she'd already known that Esme and I would do what we needed to do.

But after Seramina's breakdown, she pressed her nose to Seramina's head, pushing it upwards. "I fear dark times are coming very soon for you, young mage, and things will get worse before they get better. But if you always keep a flame burning as you swim through the darkness, and always remember the value of your friends, you will eventually learn not to falter. Light always comes after darkness, and you are needed in the grand scheme of things. Never lose yourself to *Cana Dei,* and remember that in any darkness there is always some light."

She spoke so mystically that she caused me to shiver. She was holding something back, I could tell. There was something important that she didn't want to tell us.

Seramina shook her head. She looked just as confused as I was. "But from what you tell me, Arran already has Max's soul, and with it the means to obtain the key. Without someone powerful enough to stop him, we've already lost."

Bastet rose into a straight, elegant posture. She waited as a pink, glowing cloud floated down from the sparkling canopy. This soon developed into an image that displayed above her head, showing us a vision like those we saw in the crystals.

"You still have a chance to stop the Warlock Prince," she said, "and this is what you shall do..."

30

THE PLAN

The moving picture developed further on the pink cloud above Bastet's head. It showed the character that we'd all come to hate so well, walking through the darkness: Arran, his scarlet cloak trailing behind him. Two large bottles swung on either hip, attached to loops on his belt. One was triangular and had a pink light shining from within it, clearly someone's soul. The other was empty, round, and of equal size.

After he'd helped us beat the aeriosaurs during the final battle against Astravar, we'd almost respected him, pompous as he was. But it had all been part of a grander plan to become a powerful warlock himself. It seemed that he wanted to become the most powerful warlock of them all.

The darkness through which Arran trod wasn't the kind of darkness that you'd find on a normal night in a normal world. Nor was it the comforting darkness of the Fifth Dimension where we currently were.

This darkness swirled around him menacingly, tendrils of it lashing out as if it wanted to consume his soul. As I looked closer at the image, I could see the faint blue outlines tracing the hills of the dimension. I knew where he was, and so did everyone else: Arran was in the Ghost Realm.

"*Cana Dei,*" Seramina said. "But Arran – he seems to control it."

"He merely thinks he controls *Cana Dei,*" Bastet said. "Yet he knows nothing of what it is, and how dangerous it is to him. You encountered it in the Ghost Realm, did you not?"

"We did," I said, "and it was very scary."

The force to which Bastet had been alluding for so long – this *Cana Dei* – was a great dark miasma that would have eaten us in the Ghost Realm. Before that, I'd fought back by summoning a never-ending waterfall of salmon out of an interdimensional portal. Even that had seemed to do little to stop it. We'd only just managed to escape in the nick of time when Seramina had opened a portal out of there using her native magic. If it hadn't been for her brave actions and quick thinking, I doubt we would have survived.

Alas, my worst regret of that day was not taking at least some of the salmon along for the journey. It was the tastiest food in all the dimensions, and I hadn't had any for months.

"It is good that you fear *Cana Dei,*" Bastet said. "Because it is the darkest force there is. In fact, it is the very essence of dark magic. Few dark magicians realise how the very purpose of the stuff they use is destroy their own heart and soul."

A bit like cigarettes, I thought, but I didn't offer it out loud. No one here but me would have any idea what a cigarette was.

Seramina took a deep breath, examining her staff. Her eyes had lost their fire and gone back to being grey. She kept the crystal on her staff at bay, as if ashamed of it. "It doesn't make sense," she said. "How can *Cana Dei* destroy souls that are physically here in the Fifth Dimension?"

Bastet lowered her head. "There is a dormant portal in every person's heart that leads to their soul. It's too small for any creature larger than an ant to pass through it, but still it creates an inextricable link between heart and spirit. When in the same realm as you, *Cana Dei* will latch on to a creature's breath as does a mosquito. Once it finds you, it enters your nostrils and lungs until it finds a way to your heart. That is how it gets to your soul."

"So why hasn't it already destroyed Arran?" Asinda asked. "Surely he can't stay like that in the Ghost Realm for very long. Just like we couldn't..."

"Ah, but he has Capitut's Brand," Bastet replied, and her eyes glowed golden as the words flared out of her mouth. "That allows him to choose which parts of his body exist in which dimension. If he keeps his heart in another dimension, then *Cana Dei* might never find him. But still, as he continues to use dark magic, he will eventually lose the will to keep it away. He will surrender himself to it, and then he will become its slave."

To emphasise the point, a vessel just like the ones we'd seen in the cavern wall on the way here appeared in the vision above Arran's head. As it turned slowly, it emanated much less light than the souls we'd seen before. This was because a cloud of darkness surrounded it, tendrils trying to get a grip on it, as if trying to snuff it out of existence.

"So what exactly happens if you lose your soul to Cana Dei, anyway?" I asked. "What will happen to you physically, I mean?"

Bastet looked up towards the pink cloud hovering above her. The image changed from Arran to one of Apopis, wandering through the snow. The great demon snake overlord slithered through it, melting a path as he went. Five demon dragons flocked around him, and a troop of demon foxes trailed behind, yipping as they went. I couldn't hear them in this vision, but I could all but imagine the tune to Ride of the Valkyries spreading out across the landscape as they descended the mountain.

"You become like him," Bastet said. "Apopis doesn't realise it because he never lost his intelligence. His mind works with all the brilliance that it used to, but his emotional drive serves the will of *Cana Dei*. Now everything that the Overlord of Overlords does is to spread the use of dark magic, giving the darkness more opportunity to spread across the dimensions."

"Can he be saved?" Asinda asked. "Is there any chance of redemption?"

"Not for Apopis," Bastet said, and another vessel appeared above the demon snake's head, this time containing no light at all – only swirling blackness. "Because he no longer has a soul, and that is why we must banish him to the Seventh Dimension. I see a fight between him and myself ahead, but I don't know when and how it will occur, nor do I know the outcome."

I realised we were getting side-tracked, and now with Arran on the loose and that demon force heading to whiskers knows where, I really wanted to get on with things. Most importantly, Max's life was in danger, and he needed our help.

"So, what do we do next?" I asked. "How do we stop Arran?"

Bastet lowered her head. "Your development has made me proud, Dragoncat," she said. The image above her flickered back to the image of Arran summoning *Cana Dei*. The empty bottle that had been on his hip was now uncorked, and he held this in front of him to his chest. "Fortunately for you, Arran doesn't have a key to the Fifth Dimension. He can't take any item with him that he wasn't already carrying when he gained Capitut's Brand. So he needs to travel through portals to take Max's soul with him."

The great cat inhaled, her chest rising as it filled up with air. As she exhaled, more of the pink smoke seeped out of her nostrils and rose up to join the looming cloud above her. The image upon it changed once again; this time it showed Arran with his staff drawn, the bottle now full of the evil black stuff. A purple beam was pulsing out of Arran's staff, and he was using it to open a portal. This led to a fiery land, which I knew to be the Seventh Dimension. I guessed that's where Arran was going next.

"This premonition shows a possible future to come, and one that is about to happen very soon. You will have three chances to stop the Warlock Prince. Once in the Ghost Realm, where he will soon gather a bottle of *Cana Dei*. He will need to summon a portal to leave there, and if you can catch him before he goes you can retrieve the soul and I will summon a portal to bring you back here."

"I see..." Seramina said.

The amulet on her Bastet's chest jingled lightly. More smoke pulsed out of her nostrils and mouth, and this time it was red. It rose upwards to replace the image in the cloud above her with one of a fiery land ... the Seventh Dimension.

The camera rocked slightly as if in a boat that was floating in the sky. It looked down on a great crater, surrounded on all sides by a lava lake. Strands of sharp black rock were strewn across it, and in the distance I could make out the dark volcanic crags that shaped the rest of the land.

"This is Mount Arhoom," Bastet said, "the tallest mountain in the Seventh Dimension, and the highest landmark of them all. The glass that contains souls is reinforced with magic, and only an obsidian shard from this mountain has the power to break it. Arran will need to obtain one before he feeds the soul to *Cana Dei*."

Whiskers, I didn't like this at all. We might have to travel to two of the most inhospitable places that I'd ever been to. If we got stuck in either of them, we'd die faster than a chimp could peel a banana.

"So that's it, right?" I asked. "Once Arran releases Max's soul from its vessel, he only needs to feed it to Cana Dei, and he blinks out of existence."

"No," Bastet said. "That's not how it works."

This time, purple gas seeped out of Bastet's nostrils, and it wasn't the pretty purple that painted everything in this realm in pleasant colours. This was of the same shade of purple as the crystals on our staffs – the colour of dark magic. Like all other dark magic, it stank of rotten vegetable juice.

The image changed once again to display a barren land, fringed with purple gas. In the distance, through the thick coloured fog, I could make out a familiar building. It was Astravar's tower – the place where I had been locked when the warlock had whisked me across time and space into a pentagram of red chalk on his floor.

The sight of the tower sent a shiver right down me. But the camera wasn't focused on it; rather, it spun around and whizzed over the landscape of the Darklands. It halted just before a large gothic-style building with eleven verdigris domes topped with sharp spikes that pierced the purple sky. Gargoyles guarded the doorway to the structure, but there were no doors to seal its entryway.

As the camera drifted lazily inside, I noticed the place was a temple, surrounding a large courtyard open to the flickering sky. A large, raised circular dais stood at the centre, with an altar shaped like a massive stone cat bowl. Thirteen metal rods rose up from the edges of the courtyard, pointing towards the central bowl.

"The Fifth Dimension will protect even those souls that have been stolen away from here. That's the purpose of the vessel that contains the souls; if one is broken, the magic in the Fifth Dimension will automatically teleport it back to its location on the Wall of Souls and form a new vessel around it. That's the nature of souls – they cannot be contained outside of their native realm."

"Good to know," I said.

Bastet nodded but she didn't slow her speech. "There is one exception to this rule. Above me you can see the Altar of Lore. It's older than the Pharoah Warlocks, built by the original magicians in the First Dimension – the first White Mages. It's also the one place in the realms where anything can be contained through powerful magic. Unfortunately, this structure now resides in the Darklands, where only the warlocks can access it."

"What is it?" Seramina said. "Even just by looking at it, I can sense its power." There was a slight gleam in her eye.

"It's a magical prison, capable of trapping anything inside it, including souls and *Cana Dei*. In fact, only those skilled in dark magic – those who have embraced *Cana Dei* – can enter the temple wherein lies the Altar of Lore. This will no doubt be Arran's final destination, because when used to destroy a body's soul, anything that body contains will be transferred inside the altar. It is also your third and final chance to stop the Warlock Prince."

She paused to give us time to think about it for a moment. Seramina seemed to get the implications first. "So if I'm understanding you correctly, anything inside Max, including Capitut's Key and his last meal, will automatically appear in the Altar of Lore once Arran has destroyed Max's soul."

"Exactly," Bastet said. "Which is why you cannot let Arran destroy Max's soul. Yet the choice isn't mine, but yours, and the question is – what are you going to do?"

"We don't have a choice," I said, looking at Max. Though he must have known that his life was in the hands of Arran now, he didn't seem the least bit afraid. "We must go to this Altar of Lore and stop Arran."

"Go to the Ghost Realm first. I can summon portals across dimensions, and if you can foil Arran's plans early, you might be able to bring him back to me. He hasn't yet lost himself completely to *Cana Dei*, so perhaps there is some redemption for him – maybe we can find a way to save him from the darkness yet."

Asinda stepped forwards. "So it's settled then. We should go."

"Good," Bastet said. "My cats and Esme will show you the way to the first portal. It will open as soon as you are ready. Oh, and one more thing: if the time comes, Dragoncat, you must summon me to the Altar of Lore. I can see it more clearly now, and I can only be summoned by a cat able to use dark magic. You will need me there."

I didn't have a clue how I was going to do that, but I meowed in assent anyway.

Esme licked her paw, and then blinked at me fondly when she caught me looking at her. I was still enamoured with her, admittedly, but I had started to suspect I couldn't trust her.

"It will be fun!" Max barked, and I snapped my head around to look at him, startled.

He really didn't seem to fathom the danger he was in. Part of me wanted to tell him that he should stay. But it didn't matter, because if Arran succeeded, the dog would die anyway. Bringing him along would at least show us if he blinked out of existence, and let us know we'd failed in our quest. Alas, if that happened, we were doomed.

31

PORTAL GATE

Bastet's cats led us away from her lair, along a narrow ledge that climbed the edge of the Wall of Souls. The souls themselves pulsed like pink balls of electricity within their vessels, sparks kissing the glass that contained them. Each vessel emanated a soft warmth, the effect making the whole wall feel like a radiator.

The ledge seemed to get ever narrower as we progressed, and it continued to climb until we were so high that a fall would have been fatal. A cat stayed behind each of us to let us know about any potential obstacles in each of our own languages. I'd always thought that the ability to speak all languages would be unique to me, but it seemed that every creature here could do it. I was too focused on the mission, though, to even think about quizzing any of the cats about how they'd come to be here.

Fortunately the ledge soon widened out a little, leading off to the left. A cave mouth led into a small chamber – not much taller than Seramina and Asinda. The walls were sandstone red, and a stone archway stood at the end of the room, leading nowhere, as the cavern wall was right behind it. Large loose stones stacked one on top of the other formed the two sides of the archway, and they got smaller where the arch converged towards the capstone. This wasn't made of the same granite as the other stones, but was faceted crystal just like the crystals upon our staffs, only much bigger.

Seramina gasped, and then she stepped forwards and ran her hands down the stone. "A portal gate..." she said, looking back at Esme. "I never knew such things still existed, though I've read about them in some of the history books."

Esme stepped up to join her, and she rubbed against Seramina's calf. She was purring. Perhaps Seramina's display of power had caused Esme to warm to her. She seemed to like characters with power.

"Much of the old ways have been forgotten," she said. "The Pharaoh Warlocks exterminated the ancient White Mages and their devices when they stamped their rule across the First Dimension. But since time passes slowly here, many of the cats of this realm remember how things used to work."

Asinda had also joined Seramina, and she was examining the gate without daring to touch it. "So you can just activate this whenever you want, and it will take you where you want to go?"

"Only those who know the activation spell can use it," Esme said, and she summoned her staff bearer to place her staff in her mouth. "And only white magic can activate it. The power inherent in each stone draws energy from the ground and directs it to the crystal at the top. Nothing is used up in this way as all the power is returned to the ground. Now if you'll excuse me, we must be getting on."

She sent a beam out of her staff towards the crystal, and a white light spread out beneath it, filling the archway. Time seemed to slow, and a haunting silence filled the cavern for a moment. The white at the centre of the portal dissipated to display an entryway into a dark realm. The Ghost Realm awaited us, and I really didn't want to have to step inside. But then I knew I had to – not just for Max's sake, but for the sake of all the realms.

"This way! This way!" Max barked. He bounded through the portal, and he went far enough into the thick darkness that I couldn't see him on the other side.

Seramina and Asinda followed, both seeming to want to get out of this place. How they could prefer the Ghost Realm to this cave, I had no idea, but I guess they just wanted to get this mission over with and return to the First Dimension.

I turned to Esme and pressed my nose up against hers. "Well, so long, Esme, it's been wonderful meeting you. Perhaps our paths will cross again."

She growled back at me. "I'm coming too, you nitwit. Now go, because I can't keep this open forever."

I meowed, then leaped through. Esme followed. It wasn't until I reached the other side, however, that I truly remembered why I dreaded this place so much.

32

CANA DEI

The Ghost Realm was one of almost pure darkness, with no sense of hot or cold to the air. If I squinted I could see the faint blue outlines that marked the edges of objects, and we could perhaps wander for a little while without *Cana Dei* latching onto us, depending on whether or not the spirits that inhabited the place and who knew how to avoid *Cana Dei* wanted to guide us.

Somewhere in this realm was my entire history, from the moment I was born to the time I would die. I might catch glimpses of it as I explored, but I wouldn't see it all before *Cana Dei* found me. Truth be told, I didn't know how much time we had.

The place stank of yeast extract – tons and tons of the disgusting stuff. I would later learn that this stench characterised *Cana Dei*, the darkness that we wanted to avoid. It seemed thicker than the last time I'd been here, making it difficult to see my companions.

As soon as we'd stepped over the threshold to the Ghost Realm, the portal had closed behind us. It was timed perfectly, as moments later another portal opened just in front of us, perhaps fifty metres away – distance wasn't easy to measure here. It led to a verdant world with waterfalls rushing in the distance and the scent of pollen trickling out.

Arran would come here from the Faerie Realm. It made sense, I guess. He would have been able to carry Max's soul safely through there, as no fairy would dare go anywhere near him. They were even more scared of warlocks than they were of dragons. Mind you, warlocks had proven many times that their magic could control fairies and use them to further their own foul deeds.

The Warlock Prince soon stepped into view on the other side of the portal, his red cloak trailing behind him. He turned and walked through, the staff on his crystal glowing white as it fed the portal with energy. Then he clicked his fingers, and both the light from his staff and the portal winked out of existence.

He had those two containers attached to his belt. The first was the triangular bottle containing Max's soul, which shimmered with a soft pink energy. Already the *Cana Dei* had started to close in towards it, as if it knew exactly what it was. Arran had brought the second round bottle to capture some *Cana Dei*. He unhooked this from his hip, uncorked it, and lifted it above his head. Immediately, the black gas started to seep into it, filling it as if filling a vacuum.

Arran wouldn't have noticed us, if it hadn't been for Max. He started barking at him and growling, "Bad master! Bad master! This dog and his friends are here. We will stop your evil plans."

I bristled as soon as he started doing this. Max might be a lot of things, but I never said he was clever.

"Will you shut up, Max?" I whined back at him in the dog language.

But it was too late, because Arran had already turned his head towards him. As his lips moved, I noticed his skin was starting to lose its moisture; his complexion had begun to gain those eggshell-like cracks that had plagued Astravar before I'd vanquished him. A symptom, I'd learned, of over-using dark magic.

A mirthless smile crept across the Warlock Prince's face. "Well, well, well. I went to all this trouble to acquire your soul, dog, and perhaps I hadn't needed to after all. You cannot be killed by dark magic, I hear. But that doesn't mean you can't be destroyed by *Cana Dei*."

He clutched his staff in one hand, while the other still held the open bottle above his head. It was now almost full. The crystal on his staff glowed purple, and he turned his staff towards Max, who still stood there on the spot, barking, clearly unaware of imminent danger.

"Oh no, you don't," Seramina said, and stepped forwards out of the darkness. Her eyes were raging fires, and her staff was already glowing purple.

"We came here to stop you," Asinda said, and she also stepped out, her eyes burning embers and her shining staff in her hand. "You are a thorn in my family's past, and you will be allowed to destroy no more."

"Ben, draw your staff," Esme said. "Time to make your entrance."

I didn't need to be told twice. Yowling, I summoned my staff bearer and called the staff into my mouth. This time the hand didn't place it there, but rather the staff flew over on its own accord. Energy pulsed through me, and I felt my muscles course with power, and a burning sensation formed behind my eyes.

"I defeated one warlock," I said, managing somehow to speak normally with my staff in my mouth – it must have been through magic, "and I will gladly defeat another."

Arran took one look at us and laughed, his chest heaving as he did so. "Such foolish adolescents. I have no idea how you found me, and I'm not even going to ask. Do you really think two children and a cat can beat a warlock who controls *Cana Dei*? It cannot affect me here, you know. Not while I keep my heart in another dimension."

He clearly hadn't realised that there was a fifth member in our party. Esme presently revealed herself from the darkness. She already had her staff in her mouth.

"They also have me," she said. "White and dark magic are extremely powerful when combined."

She sent out a beam from her staff, but this time it wasn't directed at us. Rather, it hit the ground, and the darkness there parted away from it, as if a massive stone had just broken the surface of a lake. The beam split and reflected upwards, hitting each of us dark mages right on the forehead.

Warmth coursed through me, and I no longer felt overpowered by the dark magic. Instead, I felt like I was in complete control.

Dark magic surged out of all three of our staffs, aimed towards Arran. It didn't cut right through the blackness, the way light would normally cut through air, but rather the darkness seemed able to push it back. Our beams met at a point, and eventually the light managed to push the darkness away.

Arran let out a loud laugh as he watched it. "Pathetic," he said. "Against the power of *Cana Dei*, none of you stand a chance."

He swept his staff around in a circle. There came a flash of light, and then a wave of darkness swept outwards, pushing back our magic. The shockwave sent the four of us off our feet. When we picked ourselves up, we could no longer see Arran, but a faint red light had appeared to the left.

"A portal," Seramina said.

"To the Seventh Dimension," Asinda murmured.

"Whiskers, he's grown powerful," I said.

"That's because the *Cana Dei* has chosen him as its subject," Esme said. "Much as it did with Astravar. Come, he has directed the darkness towards us, and so we must hurry."

I growled, not liking the fact that we had to go to the Seventh

Dimension next. Demons would no doubt be waiting for us to arrive.

Still, I didn't want to be consumed by *Cana Dei,* so I sprinted after Esme, who was leading us on a circuitous route around boulders and other obstacles barely visible within the darkness. All the while, I could feel a dark force chasing after me. It sent the hackles up on my back and pricked at my skin, like a cloud of static trying to tear me apart.

My ears were ringing, my head was throbbing, and I couldn't see a thing. Still, I did my best to focus on Esme, not letting myself lose track of her. Whiskers, she was moving so fast.

Fortunately, just as I was about to give up, a portal to a land of fire and brimstone opened up before me. I could feel the heat raging out of the portal, and it smelled like a thousand rotten eggs had just been added to a massive frying pan.

The second to last thing I wanted was to have to go back there. But then, the last thing I wanted was to have my body and soul consumed by gaseous yeast extract. There was no worst death I could imagine in all the realms.

Thus I bounded through the portal, into oblivion. Arran was waiting for us on the other side.

33

MAGMA AND BRIMSTONE

We landed in the Seventh Dimension, bang in the middle of Mount Arhoom's crater, which loomed over a red, boiling sea. Smoke drifted upwards in thick plumes from the larger bubbles that emerged from the magma. The whole effect made it look as if there were massive fish underneath the surface, exhaling smoke into the sky.

Whiskers, this was the Seventh Dimension after all, and there probably were demon fish coming up to breathe the sulphurous air. I wouldn't be surprised if there were even demon salmon in there, though if there were I highly doubted that they would have been fit for eating.

"I thought you were getting some kind of supernatural aid," Arran said. "Because there is no way in the Seven Dimensions you should be able to follow me through portals like this. Who is helping you? And don't tell me that this is the will of the crystals, because we all know that that's nonsense..."

There were only twenty feet now between us and where the Warlock Prince stood. If we moved fast enough, we could take him down. Max stepped forwards and he bared his teeth as he growled at his former master.

"Smelly evil place! Old master will die in smelly evil place!" he barked.

Arran looked down at him and cocked his head as if considering something. Once again, his fingers tightened around his staff. But Esme stepped forward before he had a chance to take Max down.

"We're telling you nothing, Arran," she said, "and take a good look around, because the view in this place will be the last one that you see."

She called her upon her staff bearer to place her staff in her mouth. This time she directed her beam at a large shard of faceted obsidian that protruded from the rocky ground. It reflected off this, splitting in three directions as before. The resultant beams darted around a little, until they finally found their way to the centre of Seramina's, Asinda's, and my foreheads.

The three of us drew our staffs as before and summoned dark magic to course through them. By the time we'd cast the beams at Arran, he'd already set up a purple barrier, curving in front of him. It was a shimmering sphere of light that gave him plenty of space to manoeuvre.

It was then that I noticed how Arran had already scattered a good dozen purple crystals around him. They fed the magical barrier with wispy threads of energy, and we would have to destroy them before we could reach the Warlock Prince. Wavy patterns of purple light cascaded over the surface, which buzzed as loudly as a thousand bumblebees.

"Just drop the soul, Arran, and we will let you live," Esme called out.

Arran let out a cackling laugh. His voice echoed around the crater as if we were in an auditorium. "If you force me to drop the soul, I will just disappear into another dimension like when your

Initiate Seramina tried to kill me at Capitut's Tomb. You wanted it, didn't you, girl? You wanted to kill me.... You are just like your father, you know that? Perhaps one day we'll find ourselves working together – at one with *Cana Dei*."

I could see the anger in the set of Seramina's jaw. The fire at the back of her eyes seemed to burn even more brightly now. She directed her beam at one of the crystals feeding Arran's shield. The crystal exploded, sending thousands of shards scattering.

"Again, you fight me at a disadvantage," Arran said. "Because, fortunately, I have allies here. Ammit, I call upon you for aid."

His voice carried the same tone of command that I'd used all that time ago to banish the demon dragon back to this dimension. There came a flash of lightning from the billowing red and grey clouds in the sky, and a voice called out across the sea – loud and clacking.

"As you wish, warlock!"

A shiver went down my spine as I watched some bubbles in the magma drift lazily in towards the rim of the crater. Asinda yelled in glee as she shattered another crystal, leaving only ten to destroy before we could reach Arran. I also had my beam focused on a crystal of my own, and I could feel it starting to split. Meanwhile, whatever had been swimming through the lava had now reached the shore.

One beast emerged from the magma, lava dripping like slaver off its long, razor jaws. Its eyes were like raging fires from the centre of the earth, and the way the cracks ran over its long back made it look as if it wore some kind of scaled armour. The space beneath the cracks glowed red, showing the beast's molten core.

It was a demon crocodile, three times bigger than any of the Nile crocodiles in the tales the Savannah cats used to tell back home. It clacked its jaws in a terrifying rhythm, as if performing the leading percussion role in a symphony. Another demon crocodile emerged from the sea, then another, and another still, until there were seven of them coming up slowly from the shore.

Suddenly the crystal I had a beam on broke, leaving nine to bring down before we would destroy the shield. But we had no time, because one of the demon crocodiles was charging. It was heading straight for Seramina's legs.

I yowled, and instinctively turned my staff towards the demon crocodile before it could snap Seramina in two. As I had when I'd attacked one of Apopis' demon dragons, I let energy surge into my staff and sent a purple spark along the ground, the smell of rotten vegetable juice trailing in its wake. The ground beneath me shook, and the spark hit the crocodile right between its jaws.

My spell didn't kill the beast, but it did send it tumbling backwards. It curled up like an armadillo and rolled quite a way before unfurling and readying itself to charge again. But now the remaining crocodiles had become much more immediate threats.

"You need to focus on the demons," Esme shouted. "Turn your attention to them."

"But Arran will get away again," Seramina said. "We have to stop him."

The fire at the back of Seramina's eyes was burning so brightly now that it had almost lost its colour, instead displaying a white flame. Her staff was brimming with magic, and I could see that once again she was losing control.

I remembered what Bastet had said about protecting Seramina from herself. Once again we didn't have Lars' shield magic, so she would kill us all, including Max. She would leave only the Key to the Sixth Dimension remaining, which couldn't be destroyed. Perhaps she'd take the key for herself then, and the way she'd been behaving lately, I wasn't sure we could trust her with it.

"Seramina, we'll stop him at the Altar of Lore," I said. "You can't lose control now. Not here, of all places."

This time, my words seemed to hit her. Her eyes didn't stop burning, but they went back to their normal amber colour. "Sorry," she said.

"Just concentrate on the crocodiles," Esme told her.

While I had been focused on Seramina's rage, a crocodile had stalked in towards Max and taken him unawares. He was now baying at the glowing demon as if he thought he could defeat it with his teeth alone. The demon crocodile charged at him, and I grimaced, fearing the worst.

But at the last moment, the brave dog leaped on the demon crocodile's back, from where he stood, still barking and baying. No matter how much the beast shook and turned, it seemed unable to throw him off.

A beam from Asinda's staff hit the demon crocodile right on the snout, and Max jumped off its back before it rolled down over the edge of the crater. Meanwhile, the other five crocs were crowding in, snapping at us. Seramina, Asinda and I huddled together, our staffs at the ready.

"Arran!" Asinda called. "He's getting away."

The Warlock Prince had taken the opportunity to transform his barrier into the shape of a riot shield and had pushed it forwards slightly. Behind it he bent down to scoop up a shard of obsidian, and then he turned to the side and cast some magic out of his staff.

He had become so powerful that it happened very quickly. The shield flickered out, as the remaining scattered crystals directed their energy into feeding an emerging portal. This appeared quickly to Arran's right. The view through the magical, glowing frame showed the Darklands in the First Dimension – purple mist hugging the horizon. Amidst the smell of sulphur, I also caught a whiff of rotten vegetable juice coming out of the portal.

I didn't waste another second. I redirected my beam of dark energy at Arran, hoping to catch him before he entered the First

Dimension. But he was too fast, and he dived through. Before I even had a chance to blink, the portal winked out of existence, sealing us in the Seventh Dimension with the demon crocodiles. They looked hungry, and it seemed they would eat well today.

I shivered and it didn't take long for me to realise that Esme had cut off her beam of white magic that augmented our power. "Retreat," she called. "We can stop Arran if we move now."

I glanced over my shoulder to see that a portal had already emerged to the Altar of Lore that Bastet had introduced to us not less than an hour ago. Esme was already running towards it.

The three of us didn't hesitate in dropping our spells and running with our staffs still drawn towards our targets. Max bounded ahead of us. He passed through the portal first, then Esme followed, before I heard Seramina shout...

"There's something wrong with that portal!"

I heard her too late, and my head was already past the threshold, the rest of my body following me through.

I didn't emerge at the Altar of Lore as I'd expected. Rather I found myself on a stone floor, surrounded by bright flashing lights. A dark reptilian creature with an extended, webbed mane hissed at me, flicking its forked tongue in front of it.

Beside me, Max had been turned to stone.

34

STONE DOG

"It's a basilisk," Esme yelled. "Don't look at it, Ben! If you smell anything funny, run!"

"A what?" But the word was already in my memory. Together with the ability to speak all languages, I'd gained an entire canon of mythology. A basilisk was a reptilian, serpent-like creature capable of turning its subject into stone. Well, that explained what had happened to Max.

Despite Esme's warning, I couldn't draw my gaze away from its green, glowing eyes. They were swirling in such a mesmerising pattern that I wanted to sleep. The floor felt so enticing. I could become part of the ground, and it would become part of me. A perfect and natural transformation, and I didn't need to do anything except gaze into those brilliant eyes.

"Hang on, Ben," said Esme, her voice sounding disembodied. "I've got this."

A flash of light, then a silver surface shimmered in front of me. I wasn't looking at the basilisk anymore, but a beautiful Bengal. He had such a beautiful, silky fur coat, and he was a fine specimen of a cat indeed.

It didn't take me long to realise I was looking at my own reflection.

Presently, the illusion of the mirror shattered, or rather it melted as if in a furnace. I was looking once again at the basilisk that had almost turned me to stone, except it was now a statue itself. Esme had been fast enough to cast a glamour of a mirror in front of it, enacting its desired effect upon itself.

I saw a shape moving behind me. Seramina stepped out of the portal, followed by Asinda. The portal closed after them as soon as Asinda's back foot had left the Seventh Dimension. The younger teenager stumbled over to Max's statue and crouched down to examine him. His skin was of a smooth shiny stone, almost like marble, except without the rich texture and dull grey in colour.

"I knew it was a trap," Seramina said, glancing at the stone basilisk.

"Did Arran do this?" Asinda asked, her gaze fixed on the basilisk, as if the creature was also about to turn her to stone.

The grunt of a condor answered the question for us. A shadow wheeled over the ground, sending the hackles up on my back. The condor landed on a stone platform raised high over the stone floor. A plume of purple smoke enveloped it. This soon faded to reveal the old lady Lasinta – the leader of the warlocks.

Beneath her, purple sparks buzzed across a ring of spires that surrounded us. They created what looked like a massive magical fence towering into the sky. I guessed it was all a part of the trap that Lasinta had set, though I had no idea how she'd known we'd come here. A bulky man-sized purple crystal sat at the bottom of each spire, casting the magic that fed the energy field.

"No use trying to fight them," Esme said. "They've set up a

magic nullification field. We can cast magic inside, but none of it can pass through that barrier."

"It must have taken them days to set up," Seramina said. She had her staff drawn still, but she held it lightly.

"I guess they've been planning this for a while," Asinda said through clenched teeth.

"Well, that means they can't cast magic at us either, right?" Seramina asked. "Because if they come in here, I'm not holding back. This time, I will find a way to destroy that crone."

"Like we saw in that vision in the Ghost Realm?" I asked. "Because you ended up destroying the world, then, and it was Lasinta you were fighting."

"Hopefully someone can rescue us first," Asinda said. "Can anyone reach their dragons?"

It was a good idea. We were now in the First Dimension, after all.

"*Salanraja,*" I called in my mind. "*Salanraja, are you out there?*"

There was no response. All I felt was that sickening emptiness. It wasn't easy being so far from Salanraja, and not knowing where she was.

Seramina was shaking her head. "They must still be in the Faerie Realm."

"Or knocked unconscious," I said, "or even killed by the demons who were hunting them. Who knows what might have happened in our absence."

"Let's not get ahead of ourselves," Esme said. "We need to find out what these warlocks want."

"Isn't it obvious?" I asked. "They're after Max and the key to the Sixth Dimension, just like Arran is. Now they have him."

No one said anything. Instead, everyone's gaze latched on to a group of birds approaching from a distance. I say group and not flock, because they were all of different kinds, all carrion eaters.

I heard the cry of a seagull, of a hawk, of a bald eagle, of a buzzard, of a vulture. These were the forms that the remaining five warlocks could take. They landed on the platforms surrounding the magical nullification field, far too high for any of us to reach.

Purple gas clouded up around them, much as it had done with Lasinta. The seagull changed first, into a fiery red-haired woman, her hair as straight as Seramina's. The vulture became a bald, tall and lanky man, and the buzzard turned into a huge, muscular man, just like Driar Brigel except with much more hair. The woman the hawk turned into was tiny in comparison – scrawny and wiry. The bald eagle transformed last, and I recognized the old man who emerged as Moonz – Lasinta's second in command.

"What do we do now?" I asked. "Are we just going to let them get away with this?"

Esme let out a long growling sigh. "There is nothing much we can do to fight them," she said, taking a quick glance over her shoulder at Max. "But I'm guessing they came here to talk..."

That sounded a little better than fighting, but we were wasting precious time.

35

TALKING WITH THE WARLOCKS

I doubted the warlocks had expected to negotiate with an Abyssinian, but Asinda, it seemed, had now accepted that Esme was in charge. Before the white cat stepped forward, I caught a flash of movement from Max's direction.

At first I thought Max had woken up, or the spell that the basilisk had cast might have worn off. Then the Sussex spaniel would be able to skip between the dimensions and perhaps find a way to get us out of here. But what I had actually seen was Max flickering into and out of existence a few times in rapid succession. It was as if the universe had decided that he no longer belonged, either in this realm or any of the others for that matter.

I stalked up to Esme. "The ritual has started," I muttered under my breath. "Max has started to disappear."

Esme turned to me and nodded. She spoke so softly that none of the warlocks would be able to hear her, except through magic, which wouldn't be possible because of the nullification field. "This may look like an imminent danger, but it will take hours for Arran to break the glass of the vessel containing Max's soul."

"But still I saw it," I said. "He flickered into and out of existence like the picture on a wonky television."

Esme looked at me, as if to ask about television. But she didn't bother. "The glitch you see is only natural," she said instead. "It's the soul's way of telling the body it's in trouble. But we still have time."

I turned away, groaning. We might have had more time than it seemed, but I didn't see any way out of this. The magical annulment barrier really looked like we wouldn't be able to cross without it cutting us in two. Even if we could cross it, we had no idea where we were, or how much distance separated us from the Altar of Lore. Something told me that it would take a lot longer than mere hours to hike out there. If we'd had access to our dragons, it might have been a lot easier. But we didn't.

Lasinta was tapping her foot impatiently on the platform. So as to appease her impatience, Esme raised her head high and shouted out in a voice almost as rich and commanding as Bastet's: "Lasinta of the warlocks, tell me your demands, so we can get this conversation over with quickly."

Lasinta put her hand to her chin. She moved slowly and assuredly, as if she had all the time in the world. Before she spoke, she turned and studied each of the warlocks in turn. They returned nods of approval when her gaze fell upon them. Indeed, they'd surely planned this moment for a very long time, but I hadn't a clue how they'd known we'd be in the Seventh Dimension at that exact moment.

Lasinta pointed her staff at the giant male warlock – the one who had transformed from a buzzard. His muscles looked so well formed that he'd have no trouble carrying the statue of Max out of this magical field.

"Allow our warlock, Ritrad, to fly down and carry the dog back out, without attempting to harm him, and we will allow you all to go free and unharmed."

Esme barked a laugh. "Do you really expect us to believe that? We are a threat to you alive, and you have no reason not to try to kill us."

"From what I understand, we would have a fair battle on our hands. Your young dark mage with the blonde hair has already demonstrated great power, multiple times."

Esme gestured back at the basilisk with her staff. "Your original plan, I see, was to turn us to stone. Did you really think that you could defeat us all with a single basilisk?"

"No," Lasinta called out. "But we knew from what we'd seen in the Versta Caverns that the dog would come through the portal first. You know, it was Ammit herself who told us that you and Arran would both be visiting Mount Arhoom. She seems to have quite a vendetta against my grandson, that one, and I personally don't blame her. No one wants to serve a fool."

Esme stopped to consider for a moment. I glanced at Seramina, who had her head cocked thoughtfully. Her fingers drummed on the wood of her staff. I knew little about magical nullification fields, but I guessed that even they had their limit, and Seramina was a potential destroyer of worlds. Perhaps then she also had enough power to get us out of this place, but the cost could be great indeed.

I caught another flicker at the corner of my vision. This time, Max's form vanished for a good half second, letting out a buzzing sound as it did so. *What if he goes and doesn't come back again?* I thought. *What if Arran is quicker at the task than Esme thinks?*

There came a smell like burning stone, and the statue of Max glowed red for a very short time. Lasinta seemed to notice it too because she snapped her gaze downwards. Though she was a long way away, I could all but imagine the wrinkles tightening on her face.

Hurry up, I thought, and I wanted to say so to Esme. I found myself growling, but no one seemed to notice.

"You know," Esme said after what seemed like a long moment, "even if you take the dog and let us go free, you will not retrieve the Key to the Sixth Dimension with it."

"And why not?" Lasinta asked.

"Because Arran is already performing what you warlocks might know as the Ritual of Souls."

Lasinta's eyes narrowed. She clearly knew what Esme was talking about, meaning someone had tried stealing a soul before, or at least considered the possibility.

"How is that possible?" Lasinta asked. "No one can retrieve a soul – we don't even know where they exist."

"I won't tell you where he got it from, but I will tell you that his ability to walk the dimensions allowed him to do it. Did you not wonder why he went to Mount Arhoom? He needed a shard of the densest possible obsidian to break the vessel containing the dog's soul."

I growled. I really wasn't sure Esme should have been telling them all this. But she seemed to know what she was doing.

Another buzzing sound, and another flicker from Max's direction. Whiskers, how long did he have, really? Meanwhile we were stuck here, engaging in this thing called diplomacy that humans, and now Esme, seemed to think was necessary.

"If that is the case," Lasinta said, agonizingly slowly, "then we are wasting our time here." She looked up at the old man on the platform across from her – Moonz.

"He will be at the Altar of Lore," Moonz offered. "It's the only place where you can trap a soul."

Lasinta's lips stretched into a grin. "That is just wonderful. We now have the perfect opportunity to stop my grandson and claim the Key to the Sixth Dimension, which is rightfully ours."

"But he has the demon lord Apopis with him," Moonz said. "We are in great debt to the Overlord of Overlords."

Lasinta cackled loudly. She put her hand again to her chin. She spoke loudly and clearly enough that if I perked up my ears, I could hear her over the din of the nullification field.

"If Arran has summoned Apopis out of the Seventh Dimension," she said, "then the Overlord of Overlords must be under his command. We only need to eliminate my fop of a grandson and control of the demon and all the forces he commands will become ours." She turned back to Esme. "Thank you for the information, fools. We shall leave you now to rot whilst we retrieve the key for ourselves. With me, warlocks!"

Purple gas arose on each of the platforms, enveloping the warlocks. I caught the whiff of rotten vegetable juice from six distinct directions. The field surrounding us might nullify magic, but it didn't keep out its stench.

Six birds arose from the platforms – a seagull, a vulture, a hawk, a bald eagle, a buzzard, and the condor herself. They lifted off, sending manic cries, grunts, shrieks, and caws in their wake. Off they flew towards the west, from where the sun had peeked out, spreading its rays through the purple mist that plagued the Darklands.

It wouldn't be long until cold darkness fell, and as Lasinta had kindly pointed out, we were trapped here. We only had hours before either Arran or Lasinta, or whiskers forbid, even Apopis, retrieved the Key to the Sixth Dimension, killing Max in the process.

Hours before the beginning of the inevitable end.

36

DARK NIGHT

The sun set fast, and then the night crept inwards. The stench of rotten vegetable juice crowded in from all around. Every so often from beyond the barrier I caught a glimmer of one of the warlocks' magical creatures – sometimes one of the wispy Manipulators, sometimes the burning crystal in the centre of a stone golem's chest. If it weren't for this magical annulment barrier, they would attack and we'd have a fight on our hands. Ironically, the barrier was also keeping us safe.

The worst part of it all was how loudly my tummy was groaning at me, as I'd not eaten for hours. Of course there was no chance in this barren and cold land of finding anything good for hunting, particularly while surrounded by a massive noisy barrier.

We did, of course, attempt to escape. Asinda started by throwing several stones at the barrier. Sparks flared up upon impact, before the stones disintegrated into dust. Seramina even tried casting some of her magic at it, and all the while I watched her eyes to check that they didn't burn too brightly.

But not even she could break the magic, or at least she didn't dare try too hard.

After several failed attempts, Seramina, Asinda, and I sat down on the cold stone floor in despair, saying nothing. Esme watched us; she clearly had something to say, but it wasn't good news, and so she wisely waited for us to cool down before delivering it.

As you've probably already learned by now, I hated waiting. So I pushed Esme to cut to the chase.

"Okay," I said. "What's the plan, Esme?"

She cocked her head slowly, her brilliant blue eyes seeming to blaze, but it was just the glow of the purple mist reflecting off them. "What makes you think I've got a plan?"

"Because since I started this journey with you, you've always had one. So why don't you get on with it and spit it out?"

The Abyssinian lowered her head. "You are starting to know me, Dragoncat. Very well, I shall tell you, but I warn you that you're not going to like it." She paused.

"She's going to suggest we kill the dog," Asinda said, clearly also not having any patience with her.

I bristled, and my back sprang up into an arch. Asinda's words hit me like a wrecking ball. I'd wanted Esme to be a friend – or even a *companion* – as noble as Ta'ra. But I didn't like this at all.

I didn't realise it at the time, but I hissed my reply in the cat language: "What do you mean, kill the dog? We can't kill Max. He hasn't done anything wrong."

"I told you you wouldn't like it," Esme replied in the human language. "Anger isn't going to get you anywhere, Dragoncat."

"But you're a powerful white mage," I protested, also this time in the human language. I was still shouting. "That evil basilisk turned him to stone, but can't you just turn him back or something?"

"No," Esme said. "No human magic can undo a basilisk's spell."

"So what about a cat's magic? After all, you're the daughter of Bastet. That makes you all powerful, doesn't it?"

"I'm sorry, but it cannot be done. I know this is hard for you, Ben."

Perhaps Esme's voice did actually have a soothing quality to it, or perhaps I just started to realise getting angry was futile. I dug my claws into the ground, pulling on the rock to help relieve some of the tension. Soon, my rage subsided a little. It didn't change how I felt about Esme's decision, but who was I to stop her?

"I'm guessing Ben said that you can't just go ahead and kill Max," Seramina said. "Because you can't. He's our friend." Her voice trailed off, as if she also thought her efforts were futile. I guessed she was afraid that she might blow up again and end up killing us all just to save some stupid dog.

"How do you plan to kill him anyway?" I asked. "If you've failed to notice, he is a statue right now."

I worried that Esme would suggest that one of us should use our dark magic to shatter him to pieces, because White Magic can't be used to destroy. Bastet had already warned about the danger of using the stuff, and of *Cana Dei* consuming us as a result. But to use it for such a malevolent deed would make the caster no better than any of the warlocks. Such evil could start a long chain of dark events in any one of our minds.

Her plan became more apparent when Asinda picked up a much larger stone than before and threw it right at the barrier. It disintegrated instantaneously, letting out an awful, odious smell.

Esme watched it then turned back to me, still speaking in her treacly voice.

"If you think about it, it's our only way out. We disintegrate him using the barrier, and the Key to the Sixth dimension drops at our feet. Yes, a life will be lost. But it would be for a noble cause." Esme looked over her shoulder at the statue and bowed her head as if she were at a funeral. "Max would be happy to make this sacrifice, I'm sure. He would be honoured, in fact."

I bowed my head to mirror Esme's. She was right, in a way. Max could save us all, and it would be so easy. He would forgive us, when he looked down from dog heaven – wherever that was – and saw what we'd done. We'd never see him again, but I guess there was a cost to everything.

I was about to say that it was fine, that we should go ahead with it. But then I turned, and I saw Max's face frozen on the statue. He looked so innocent, with his tongue hanging out and his eyes wide. He'd always been loyal to a fault, and he certainly didn't deserve this.

He'd told me once that his first master had thrown him out on the streets in his old home in Sussex. He'd had to fend for himself for a while then, picking scraps out of dustbins, and fighting with other stray dogs for territory. Then Arran had reached out through a portal and pulled him into this dimension, just like Astravar had done with me.

Whiskers, he was just like me. An innocent creature who had been thrust into this world and hadn't asked for any of it. But unlike me, he'd accepted the changes quickly, and he had always been fighting, always trying to protect others until the very end.

Seeing him like this, and remembering what he'd told me, caused me to spring into action. I summoned my staff bearer who plunged the staff into my mouth. I turned around and stared at Esme, an intense burning sensation in the space at the back of my eyes.

"I will not let you hurt Max. He would protect me if he were in my position, and so I will protect him from you."

Esme growled, and she circled around until she was facing me. "You would save one life, though his fate could protect worlds? He isn't even a cat, or a dragon, or a human for that matter! Would you protect mice, or cockroaches, or ants as well?"

"It doesn't matter what species he is. He is our friend. Look, if we end up killing him to get what we want, we're no better than those warlocks. We're meant to be the good guys here."

"Have you never heard of the greater good?" Esme asked. "Harm one to save thousands, utilitarianism and all that. Once upon a time, they said cats were good at philosophy. Bastet once told me the tale of a cat belonging to a kooky scientist in the Fourth Dimension. It spent all its life in a box, that one, contemplating the nature of its existence. That's what cats are meant to be like – all thoughtful and contemplative."

Poor cat, I thought, then realised that I really didn't want to get side-tracked. "It doesn't matter. It's just not right, and I won't let you hurt him."

"Well," Esme said as she summoned her staff bearer, which consequently placed her staff in her mouth. "I'm afraid there's not much you can do to stop me, Dragoncat."

"Maybe not alone," Seramina said, and she stepped up beside me, her staff already drawn. "But you won't get through the both of us."

"Seramina," Asinda said. "This is stupid. It's our only way out and you know it."

"Is it?" Seramina asked. "What would Lars think if he saw you behaving like this? Do you really think he'd go ahead and let you kill your friend?"

"Don't you—" Asinda started, then stopped herself. "Just leave my boyfriend out of this."

"Don't let her get to you," Esme said. "Remember, you and High Prefect Lars won't last forever. You need to learn how to forge your own path without him, if you are going to learn how to survive in this world."

But Seramina had realised she'd opened a vein and continued to exploit it. "What does it matter what the future holds? Lars completes you now, and you know that he wouldn't let you do this. He'd tell you that it isn't the right thing ... that you're better than this. And what about your dragon? What would Shadorow say if he saw you behaving this way?"

One of Asinda's hands was holding her staff tightly. The other formed a fist, clenched tightly by her hip. The features on her face tightened, and her hard stare seemed intent on boring into Seramina. But Seramina gazed back, this time no fire behind her grey eyes, only compassion. This was the Seramina I knew and loved.

There was only silence, and no one moved except Esme, who kept turning her head between Asinda and Seramina as if wondering how this would play out. Up to this point she'd always seemed to know the future. But I guessed Lasinta had thrust a knife into her plans, and for the first time she didn't have a clue what would happen next. She was merely improvising, because she thought she had to lead, but for a change her decision was wrong.

Eventually Asinda lowered her staff, and the expression on her face softened. "You're right – we cannot harm Max. Not after all we've been through together."

Esme now had her back arched and she hissed at Asinda from behind the staff that she still clutched in her jaws. She spun around and turned her hissing upon me. "So what do you propose we do? Come on, Dragoncat, you seem to have all the answers here. What's the plan?"

I hissed back at her, not liking being talked to like this, especially by her. Then, I let the anger seep out of me, and I dropped my staff to the ground. My staff bearer swooped down to pick it up and vanished into thin air.

"We wait," I said, and as I did I felt something happening. My fur pricked up as I sensed the fabric of space beginning to change. Time started to slow, and I knew then that everything was going to be okay. Someone had come to help.

"What are we waiting for?" Esme asked. Clearly, she hadn't sensed it.

As if in answer to Esme's question, there came a flash of light from my left. Time seemed to slow even more, and static pulled at my fur. I turned to see a portal opening to a verdant land.

Whiskers, after passing through portals to three of the smelliest places in all the dimensions, I'd thought I'd had enough of portals. But I was more than happy to see this one, particularly when I heard the swishing of waterfalls and smelled the pollen pushing away the stench of rotten vegetable juice.

I was even happier to see who stepped out of it. She wasn't in her feline form, but it didn't matter. She wasn't in her fairy form either, but glamoured to look like a human. Her dark raven hair cascaded over each side of her pale face, and when she saw me, her green eyes lit up like bright gems.

"Ben," Ta'ra said. "I thought we'd never find you. Come on inside, your friends are waiting." I ran over to her, purring louder than I can ever remember purring. I chirped gratefully when she reached down to tickle my chin.

37

SHADES OF FRIENDSHIP

Ta'lon stepped out of the portal behind Ta'ra, and he was also glamoured in his human form. He ordered some golden wisps to take Max into the Faerie Realm. There must have been dozens of them, swarming out of the portal and then starting to spin around the statue, sprinkling fairy dust onto the stone.

Despite the arrival of our saviours, I still couldn't help worrying about Max. He was still flickering in and out of existence, flashing into nothing and then returning to being a statue again. At first I had hope that the fairies might know a way to turn him back to his normal self. But instead, their magic lifted him off the floor and floated him over through the portal. He would be safer in the Faerie Realm, I guessed, than stuck all alone in this magical cage.

Ta'lon saw me looking at Max. He strolled over to me. "You know, if what the Oracle Fairy tells me is true, it's better for him that he's turned to stone right now."

My ears twitched, and I looked at Ta'lon in disbelief. "You can't possibly think this is good for him. Let me guess, you like dogs even less than cats. You want his life to end, don't you?"

Ta'lon shook his head. "I know you don't particularly like me, Ben. But I, and all the fairies, have everyone's best interest at heart. The Oracle Fairy told me that so long as his skin is stone, so will be the material of the vessel that contains his soul – the one that Arran is currently trying to break. It will make it a lot harder for him to feed the dog's soul to *Cana Dei*, delaying his plan."

I really didn't want to think about the moment that Prince Arran broke the barrier. I didn't want to think about the inevitable moment that we lost Max.

"Who exactly is this Oracle Fairy, anyway?" I asked, trying to change the subject.

"You will meet her soon," Ta'lon said, and before I could say anything else, a cloud of golden dust rose around him. In seconds he was a golden wisp darting back into the Faerie Realm. Which was fine by me – I hadn't wanted to stand around talking to him anyway. I took another look at Ta'ra.

"Come on," she said, and also stepped through. I followed her.

The air had never tasted so fresh as it did in that moment. It was as if I'd just stepped out of a vacuum, and I spent several moments taking deep breaths and letting my lungs fill up with oxygen. I didn't even stop to look around. Instead, I kept my eyes closed – appreciating the warm kiss of the sun on my fur, since night had not yet fallen in the Faerie Realm.

I breathed in all the smells of nature. There was thyme, and oregano, and pine, and the heady pollen of poppies. There was the scent of long dewy grass and ... catnip ... the fairies had planted catnip in the vicinity. Maybe it had been Ta'ra's idea. Did that mean she was here to stay?

I opened my eyes and looked up at her. Esme hovered nearby, her ears raised and twitching as they rotated towards us. I didn't care. She could listen to what I had to say to Ta'ra and how I felt about her. I was done with Esme.

"You still smell like a cat," I said, in the cat language, because I knew Ta'ra could still speak it. I rubbed my head against Ta'ra's calf so some of my scent would also brush onto her.

Ta'ra giggled and she placed her hand over her mouth. Fairies seemed to like to giggle a lot. Cats, on the other hand, didn't. This wasn't a giggle of laughter anyway, but a nervous giggle – one of embarrassment, I guess.

Ta'ra lowered her hand, then took a deep breath. She didn't give me the honour of speaking back in the cat language. Instead, she spoke in a language even more ancient the human one ... the Faerie Tongue.

"This is my life now, Ben. Ta'lon said he'd give me another chance. That even if I was a cat, he could glamour me as a fairy. I can't use magic anymore, but it doesn't matter. Ta'lon said that he had a good talk with the So'ta, our Faerie King."

"Ta'ra, I'm sorry ... I shouldn't have run off with Esme like that. She isn't for me, and I've learned that now. I was being stupid. You're the one that I want to spend my life with. You mean every-thing to me."

I gave Esme a cursory glance. She still had her ears turned towards us, though her eyes weren't watching us, but instead tracing the flight of a blackbird crossing towards a distant oak.

Ta'ra shook her head slowly and let out a long sigh. Her gaze roved over to Esme, then returned to me. "It doesn't matter now. Ben, you might not have meant it, but when I saw you and Esme together, I realised something. Cats aren't meant for only one companion. They never were."

"Ta'ra, I—"

"Just let me finish Ben, please."

I paused and waited, my tail thrashing anxiously over the mulchy ground.

"I grew up in humble circumstances, and I knew I would only take one husband. Then, when I learned it would be Prince Ta'lon, my grandfather – Be'las, you've met him – was so happy. But Astravar turned me into a cat, and cats don't belong in this realm. It looked for a long time like it would never be." She sighed. "Things are just different here. Ta'lon never took another partner after me, and he just couldn't stop thinking about me. He's convinced his father, King So'ta, to allow the Cat Sidhe to live in this realm so long as they have a fairy close by who can keep them glamoured. We're allowed to go back to who we were, Ben. Do you know how that feels? It's a huge change for all of us."

I growled. I really wasn't liking this. It wasn't just because of Ta'ra's decision to leave me; I guessed I deserved that. But she couldn't trust Ta'lon. He wasn't a good fairy – he'd betrayed her too many times.

"Ta'ra, I care about you," I said.

"And I care about you, Ben. But you're not meant to be tied down; it's not in your nature. And this is the life that was meant for me. I can see that now, and I'm sorry if you feel differently, but this is just how it is."

"And what about your dragon?" I asked. "What will happen to your bond with Kada?"

She smiled. "She never really wanted to stay in Dragonsbond Academy anyway. So the fairies have agreed to let her stay here. She'll be the first dragon to live in the Faerie Realm, ever. Maybe she will finally help broker peace between fairies and dragons. It's not as if we're at war, but there's still a lot of enmity between us."

"But you haven't even received your gifts yet, Ta'ra. Your crystal must have plans for you."

Ta'ra shrugged. "You know, maybe I wasn't meant to get any gifts in the first place. It doesn't matter now – I don't belong in

Dragonsbond Academy. I'm a fairy by birth, and I belong here. The crystal will come too, of course. The fairies think it'll be a great honour to have a crystal in this realm, in the king's palace. Its forecasts may even help protect the kingdom."

Just as she mentioned the crystal, I realised exactly what was going on. This was political, and Ta'ra was too blind to see it. Ta'lon didn't want Ta'ra because of who she was, but now that she had bonded with a dragon, the realm wanted her crystal.

But who was I to steal Ta'ra's thunder? I didn't want to break her heart for a second time.

Ta'lon called Ta'ra over. He was standing just in front of my friends, who were sitting at the edge of a thick forest. We were on a plateau that looked down into a valley, a long silver river stretching from one end of it to the other. If I listened hard enough, I could hear the gentle swishing of it running over the rocks, and I could see the dragonflies that swooped down low to drink of its waters.

Ta'ra looked at me, apology in her eyes. "I should go. There's a lot going on in Faerini. Announcements to make and all that." She showed me the polished ring on her finger with a ruby in its centre. Her cheeks went almost as red as the gem. "We're getting married." She squealed. "It's finally happening. Anyway, I guess you didn't want to hear that. But Ben, really, it was good to see you again."

She reached out and touched my cheek with the tip of her finger. She still definitely smelled of cat, and she'd never change that. After taking one last look at me, she skipped off towards Ta'lon. She still had a cat's grace in her step, even when she was in her human form. I hoped she would never lose that.

I turned my attention back to my friends. They were all there – the dragons, the unicorns with their riders, Rine and Ange....

I suddenly found myself blinking in disbelief. Rine and Ange were sitting together on a lone mossy boulder, and they were very close.

Ange was nestled in the crook of Rine's elbow, giggling while Rine was feeding her an awfully ripe looking strawberry. Whiskers, I guessed they'd had plenty of time for bonding, this time without Bellari around to spoil everything. It seemed they hadn't needed me around to bring them together after all. Below them, Palimali lay in the shade of a willow tree, pawing lazily at one of the branches that dangled overhead.

A wave of elation washed over me. But it was short lived, as I saw Max's stone body hovering towards them, guided by a ring of circling fairies. A heavy sigh passed through my chest ... I'd lost Ta'ra, and I'd soon lose Max too.

"*I'm sorry, Ben,*" Salanraja said in my head, and I looked up to see her standing above the other dragons. "*But you need to have faith. We'll find a way to save Max, I'm sure.*"

"But Ta'ra," I said. "*I pushed her away, Salanraja. Because of who I am.*"

"*Just let's focus on saving Max, shall we, and you can maybe patch things up with Ta'ra later. You never know how it's going to turn out between her and Ta'lon. Anything could happen.*"

"*I guess.*" I stopped to think for a moment. "*How much do you know of what just happened?*"

"*Alliander explained everything,*" Salanraja said. "*You went on quite an adventure through many portals, I hear, and you even got to meet Bastet herself. It sounded like it was going so well, right up to the point that you came face to face with a basilisk. It was lucky you had that Abyssinian, with enough wit to cast a mirroring glamour. I don't know what I would have done if you had been turned to stone. I don't want to lose you, Ben.*"

She glanced over at Corralsa. The fairies had deposited Max beneath the massive jet dragon. She had lowered her head so that her neck folded over him, as if to guard him. She looked so sad with her head draped on the ground like that.

"*Wait a minute,*" I said. "*How exactly does Alliander know all this? Please don't tell me she's a daughter of Bastet, too.*"

Salanraja let out a roar that shook the ground and sent the fairy wisps around her scattering. There was a reason that fairies didn't like dragons, but I knew well enough by now that she was only laughing. "*Oh, how I've missed you, Ben. You know, it's a lot easier to handle your excursions across the dimensions when I have at least a single ounce of faith that you'll return again.*"

"*You didn't answer the question,*" I said, the tip of my tail twitching in frustration.

"*Don't you remember? Just before you dark magic users decided to run away, Alliander went to speak to the Oracle Fairy – who is apparently the wisest of all who dwell in this realm. The White Mage captain learned a lot, and she has a very good memory, so she has told us everything. Oh, and that reminds me; I was meant to pass a message on to you. The Oracle Fairy told Alliander to tell me to tell you – because the Oracle Fairy doesn't talk to dragons. She finds us a little too, well let's just say, 'risky'—*"

Whiskers, Salanraja could rattle on sometimes. "*Just get on with it. Because every moment we delay, Arran gets closer to destroying Max's soul.*"

"*Very well,*" Salanraja said, "*although the Oracle Fairy told us we have a lot more time than we think we do. Like Bastet, she can also read the future.*"

"*Salanraja,*" I said. "*Please ... I haven't got the patience for this right now.*"

"*Fine,*" Salanraja said. "*The Oracle Fairy suggests that you go and see her before you go and talk to your friends, and she says both of you must go.*"

"*The both of us?*" I asked. "*Who else?*"

I bristled when I smelled Esme approaching. She brushed gently passed me, and I swear I literally took a swipe at her, hissing as I did.

"Calm down, Dragoncat," she said. "Gratis has already told me that we need to go and see the Oracle Fairy. It looks like it was fate all along."

She sauntered off into the forest. I paused only for a short while before deciding I had better follow her. Not because I particularly wanted to, but because she seemed to know where to go.

38

ORACLE FAIRY

I used to live in a small village in South Wales in the Fourth Dimension, where they didn't really have forests. They had woods alright, but woods were always kind of safe. The worst thing you might find in one was a fox or a badger, and you only tended to see them at night.

It wasn't until I reached the First Dimension that I learned how different and more dangerous forests were. Honestly, every single one that I'd visited there seemed to have been designed to creep me out. The shadows were darker, the creatures scarier, and there were things like fields of magical mushrooms whose spores would send you into a permanent sleep.

But nothing was creepy in the Faerie Realm – it just wouldn't have suited the character of the place. The forest we entered was rich in vegetation, and trickling streams danced through it everywhere I looked. Fluffy moss grew over the rocks, and the ground was crisp with fallen leaves. Though the canopy above looked thick, plenty of light still seeped through it. But it wasn't a harsh light, and the shadows remained soft.

Honestly, I wondered if Rine and Ange and I could set up a cottage here where we could finally retire. There were so many places to explore, so many rich smells and tranquil sites that you could just sit and stare at for hours. In a way I could see why Ta'ra had wanted to return here.

Fairies certainly didn't seem scared of the place, and their golden glows darted in and around the trees. Butterflies also danced around the flowers and colourful mushrooms that grew on the forest floor, and bees buzzed around hives in the branches that were always a good safe distance away.

Still, despite the tranquillity of the place, my company was far from pleasant. I really wasn't in the mood to talk to Esme, so I let her stay a good dozen paces ahead of me as she meandered through the trees. I tried not to look at her either, but rather just followed her shadow and traced the path of her paws through the soil.

Alas, I couldn't ignore her forever, and she wouldn't let me, because she eventually turned and creeped up to me. I stopped in my tracks, staring with my back arched.

"Stay away from me," I hissed in the cat language. "If you come any closer, I swear I will use my claws."

Esme honoured that and kept a respectful distance. "Look, I know you're angry, Ben, and you didn't understand my decision back in the Darklands. But I was only doing what I thought was right."

In truth, she didn't actually call me Ben, but used my name in the cat language, which is incomprehensible to the human tongue. But it was the first time she'd used it, and I hadn't even realised that she knew it. Still, I wasn't going to fall for any of the cheap tricks she was trying to use to endear me to her.

"There was nothing good about it," I said. "You wanted to kill my friend."

"I wanted to save the Key to the Sixth Dimension in the most efficient way possible. I wanted to ensure it didn't fall into the wrong hands."

"Then why are you slowing us down now? Max's life is in danger, and if Arran gets the key because you delayed us, then it will be all your fault."

Esme hissed. "You're impossible!"

"Fine, I'm impossible, and you're evil. Now let's just go and meet the Oracle Fairy, shall we?"

Esme turned away, growling. I felt slightly bad for holding a grudge. It didn't feel a particularly feline thing to do. But as Salanraja and others had pointed out many times, I was becoming more and more human, and humans were allowed to hold grudges.

I let her get ahead of me again, and I continued to follow in the same way as before. The forest got a little denser, and the shade deepened, but still not to the extent where I'd call it scary. Not long afterwards, we reached a section where the trees seemed to peel away, a blue glow poking through from the horizon. As in all this Realm, I could hear rushing water, and a cooling freshness gusted back from the clearing.

I saw the waterfall when we passed through the trees – a spectacular foam of raging white that dropped down into a blue lagoon below, stretching out as far as the eye could see and lit to amber by the waning sun. It was so beautiful that I almost missed the massive tree that hung over the waterfall.

It was an ash, taller and wider than any tree I had ever seen. Its branches were knotted together so tightly that it was impossible to see the top of it. It had an incredibly wide trunk, more so than any tree I'd ever seen. But what I found most curious of all was the face that peered out from the bottom of the tree bole. An old and wise face, that creaked gently as it moved its lips.

I walked up to it. I'd seen so many strange things in the past year that a talking tree couldn't scare me one bit. "You're not going to tell me that you're the Oracle Fairy, are you?"

"Why…" the tree said. Both its lips and voice moved agonisingly slowly. "I never knew that the fabled Dragoncat was so rude!" Its language was old and ancient, and I don't think I understood it because of my gift of languages. Rather it was the kind of language that you didn't think you should understand before you encountered it, and once you did you wondered what you'd been missing all this time.

"I'm not rude," I said. "I'm just having a really bad day." I glared at Esme as I thrashed my tail, so she would understand this was all her fault.

"Very well," the tree said, still drawing out every single syllable. "Then to answer your question, I have many names. In an ancient land, I was once called *Yggdrasil*. And in many languages, I'm simply called the Tree of Life. In another dimension, a botanist might see me and label me *fraxinus maximus*. That hasn't happened yet, but I predict it will in the future. But here, they decided to name me the *Oracle Fairy*. I think I like that name best, don't you?"

"But you're not even a fairy," I pointed out. "Or maybe this is a glamour. Maybe you are a fairy just like Ta'ra is a cat, and that waterfall behind you is probably an entire city."

"This isn't a glamour," the tree said, and it curled some of its branches towards it, rolling its eyes towards them as if examining its form. "I'm an honorary fairy, apparently. Trees are older than fairies or humans, or even cats, you know. Surely that means that I can be whatever I like?"

Come to think of it, it did make sense in a way. Not that the tree was a fairy – I was still having trouble wrapping my mind around that. But that it had preferred to see Esme and me instead of our dragons. After all, dragons breathed fire, and fire burned trees. What it might have forgotten, however, is that cats liked to use trees as scratching posts.

"Okay, honorary Oracle Fairy," I said, my whiskers twitching. "I'm sorry if I offended you. Perhaps you might tell us why you summoned us here today?"

Esme was staring at me, blinking her bright blue eyes in disbelief. "I'm sorry for my *companion's* awkward behaviour—"

I spun around to face her, displaying a snarl and a hiss. "I'm not your *companion.*" I said it in the cat language, not wanting the tree to understand.

"Now is not the time, Dragoncat. We have more pressing issues, do we not?"

"Will you two stop behaving like kittens who have been dropped into the wrong litter?" the tree rumbled. "You came to speak to me, did you not? Or did you simply want to come into the forest to argue?" A wind came up from the waterfall as it spoke, carrying soft and soothing smells.

I turned back to the tree. I certainly preferred to speak to it and not to Esme. "Our friend is in danger," I said, "and something tells me that you might be able to help."

The tree paused for a long moment, as if it needed time to think. "You're talking about the dog, no doubt," it said eventually. "For my roots spread across dimensions, and I can read the threads of space, time, and destiny."

Esme stalked forward as if she wanted suddenly to control the conversation. "So tell me, great one. Should we refer to you as he, she, or they?"

A rumbling laughter came from the tree's massive mouth. "I have lived many years, and I have seen conventions change across generations. My gender of the year depends on the weather, the seasons, the warp and weft of time, and the current needs of the forest. But for now, I am a she."

"Glad we cleared that up, then," Esme said, looking back at me. I blinked in confusion. "What? It's important!"

"What's important is saving Max," I said, and I turned my attention back to the tree. "What can you do for him?"

"That's where you're wrong, you see. What I *can* do is not important. What's important is what you *should* do."

This time I need to pause to think. The tree reminded me of the sphinx in a way – it seemed to want to tax your mind. "Look," I said. "I believe no human magic can turn a creature back from stone. But maybe the magic of the forest can help? Because I'm guessing a talking tree must have certain powers."

The Oracle Fairy paused for a moment, and the whole forest seemed to go silent in response. The only thing I could hear was the rushing sound of the water falling off the rock, so clear that it was almost deafening.

"So can you save Max?" I asked. "Can you make him a dog again?"

"I can..." the giant ash tree said. "But I shall not."

"Why not?"

"I believe Ta'lon has already explained this to you. The dog is safer in his stone form for now. Right at this moment, the Warlock Prince is hammering at a vessel of stone to try to feed Max's soul to *Cana Dei*. All the while, the warlocks are flying to the Altar of Lore to do battle with him, and Apopis is traveling through the Wastelands with his demon army. But what, I ask, are *you* going to do?"

I raised my head in pride. "That's that, then. We've done our work in setting Arran against the other warlocks. They'll destroy each other, and Max will be safe, and then you'll turn him back into a dog. Is that what you're saying?"

"No," and the whole forest seemed to shiver as the tree roared out that single word. "You still must play a part in this, Dragoncat, as will you, Esme, Dragon Rider of the White."

"So tell us," Esme said. "Because destiny seemed to change when the warlocks foiled our plans to stop Arran, and I've not had a crystal available to look up what to do next."

Honestly, I was getting a little sleepy. This whole debacle had taken its toll on me. A wide yawn overcame my body, and my eyelids became heavy.

The tree brought down several of its branches to thump the ground around us. The waterfall whipped up some heady foam, and for a very brief moment the forest did indeed seem scary. I jumped to attention, ready fight or flee.

"That's better," the Oracle Fairy said. "Because the two of you seemed to be getting quite lethargic. Since you seem unable to answer my question, I shall do it for you. You must gather your allies and join the battle. Because destiny dictates you will all play a part."

"But how will we know what to do, O great one?" Esme asked.

"When the time comes, you will know. The only thing, I must say, is that the two of you must work together."

I glared at Esme, and she glared right back. But soon her glare softened, and I guess mine did too. She wasn't a bad cat, and I guessed we could help each other. The Oracle Fairy was right – we did have to find a way to get on, somehow.

"I'll work with you," I said. "But don't think that means you're my friend."

"Then we have something passable," Esme said, and she turned her head towards the waterfall and licked her paw.

"That's good to see," the Oracle Fairy said, and her voice was no longer slow, but had an urgency to it. "Because we have spent enough time talking, and I believe the mighty Matharon wishes to make a speech."

39

MATHARON'S SPEECH

I'd come to learn that it was traditional to make a speech before a big and climactic battle, and in this instance I was glad that Matharon was to make the speech and not Alliander. For one, I didn't value any of what the pompous Captain of the White Guard had to say, and for another, she had an incredibly boring voice.

Of course, neither the humans nor the fairies could understand Matharon, which meant that they needed an interpreter. To encourage our friendship, Esme suggested that we work on interpreting together. After remembering what the Oracle Fairy had said about us having to work with each other, I reluctantly agreed.

Matharon stood between Esme and me, his head craned as high as possible. We were standing on tall mushrooms that the fairies had grown. They had strengthened the stalks so we wouldn't tip off them. Mine was red with white polka dots underneath, while Esme's was more pinkish.

Night was catching up with us in the fields outside Faerini City, and the sun was starting to set behind us. Still, the land didn't lose its pleasant warmth, and part of me really didn't want to leave.

Everyone was situated below us, arranged in neat rows. Alliander and the other White Mages sat on their unicorns at the front, and behind them, Seramina, Rine, Ange with Palimali, and Asinda sat on their dragon's saddles, looking up at Matharon. The dragons each stood with his or her head craned up at him as if scared to break eye contact with the great bronze dragon.

Salanraja stood on my side of the other dragons. Gratis stood on Esme's side, but he was closer to the unicorns than the dragons, as though he didn't feel he belonged to the dragon party. Behind them stood what I'd now counted to be thirteen of Matharon's Guardians. The sun glinted off their scales, and they had their blazing eyes locked on Matharon, looking genuinely interested in what he had to say.

I surveyed them all for a moment, thinking we had gathered an impressive force. We didn't have the magical power that the warlocks did, or the help of a massive demon snake. But we did have pluck and spirit and, most of all, the will to win. We also, of course, had the largest dragons of them all.

In the centre stood Max – a lonesome statue who'd been arranged to face the same direction as Matharon. Some fairies had also gathered, but none of them were to join in the battle. Still, they buzzed around curiously.

Matharon let out a loud growling cough that seemed to shake the ground beneath us, and also the spongy mushroom surface on which I sat. Fortunately the fairy magic that had reinforced it also meant there was no chance of me tumbling off my perch.

The great bronze dragon spoke out in a booming voice, capturing the attention of all the dragons below him. He paused at the end of each sentence to give me a chance to translate what he'd said.

"The night has come; the darkness is upon us. We have had a time of repose in the Faerie Realm, whilst our brave dark magic users have traversed dimensions and gone through many portals to learn of the dangers that assail us. But perhaps the bravest among us is this stone dog you see standing resolute beneath me. This noble creature came from a dimension that is not our own, and he didn't ask to have the fate of worlds resting upon his shoulders.

"Despite learning from the crystals what dangers lay before him, and even knowing – according to the Oracle Fairy – that he might be turned to stone, indeed even in the knowledge that he might have to sacrifice his life, still he chose to persevere. Why did he do this, you might ask? I tell you why: he did it because he has absolute faith in his friends."

Matharon took a deep breath, and he turned to Esme to prompt her to continue. I was mostly glad, because I'd been trying to interpret at the same volume as Matharon, and I'd ended up giving myself a sore throat.

"We will now work together," Esme shouted, and her voice was even louder and more confident than my own. "We have one thing that the Warlocks don't have – neither does the traitor that we've come to know as the Warlock Prince – and nor for that matter do the demons. Each one of us cares deeply about his or her comrades, and none of us are in this for ourselves – for our own best interest. None of us wish to serve the darkness that wishes to consume our souls.

"We do not strive for the sake of greed. We do not strive to better another man or woman, or dragon or cat or unicorn or dog. We strive for each other, and no matter the outcome of this battle, that is what makes us strong. We are comrades, I tell you. We are companions. We are a team. So, let us go out and show our enemy who we truly are. Working together, while they shall always, on some fundamental level, work apart."

Whiskers, I wanted to have been the one to deliver that finale.

But Esme had probably delivered it with greater finesse than I ever could.

That then was it. We'd already taken time to discuss our strategies and tactics; each one of us knew what we had to do, and we were ready to charge.

Beneath us, the crowd whooped and cheered. Fists pumped the air, and unicorns whinnied and reared. Dragons roared, letting jets of flame out into the sky. Even the fairies glowed brightly, and I hoped for Matharon's sake that they'd stayed away from the flames.

The fairies ducked past the crowd, disappearing from sight. Soon afterwards, a portal opened behind Matharon's Guardians. The elder dragons turned first and flew through it. The dragons of Dragonsbond Academy followed, with the exception of Salanraja and Gratis, and then the unicorns. Matharon gave a triumphant roar and launched from the ground to charge over the threshold. I took one last look at Esme, and together we leapt off our mushrooms and onto our dragons' backs.

"*Great speech, Ben,*" Salanraja said.

"*It wasn't mine, it was Matharon's.*"

"*Yeah, but you made it sound less scary.*"

Before I could chide her for mocking me, she lifted off the ground and flew through the portal into the barren Darklands, where the largest battle I had ever seen, would soon commence.

PARLEY

The temple that contained the Altar of Lore stood before us, lit purple with the ambient glow from the horizon. The stench of rotten vegetable juice was so thick that I thought I would suffocate. I hated this place even more than the Seventh Dimension.

All kinds of magical creatures lay in wait. There must have been hundreds of Manipulators, glowing white like ghosts, with their spectral staffs held high above them. Bone dragons kept vigil from the air. Stone golems shook the ground as they trod each heavy step, and I could see the flame golems burning on the horizon, ready to attack.

But they were still far away, behind the temple that greeted us with its thirteen towering spires. Their bases were concealed by the structure's stone walls and eleven verdigris domes. Even from this distance I could make out the gargoyles, twisted into grotesque shapes. We weren't facing the main entrance, but rather the back door, a narrow slit between too columns that supported the smallest of the domes.

In the shade of the thin doorway stood Arran, his scarlet cloak whipping behind him in the night wind. He held something above his head, which looked to be a bottle made from stone. Two objects lay at his feet. I couldn't see them in detail from where we stood, but I guessed them to be the obsidian shard and the vial of *Cana Dei*.

It seemed that Arran hadn't prepared an army himself – or rather, the army behind the tower didn't belong to him. On further inspection, I noticed that this army was still marching towards us, but it hadn't reached us yet. It must have belonged to Lasinta and the other warlocks.

Meanwhile, Arran hadn't set up defences of his own. It was such a strange thing; I'd expected a huge battle to be raging against Arran as he did everything in his power to complete his ritual of destroying Max's soul. Now it seemed he didn't even want to destroy the soul in the first place. Rather, he was holding out his arm and beckoning us forward with the back of his hand.

We'd already agreed in advance that if a parley – in other words a talk between the two sides – were possible, then the cats would represent our side. The reasoning was simple. It would be easier for us to get away than anyone else. Also, Palimali might be able to charge at cheetah-speed and knock Max's soul out of Arran's hand.

"*Gracious demons,*" Salanraja said. "*What is going on?*"

"*I don't know,*" I said, "*but I'm guessing Arran wants to talk to us.*"

"*Just be careful, Ben...*"

"*When am I not?*"

I scrambled down Salanraja's tail and joined Esme and Palimali. Together we stalked – or rather the cheetah stalked, and Esme and I had to hurry to keep up with her – towards the temple entrance. We arrived in front of Arran. Palimali immediately took a defensive posture and lowered herself in a crouch, ready to pounce if need be.

Now that I'd had a chance to examine him up close, I realised Arran looked different – and much more terrifying than before. His skin now resembled Astravar's, with cracks across every inch of its surface, as if it were made of eggshells. It also had a pale blue sheen to it. This meant that Arran must have been drawing off an awful lot of dark magic recently – more it seemed than was humanly possible.

"A parley with three cats," he said, shaking his head. "What is the world coming to?"

"Usually, a parley is between representatives of two armies," Esme replied. "But you seem to be alone. Or are you representing that force in the distance? Maybe you've been working with the other warlocks all along."

Arran looked over his shoulder, then chuckled as he turned back to look at Esme. His expression twisted. "I would never work with my grandmother again. Not now I've come so far."

I growled at Arran impatiently. "What are you up to, Arran? You've been trying to destroy our friend's soul so that you can get the Key to the Sixth Dimension, but now you've stopped. Bastet showed us what you were trying to do."

Esme hissed at me as soon as I mentioned Bastet's name. I shrunk back, my tail folded between my legs as I realised my mistake.

Arran cocked his head. "So that was who you were working with. The great Bastet herself."

"That is none of your business," Esme said. "Just hand over the soul, and then we'll work out what to do with you."

Arran checked over his shoulder once again. He was tapping his foot impatiently, as if waiting for something. "You can have the soul. But if you must know, we've all been tricked. Max doesn't have Capitut's Key inside of him as we all thought. I saw a glimpse of the truth when I was trying to break open the soul container. *Cana Dei* can reveal a lot more than you realise, particularly with its link to the Ghost Realm. So why don't you make it easier for everyone and tell me where he hid it?"

I looked at Esme in surprise. At first I thought he was playing games with us, but I saw no other reason why he would stop the ritual.

"Don't show him anything," Esme hissed at me in the cat language.

"It doesn't matter," I replied, "he wouldn't be able to read my expressions anyway."

She growled at me, then turned back to Arran. "You will not get anything from us."

Arran nodded slowly, and I noticed a gleam in his eyes as he studied each of us in turn. Whiskers, Arran was a mind mage, and if he caught us off guard he could extract the information from us with a click of his fingers. He looked first at Esme, then at Palimali, and finally his gaze settled on me. He stared at me for the longest time, as if thinking I'd be the easiest to read.

I willed myself to think of all the mutton sausages I'd been missing out on lately. I regretted it immediately, because it just reminded me how hungry I was. So instead, I thought of Ta'ra, but that only made feel sad. Finally, I settled on remembering the meal of milk and salmon trimmings that I'd been eating before Astravar yanked me into the First Dimension, which set my tummy to rumbling again. It worked though – through all these memories, I had completely avoided thinking about Max.

I'm not sure Arran would have found what he wanted in any case, because we'd all genuinely thought that Max still carried Capitut's Key. Or at least *I* had.

Eventually, Arran took his gaze off me and looked up at the sky. "I guess Alliander was wise in sending cats out to parley after all; I can't read anything from you. Ah, well, at least I can get a head start on finding where your dog kept the key. All the while, I'll leave you to fight the warlocks that I believe you tried to set on me, and it won't be long until Apopis arrives with his minions, too."

He glanced down at the vessel containing Max's soul and then abruptly dropped it. I bristled as I saw it fall. It tumbled over the ground as a cloud of purple mist rose around Arran's feet. A whiff of rotten vegetable juice was carried upon the breeze.

Esme immediately called out a command in the cheetah language. "Palimali, now!" Then in the cat language, "Ben, draw your staff!"

Before she had barked out the second command, Palimali had already charged. She leapt just before she reached Arran. At the same time, both Esme and I summoned our staff bearers, two giant hands wavering in front of us. Together our staffs glowed – Esme's along the length of it and mine at the crystal.

Palimali broke her charge at the purple plume that had gained density quickly. She scuffed the ground, turned around, and she lifted herself on two legs as she stretched as high as she could with her paws.

A claw hit an emerging blue jay, but she only managed to graze it, bringing down a clump of blue feathers. The rest of the crested bird got away, shrieking loudly as it headed east. I sent off a red beam after it, but Arran was already too far away for me to do any damage. In all honesty, I don't think I even hit him.

"So Arran has finally become powerful enough to complete a transformation," I said. "But a blue jay? I thought warlocks were meant to transform into carrion eaters."

"Jays will eat anything," Esme replied, letting out a deep growl from the pit of her stomach, and I didn't have to be a genius to catch the irony of her statement.

Indeed, Arran would do anything to get what he wanted.

41

DESERTER

Usually battles against warlocks involved a whole lot of Manipulators. Clearly, from the shimmering forms that we'd seen approaching before, this battle would be no different. The standard strategy in such battles was for dragon riders to take down the Manipulators from the ground, leaving their bone dragon cohorts to the dragons themselves.

Fortunately, we now had a whole troop of the White Guard at our disposal. Thus, Alliander and Matharon had together decided that it would be better if the dragon riders fought from the air.

From my perch on Salanraja's back, I watched the purple mist seep along the ground, grateful that I wasn't in the thick of it. Below, the unicorns charged through fields of purple mist and over barren land, their horns glowing as they went. The White Mages on their bare backs had transformed their staffs into magical scythes, which they used to cut swathes through the thorny mandragoras that the Manipulators had summoned onto the ground. The disgusting plants had huge heads like Venus flytraps, which could snap you in two. Not to mention their sharp and venomous thorns.

Suddenly I spotted an eldritch tangle of bone and sharp, terrifying talons coming at Salanraja from the side. I ducked down into Salanraja's corridor of spikes as the bone dragon attacked. But they offered little cover from the acidic flame, which washed over me, burning with pain.

The same stuff had sapped my energy before, near Bestian Academy. If I didn't do something, I might not last long. My staff in my mouth, I sent out a purple beam after the bone dragon, missing completely.

I looked back at the construct, tracing its movement. I really hadn't seen it coming. It must have literally swooped down from on high. Salanraja turned and chased after the thing.

She veered so hard that I was almost sent tumbling off her back. Usually I would have corrected myself, but that unexpected spray of acid had disoriented me. A jet of fire leapt out of Salanraja's mouth, and it washed over the bone dragon. But its skeleton only shimmered beneath the flame – any damage that Salanraja did being automatically healed by the beam of energy from its Manipulator's staff feeding it from the ground.

My friends up in the air weren't faring much better. Matharon and his Guardians kept ramming into the bone dragons with their bulk and breathing heavy flames on them. But they did nothing but knock the bone dragons around in the sky, as if playing an elaborate game of snooker.

From the emerald dragon Ishtkar's back, Rine shot shards of ice behind and around him, but he didn't seem to be able to hit anything. From the sapphire dragon Quarl's back, Ange whipped heavy vines out of her staff, but they simply glanced off the bone dragons without doing any damage. Beside her, Palimali sat with her lip curled away from her teeth in a snarl. She was crouched down as if ready to pounce on one of our enemies. But nothing seemed to come close enough for her to do so, and even it if it had, the cheetah wouldn't have been able to do much damage.

Asinda also whizzed around on her grey dragon Shadorow's back, and she was doing more damage to the dragons than Ange or Rine, tearing great chunks of bone off of her enemies. But whatever she knocked off, the Manipulators immediately replenished with their spectral magic. I wondered if we should have been fighting on the ground, and Salanraja seemed to share that opinion.

"*Gracious demons, those White Mages are useless,*" she said. "*Whiskers, are you okay, Bengie? You took quite a hit.*"

"*Salanraja, you said whiskers,*" I pointed out.

"*So I did.... Obviously, I am picking up your vernacular.*"

I was stinging, but the dark magic coursing through me continued to heal me. I drank up the power, wanting more of it. Then I remembered – this stuff would destroy my soul.

"*I'm fine,*" I said.

"*I wish you were down there fighting the Manipulators. I could tell you which one to take down so there wouldn't be so much guesswork up here.*"

"*Perhaps you're right,*" I said, then spotted another bone dragon darting up toward Salanraja from below. "*Watch out!*"

She swerved just in time, and I managed to brace for the turn. She chased after the bone dragon, which didn't have any magical beam connecting to it this time. Salanraja took it out in one swift fiery breath, burning it to meal.

"*That's better,*" she said.

But my eyes had already latched on to something that had distracted me: I saw Seramina on her dragon. The teenager's eyes were burning brightly, and a white beam was being directed from her staff right into the back of Hallinar's head. Together, teenager and dragon descended away from the battle up here in the sky.

"*What is she doing?*" I asked Salanraja.

"Who?"

"Seramina ... can't you see?"

Salanraja turned her head. *"Gracious demons, she's controlling her dragon – forcing it down to the ground. She's deserting us."*

"But why—" I hesitated as I remembered something Bastet had said back in her lair.

Only those brimming with Cana Dei can enter the temple wherein lies the Altar of Lore, and anything that leaves must be carried by those who can use dark magic. In other words, only dark magic users like Seramina could go inside. But what did she want there? What did she hope to gain?

All of a sudden, an orb of fire separated itself from Seramina's staff. It drifted up above her head and seemed to hover there, undisturbed by Hallinar's flight path.

"Gracious demons, she's sending up a challenge," Salanraja said.

"A what?"

"I've heard about these in training. Sometimes warlocks will challenge each other with a ball of fire, just like that one. She's saying she's ready to fight the warlocks; she probably thinks she can take them all out. With her power, maybe she can."

"But she'll lose. She's not ready..." Then an even more terrifying thought came to me. *Or she'll end up destroying the world.*

"Clearly she believes she is," Salanraja said.

"And no one but we dark mages and the warlocks can go in there. Whiskers, she means to try and take them all out alone."

I still wasn't sure I could believe it; it seemed like I was living a dream. I remembered the premonition that I'd seen in the Ghost Realm, how Seramina had driven her staff into the ground while fighting all six of the warlocks. She had split the world apart.

Could this be it – could this be the day that Seramina destroyed us all?

"We need to follow her down," I said. *"You need to drop me off down there."*

"Bengie," Salanraja said. *"Do you know what that place is? It's the temple that contains the Altar of Lore. I can't go in there to protect you. No dragon can, and neither can your friends."*

"No," I said, and my jaw was clenched with determination. *"But I can, and Asinda can if she so chooses. Bastet told me to do this, Salanraja. It's my destiny."*

"You already fulfilled your destiny..."

"But I have a new one. I'm the only one who can keep Seramina safe." Still, though the words had tumbled through my mind, I wasn't sure I really believed it. Was there really anything I could do?

Salanraja groaned loudly, but she also she knew she had no choice. Without further ado, she swooped down towards the temple.

As we sailed over the courtyard, I looked down to see that the thirteen spires had started to glow, as if they were indeed summoning me towards my destiny.

42

BATTLE OF THE WARLOCKS

Since Salanraja couldn't enter the temple, she dropped me off at the narrow entryway where we had previously encountered Arran. The obsidian shard from Mount Arhoom, the bottle filled with *Cana Dei*, and the vessel containing Max's soul still lay there on the ground – no one had dared to touch them.

Around us, the air had a rich and evil thickness to it, with that horrible stench of rotten vegetable juice pervading every inch of the landscape. Lights from the battlefield flashed all around us, and neither the White Mages nor the forces of the warlocks seemed to be gaining any ground.

Salanraja had managed to cut ahead of Seramina and the hypnotised Hallinar. The teenager had been so enthralled by what she was doing that she hadn't seemed to notice us come in to land. I quickly rolled off Salanraja's tail, the way that I'd practised so many times. Salanraja left me there to give Hallinar room to land.

Seramina didn't jump off Hallinar's back, but rather floated down as if on an invisible magical platform. Her staff was blazing and her hair whipped around her. Her skin gave off an ethereal glow, and she almost looked like one of the Manipulators herself. Her eyes were raging fires, her gaze set on the temple's entrance.

I watched her drift inside for a moment, and then I stalked after her. She didn't seem to notice me, or if she did she didn't seem to care. Instead, she was apparently focused only on one task: to destroy the warlocks, and perhaps in the process destroy the world.

There was only a short, wide corridor between the entrance and the room that contained the Altar of Lore. As Seramina entered, with me following close behind, the thirteen metal spires glowed even more brightly. There was a strange thrumming sound emanating from every direction. It wasn't loud, but it somehow cut off the sounds of the battle outside, as if not even sound itself was allowed to enter the temple.

"Seramina, you are losing control," I told her. "Remember yourself."

The voice that responded wasn't quite her own. It was of her distinct pitch and rhythm, but it also sounded disembodied, and it was more monotone.

"In the darkness, I have found myself," she said. Really, it felt like I was talking to a ghost. "The warlocks must learn the way or be destroyed. Then you, Dragoncat, will also need to make the same choice."

I hissed at her, fluffing my body up and feeling the hackles tear at my skin. "Seramina, this is not what we came to do. We came to stop Arran, and we did that. Now we should aim to take Max's soul from here and get home as quickly as possible."

"No," she said, and her face suddenly snapped around to look at me. Her skin looked like a porcelain doll's, with slight cracks developing on her cheeks. "Arran is with us, too. He, Apopis, Ammit, and I. We are all to become one. Don't you see how beautiful this is, Dragoncat? Every single creature, united and evolved. Everyone working together towards a single purpose."

That was when I realised what was happening. *Cana Dei* was starting to take over Seramina's soul. Bastet had warned us about it many times. If we let the stuff in, then it could consume us. Seramina was going right down the track that her father had, and I needed to find a way to stop her. Yet how, I didn't know.

"Seramina, you have to stop this."

"No." Seramina pointed to the sky with her glowing staff. "I must destroy them." I craned my head to see what she was pointing at.

Six birds of prey shot out of the sky, diving towards us: a condor, a bald eagle, a hawk, a buzzard, a seagull, and a vulture. Shrieking and cawing and crying at the tops of their voices. The temple, it seemed, would allow their voices to enter, as they were advocates of dark magic themselves.

The birds landed on the other side of the altar, and purple clouds of gas arose around them. The clouds subsided quickly, and the six warlocks emerged with their staffs drawn, their crystals glowing brightly.

They all had that same fire in their eyes. Their hair – of those who had it – flailed in all directions. For those who didn't, their cloaks thrashed above the ground. The verdigris domes glowed even brighter, and the buzzing intensified. Sparks lashed out along the spires from tip to tip, forming a ring that danced and sang to the sky above, of the battle to come.

"You called us to enact your death," Lasinta croaked. "Initiate Seramina, you think you are destined to be an all-powerful warlock. Yet these grounds – the Altar of Lore – shall do you no favours."

Seramina's lips stretched into a mirthless grin. I'd seen that same expression on Arran's face, and on Astravar's. It didn't belong to a human; it belonged to *Cana Dei.*

"I am no longer an Initiate," Seramina said. "Not in this form. I have brought you here to finally pay the debts you've accrued over the years. You have worked too long for your own interests, and if you don't join us now your lives shall be forfeit."

The warlocks didn't waste any more time on idle chatter. Instead, they lifted their staffs high above their heads. Wispy lines of purple energy spiralled out of them, leading up into growing balls of white light at their crystals' tips.

In response, Seramina thrust her staff into the ground. The ground shook – much like I'd seen in that vision in the Ghost Realm. Cracks started to run out from her staff, one leading right under my tail. I yowled and leapt out of the way, still staring at Seramina and absolutely unsure of what I was meant to do.

A ball of magic grew from her staff. But it wasn't white and pulsing with heat, like the warlocks' magic. Instead, she'd created a dark disc with a purple glow surrounding it. It sucked in the air around it, as if it were a black hole. Bits of dust and debris lifted off the ground, spiralling towards it.

"Seramina, this isn't you!" I shouted. "Where are you right now?"

"This is the way," Seramina replied, as if her words had been rehearsed. "*Cana Dei* is our future. As for you warlocks, for years the six of you have been resisting the darkness, trying to walk as delicately as you can on the edge. Now you must either submit, or let it consume you. There is no other way."

As the purple glow above her spun faster, a dark cloud seeped out of the hole she'd created above her head. It moved as if it had intelligence, creeping outwards with dark tendrils that probed the air, searching for the breath of any creature – the very tunnel that would lead ultimately to a soul. The surroundings no longer smelled of rotten vegetable juice, but instead of yeast extract.

"She's summoning *Cana Dei* from the Ghost Realm," the oldest male warlock screamed. "She wants to destroy the world!"

Lasinta glanced up at the miniature portal above Seramina's

head. Her brow furrowed and her eyes narrowed to slits. "Get out of here!" she called. "Retreat or die!"

None of the warlocks hesitated. They cancelled their spells, and clouds of purple gas rose from their feet. This spread and faded quickly. Soon six birds of prey were lifting off into the air.

"You are going nowhere," Seramina screamed. With each word she spoke, her hair lashed like thousands of tiny whips, and her eyes pulsed with white light. There was no amber left in there anymore. Her spirit dangled at the extremes of light and dark, with no room for shade or colour.

Another ball of white light emerged from the tip of her staff, without interrupting the flow of energy to the portal. It grew as it shot upwards, halting at a point high above the courtyard. A dome of sparks spread out from it, looking just like that magical nullification field that the warlocks had trapped us with not long ago.

"Nothing can leave," Seramina said. "But don't worry – it shall not be this girl that destroys you. I am *Cana Dei!*"

At the same time, there came a massive roar from outside. It rumbled like a thousand thunderstorms, once again shaking the earth.

Many things happened at once. The dome of sparks fell down against the walls of the courtyard. A cloud of rubble and ash roiled at the base of it, consuming the temple as its walls went crashing down. This was brought about not just by the force of the sparks, but also the continued tremors that Seramina's magic was sending across the earth.

Momentarily I felt a weakness in my wings. Not my wings, but Salanraja's – I felt them through our bond. She'd been hit by the flame of a bone dragon so powerful, the acid had scorched her wing. I saw flashes of what she saw: the other dragons falling, tightness and worry upon my comrades' faces. Something was pulling them down, a darkness that stretched out across the landscape. It seeped out of cracks in the ground – the cracks that Seramina had created. A field of darkness expanded outwards through these cracks, seeping upwards. A field of *Cana Dei*.

In a way it looked inviting. It would send its subjects into a permanent sleep, and they would wake up renewed – a more powerful version of themselves. Before Salanraja hit the ground, I saw that the demon dragons had joined the battle, their wide-open maws leading to their molten cores.

Back in the temple, I saw through my own vision the movement of something massive through the sky. Suddenly, a gigantic snake head crashed down from above, connected to a long body that looked like volcanic rock, with a crisscross pattern of lines seeping into a fiery core.

"Welcome, Apopis," Seramina said. "Fellow servant of *Cana Dei*."

"The darkness will soon serve us all," Apopis replied.

Whiskers, I didn't like this at all. Bastet had already explained how the Overlords of the Seventh Dimension were once warlocks who had been consumed by *Cana Dei*. Now it seemed both Apopis and Seramina were working together, and I still had no idea what I could do to stop them.

43

THE RETURN OF CANA DEI

The cloud of *Cana Dei* continued to flow outwards from the portal above Seramina's head, limiting the space in which I could move safely. It seemed to swallow the light wherever it went, sucking it in and causing the air around it to shimmer.

Seramina controlled it, her eyes and skin glowing bright white. She inhaled great breaths of the stuff, then blew it back out through her nostrils, as if she were a dragon brewing the darkest fire.

I now had my staff in my mouth. My staff bearer had balled itself into a tight fist, not in aggression, but to keep in as tight a space as possible so *Cana Dei* couldn't find it. I let the magic surge through me, ready to fight. It made me also want to draw the darkness in, to breathe it and let it wrap around my soul, as it was no doubt doing around Seramina's.

Outside of the domed barrier that buzzed and raged above and around us, I could also see the darkness flowing outwards from the tight cracks in the ground. I couldn't see any creatures there anymore. The unicorns, the White Mages, the magical creations of the warlocks, the dragons, and the dragon riders, were all becoming the property of *Cana Dei.*

Through my bond, I could feel the darkness spreading through Salanraja's body. It coursed through her veins and seeped into her lungs, burning as it did everything in its power to find its way into her heart. Once it found it, it would enter that microscopic portal that linked her substance and Salanraja's soul in the Fifth Dimension.

I didn't know how long we had until my friends and my dragon were doomed. Whiskers, even Esme must have been out there somewhere, struggling. No matter how little I trusted her, she didn't deserve this. Not even the warlocks deserved this....

Meanwhile, the warlocks – now in their flying forms – circled around the roof of the dome of magic that contained us. The black cloud hadn't yet reached them – it still had to fill the ceiling of the dome, but there was plenty of it coming. Enough, I knew, to flow out across the realm.

Right now, however, *Cana Dei* wasn't the warlocks' primary opponent. Rather, Apopis had coiled his body around the base of bowl that was the Altar of Lore. His head was as high as possible above it, and he kept snapping out at the birds, trying to catch them within his great mouth. Given enough time he would do so – the warlocks had nowhere to go.

The only place where *Cana Dei* hadn't seemed to enter was the gigantic stone bowl – the Altar of Lore. Rather, it seemed to have an invisible field of energy around it, as if High Prefect Lars was right at the centre casting a shield to keep the darkness away.

I turned my attention back to Seramina, who was even more difficult to see within the swirling clouds of darkness. My fur prickled as I noticed *Cana Dei* creeping ever closer to me, searching as if it had whiskers in every inch of its fabric. The sensation of hot and cold had left this place, and it was looking more and more like the Ghost Realm.

I was trapped. The more magic I cast, the more I would draw it towards me. But if I didn't do anything, time alone would be my enemy.

I summoned some energy to my staff, my tongue burning. Whiffs of both rotten vegetable juice and yeast extract filled my nostrils, seeming to battle each other for dominion. I let out a red beam of magic, directed right at the portal above Seramina's staff.

It did nothing, just entered the darkness like a beam from an electric torch entering a dark room. But it seemed this room had no end to it, and so the beam was eventually swallowed by the blackness.

I still had another option, but I hadn't wanted to use it. Increasing my size also increased the chance that this dark seeping force would find its way inside of me. But I really didn't have much choice.

I willed my staff bearer to take the staff from my mouth, and then allowed it to vanish, hoping the darkness could no longer touch it. I'd already learned from failed experiments that I could not use my staff in my chimera form.

My muscles burned and tore and I yowled out in pain as I transformed. Muscles popped, joints creaked, bones expanded, and soon my yowl became both an ear-shattering roar, a high-pitched bleat, and a hiss that could send terror across dimensions. I emerged with a lion's head, a goat's head protruding out of my neck, and a snake's tail.

I didn't waste another moment. I used my hind hooves to charge at Seramina, as my snake's tail lashed out in as many directions as possible, like a flailing whip trying to lash the *Cana Dei* away. I was heading right for Seramina's staff, my lion's teeth bared, and my jaw ready to snap it out of her grasp.

Instead, I hit a wall of magic, set up a good foot's radius all around Seramina. It was the ultimate resistance, and I bounced off it, my head pounding as if I'd charged head-first into a wall.

I lay on the ground, breathing heavily. There was no way out of this. Seramina was too powerful, and she would soon win.

Suddenly, I saw a flash of white dart out from behind me. The body it belonged to stopped. A pink nose, and the brilliant blue eyes of an Abyssinian stared up at me. Esme's ears twitched.

"Dragoncat, into the Altar of Lore," she said. "It's the only place you're safe."

I blinked in disbelief. "Esme.... But how?"

She didn't answer. Instead she dashed forwards, and with a dexterity only available to cats, she leapt up four times her height into the great stone bowl. I'd expected the force field to stop her, but she sailed right through.

It made a lot of sense when I later had a chance to think about it; Bastet had said that the altar could be used to contain a soul and stop it from finding its way back to the Fifth Dimension. It also seemed that it could stop *Cana Dei* from entering.

I turned back into a Bengal as I sprinted towards the great stone bowl. It always hurt less when transforming into a regular cat – shrinking was a lot less painful than stretching. When I reached the altar I was normal again, and I could swear I jumped even higher than Esme had as I sailed through the protective barrier.

Esme was waiting on the other side with her staff clenched in her jaw, glowing with white magic.

SUMMONING

"You work on stopping Apopis," Esme said in the cat language. "I'll work on stopping the teenager."

I blinked rapidly at her a few times as if to ask what the whiskers she was talking about. She didn't seem to notice, rather focusing on the energy pulsing into her staff. "Esme?" I asked. "What do you mean? Nothing can defeat Apopis except another immortal."

She didn't turn towards me but growled, "Have you forgotten what Bastet told you? You need to summon her into this realm."

"But only those who use dark magic can enter this temple. Only those who have embraced *Cana Dei*."

"How do you think I got in here?" Esme snapped back. Her speaking didn't seem to break her concentration, and a stream of white energy was surging towards the top of her staff. "Look, there's no time to explain now, but I will later. Just know that both Bastet and I were once dark magic users, and I'm much older than you think. Now open a portal using the altar, otherwise either Seramina or Apopis will destroy us all."

Because they've both been consumed by Cana Dei, I reminded myself, and then I had to tell myself that Seramina wasn't Seramina right now. She wasn't the girl who had protected me so many times, and who I was fated to protect. Still, I had to bring the real Seramina back. I couldn't let her get lost to the darkness.

Whiskers, was there any way back for her? Maybe the *Cana Dei* had already consumed her soul. But I had to believe that she had time; I had to believe there was still a part of her clinging on.

"Don't think about it too much and you'll work it out. Now focus!" Esme said.

No matter how much I pushed her, she didn't seem to be of much help. But there was another voice, one in my head. It had been pinging on the sides of my brain, trying to get my attention, but I hadn't been listening. Or rather, I'd let it become part of the environment, like distant wind chimes. I'd been too concerned with keeping away from that horrible dark gas and surviving.

"*Dragoncat,*" it said, and it spoke in a soft Welsh accent. "*You have finally let me through.*"

The voice of my crystal…. But no, it was more than that. This was Bastet speaking to me herself, from the Fifth Dimension.

"*Bastet,*" I said in my mind. "*What must I do?*"

"*You know what to do,*" she replied. "*It's already within you. But if you don't hurry, then the opportunity will be lost.*"

Just like that, Bastet's voice faded away, tinkling like the sound of wind chimes drifting on the breeze. But she was right; I had power within myself, and she'd said that I had to do this. I just needed to believe.

At the centre of the bowl there was a crystal, and a large one at that. I could see its aura, brimming with power. It had enough strength in it to open a portal to anywhere. Perhaps it was the most powerful crystal I'd ever encountered.

I closed my eyes, and I summoned my staff bearer to place the staff into my mouth and willed power into it. It burned at the back of my tongue, but for the first time I knew that the darkness couldn't find me here. *Cana Dei* had no way through to this altar. I could cast the most powerful spell of all, and it wouldn't change me.

I wasn't sure what I was doing at first, so I just focused on the flow of energy to my staff, letting it pulse softly as it thrummed with increasing power. But soon I saw a white light in front of me. It wasn't there physically, but I still saw it in my mind's eye.

I focused on drawing the energy into my mind, on letting the fire burn at the back of it, as I focused all my attention on that pulsing light. When I opened my eyes, I realised I had cast a beam of purple energy from the crystal on my staff to the crystal at the centre of the bowl. A disc of white light started to grow across the surface of the bowl from the larger of the crystals, pulsing with energy.

"That's it, Dragoncat," Esme called. "You're doing it."

She already had white light surging out from her staff, directed at the portal that Seramina had used to summon *Cana Dei*. Her beam seemed to be consumed by the darkness in the portal, just as mine had been. But unlike me, Esme didn't seem ready to give up. Slowly, I could see that the purple light surrounding the portal was being replaced by a white one.

Whiskers, maybe Esme could close the portal. But then what?

The teenager's eyes were still glowing with furious fire, but she hadn't yet seemed to notice Esme's interference. All the while, I continued to feed the disc at the base of the bowl, which gathered brightness as it grew outwards.

There suddenly came a boulder-splitting roar from above us. It was coming from Apopis, who had stopped snapping at the shrieking birds of prey. The six warlocks were circling the upper perimeter of the dome of energy, still trapped. Somehow they had managed to evade Apopis all this time.

The snake turned his head towards us. Two massive red eyes assessed Esme and me. A long flaming forked tongue lashed out of his mouth, seeming to taste the Cana Dei. Then, the snake's great craggy head began to roll slowly towards us.

"Apopis has noticed us," I said. "He's coming this way."

"Don't break your focus," Esme replied. "He won't be able to see inside this altar. We are invisible here to the influence of *Cana Dei*."

But I wasn't so sure about that, as I watched Apopis' head looming ever closer. His tongue continued to taste the air, as if he had latched onto a scent.

"He can sense us, though," I said.

"He's searching, but he shall not find us. Now concentrate!"

I didn't let the stream from my staff cut off. The white light beneath us had now reached our feet and was continuing to grow outwards. I knew instinctively that as soon as it reached the edge of the bowl, Bastet would be able to break through and battle Apopis.

But still time seemed to pass agonizingly slowly as Apopis continued to edge closer. I could taste the sulphur on his breath now, and it would only take one lash from that fiery tongue to end my life. Another to end Esme's. I could try casting magic at him to push him away, but that would just end up alerting him to our location.

Whiskers, I had to be patient and I had to have faith, and I did neither of those very well.

Time slowed around us as the portal opened beneath our feet. It was a one-way portal, and so Esme and I didn't fall into it. All I had to do was make it large enough so that Bastet could leap out.

I watched in horror as Apopis opened his mouth. Between his two massive lava-dripping fangs, I could see the great fires burning in his core. His gaze swivelled downwards, and I knew then that he had detected me. Ever so slowly, out came that forked tongue, slowed by the space-time rift caused by the bridge between the dimensions.

Moments passed, and I willed my legs to run out of the way, but they were also affected by the slow motion. In seconds I would be dead. Except those seconds would last minutes from my current frame of reference.

I saw it all, then: the darkness still roaring out of Seramina's portal, despite Esme's best efforts to stop it; the birds hopelessly flapping to try and escape this place, reduced from powerful warlocks to creatures of instinct; the darkness spreading out across the landscape, that had consumed, and would continue to consume, until there was nothing left in this or any of the realms it found its way into.

The final moment of my life, and it was over, and I had lost. *Goodbye, cruel world*, I thought. I had fought bravely, and I had done my best to save it, and all the good humans, cats, dogs, dragons, and even unicorns upon it.

But it wasn't over, because Bastet took that opportune moment to launch out of the one-way portal that I had opened to the Fifth Dimension.

45

SUPERNATURAL AID

The giant cat sailed out, stealthy and panther-like, from the portal, sharp claws extended and even sharper teeth bared. Her silent hiss seemed to push the darkness away. Just before Apopis' tongue slid over me, her paw pushed his neck away, bringing him downwards with the strength of the giant cat's pounce.

Bastet hit the ground and rolled twice. The dark miasma of *Cana Dei*, which had almost concealed the courtyard outside of the altar completely, puffed outwards as if someone had blown a gigantic bellows through its path. It made room for the giant cat and snake to battle.

Everything seemed to have happened so far in slow motion. But now time sped up once again, as the portal beneath my feet winked out, revealing cold grey stone. Apopis tossed his head upwards and roared with such force that the ground and the altar shuddered violently. My teeth chattered, but I managed to stand my ground.

"My old friend," Bastet said to Apopis, but her snarl told me she thought Apopis anything but a friend. "The legends seem to repeat themselves, and somehow I always win."

"This time will be different," Apopis snapped back. "For I have grown in power during my time in the Seventh Dimension."

"And so have I," Bastet said. She no longer spoke with the lilting voice of the crystals that I'd come to know so well, but in a deeper, feral tone – one that seemed as old as time. On this note she pounced, and Apopis lurched in to defend.

There came a flurry of claws and teeth. Loud hisses filled our surroundings, and as Bastet and Apopis writhed and turned – Apopis twisting each segment of his fiery body, and Bastet leaping away from the snake's attempts to strangle her and striking back with diamond-sharp claws – it became apparent that I didn't know who would win.

"Ben, I could really do with your help here," Esme shouted.

I snapped my head around to see her jaw clenched and eyes tight in concentration. She was still casting that white beam out of her staff, but now it was being met with a stream of *Cana Dei* that came out of Seramina's staff. Seramina's fiery gaze was focused right on Esme, and it seemed that this alone could burn her to a crisp.

"Cast that magic on me," I said to Esme. "I'll fight back like I did before."

"No, it won't work – you need to tell her to stop."

"But how?" My words were lost to the darkness, because as soon as I'd spoken them I had a flash of inspiration. Just as the crystals had spoken in my mind many times, so too had the darkness. But it had been in such disembodied whispers that I hadn't noticed it existed until now.

Join me, Dragoncat, it was saying in its dark and ancient tongue. Strangely, it sounded exactly like Astravar.

Cana Dei was a creature, albeit an incredibly complicated one, and right now its voice would also be whispering in Seramina's mind. All I had to do was insert the right message – one that would bring her back to us. Only in that way could I break through the darkness.

Out of the corner of my eye, I could see that Esme was losing. Seramina was pushing her beam back towards her with an incredible strength. In moments the Abyssinian would die, and so I only had one chance.

I swallowed my fear, and I opened my mouth, and I spoke the words in as commanding a voice as I could muster. "Seramina, you do not have to lose yourself to the darkness. There is always a light! Find it within you."

These words were enough; nothing more needed to be said. The language was so powerful that it seemed to still everything around it into silence. For a moment, nothing happened. Seramina's eyes still raged with fire, and the *Cana Dei* still surged towards Esme, getting so close to her face that it was about to break her.

"Do not lose yourself!" I repeated again, even louder now. "There is always a light!"

My words seemed even to catch the attention of *Cana Dei*. For a moment the tendrils of gas stopped moving, and then the whole cloud tremored as if in fear. The crystals had once told me that the gift of languages was the most powerful of them all, but I don't think I'd ever believed it until that moment.

The fire faded from Seramina's eyes, and she blinked a few times and shook her head hard as if remembering herself. She looked around, seeming to notice the dark cloud for the first time, then she gasped. But she didn't stop casting her magic just yet. A new light emerged from the crystal on her staff, a white one which floated upwards towards the centre of the disc. This swirled around rapidly and proceeded to suck the *Cana Dei* back into the Ghost Realm.

From behind me, there came a screech ten times as loud as

might be made by two of the largest Maine Coons in a catfight. I turned to see Apopis' head lunging down towards Bastet, his jaws wide open and ready to sink his fangs into her skin. At the same time, she had her jaws wrapped around a section of Apopis' spine, and she clenched them tight.

Lava spouted up out of Apopis as Bastet rolled out of the way to avoid his bite. The demon snake tossed his head up to the sky and roared in pain.

The *Cana Dei* rolled back from the landscape outside and over Apopis' body as Seramina continued to suck it back through her portal. She was drawing it in faster and faster, her eyes and staff brimming with a new kind of power. The eggshell cracks had left her skin now, leaving her with an image of renewed vitality.

At the same time, the dome of magic above us winked out of existence, and the birds of prey above screeched and flew away to the south. I watched them for a moment, doubting that this would be the last we saw of the warlocks. We still had battles to fight, I was sure.

Meanwhile, the black cloud had masked Apopis so completely that I couldn't see what was happening to him. It soon washed over him utterly, revealing a smouldering husk of rock, with no sign of the demon snake underneath it.

I caught sight of something dark, long, and incredibly thin – looking like the world's longest worm – slithering off into the distance. It moved so fast across the ground that I doubted anything could catch it.

But I did see five demon dragons following it, lines of red energy leading from them towards the snake as if trying to heal it. A sea of demon foxes followed Apopis, yipping out the Ride of the Valkyries. Yet their notes were now completely out of key and the same lines of red energy seemed to lead out of them into Apopis' nearly dead inner husk.

Bastet had lain down on the ground and was panting heavily. She noticed where I was looking and turned her head towards the retreating army of demons, and what was left of Apopis. "He will first draw power from his minions in an attempt to heal, but they don't have enough inside them to restore his vitality. He will need to return to the Seventh Dimension to fully regain his strength, and that will take a while. But I fear this won't be the last we see of Apopis."

"Still, we have won for now," I said, and I looked over at Esme, who gave me a slow blink.

Meanwhile, Seramina continued to suck in the last vestiges of *Cana Dei,* and I looked up at the landscape as unicorns and dragons lifted themselves up off the ground. There were humans there as well, most of them dressed in white robes, but I also spotted my friends Ange, Rine, and Asinda amongst them. Thousands of dormant purple crystals surrounded them – the previous hearts of the Manipulators and golems that had attacked us, and which I hoped would never see life again.

Seramina let out a heavy sigh, and the portal winked shut above her head. Once her spell was complete, the fire left her eyes and all colour blanched out of her cheeks. Her legs and arms went limp, and she collapsed. Bastet bounded forward so that she had a soft body to fall on. The giant cat lowered the teenage girl gently to the ground, where she lay looking so innocent and frail that you'd never think she'd played such a big part in the recent chain of events.

Before Bastet left her, she pushed her head forward to talk into her ear, as if wanting to speak into her dreams. "Don't see this as the end, young mage," she said. "For the journeys towards greatness often begin in our darkest hour, and you still have the grandest of parts to play."

She left Seramina there to sleep, and she stopped beside the altar and summoned a massive portal into the Fifth Dimension right in front of her, without any visual indications she was casting magic at all. Before Bastet stepped through, she looked at Esme and I, who were lying down nestled up close to each other.

"Take them to the School of the White, Esme," she said. "Train them away from the darkness, just as you were trained all those hundreds of years ago."

Esme stood up and nodded to Bastet in acknowledgment. "Goodbye," she said.

"Goodbye ... for now." Her words trailed away as she stepped through the portal, leaving the First Dimension to be governed by mortals once again.

46

BACK AT THE ACADEMY

The journey home on our dragons through the darkness was gruelling for two reasons. First, all this exertion and magic meant every single muscle in my body was aching. Honestly, I could hardly move. Second, there didn't seem to be any food for miles, and Alliander had ordered that there wouldn't be any stops until we reached Dragonsbond Academy.

The last good meal I'd eaten had been those rabbits, and that now seemed like days ago. But as the cold and the high wind lashed at my sore ears, I tried to keep my grumbles to myself, even if Salanraja could no doubt hear them inside her head.

Captain Alliander was in charge again, since Matharon and his Guardians had left us to return to Bestian Academy. They had a new class of dragons coming in in a couple of days, and they needed to be there to greet them. Alliander had also confiscated the dark mages' staffs, including mine. She'd tried to confiscate Esme's, too, but the Abyssinian had run off so fast and on to Gratis' back, she hadn't had a chance. As an extra measure, Tanni carried Seramina strapped back-to-back with Alliander. Hallinar therefore flew in formation without a rider.

Salanraja didn't talk to me until we had left the miasma of purple rotten vegetable juice behind and flown into the Wastelands – the no man's land that stretched between the Darklands and Illumine Kingdom. I don't think she was angry at me, as such. But she, and the other dragons with us, seemed absolutely exhausted.

After everything that had happened, mind, I didn't blame them. When we got back to the castle I was sure we'd all sleep for hours.

"*You know, there is some good news that has come out of this,*" she said. "*I think you'll be glad to hear it.*"

"*What's that?*" I asked. "*Are they going to prepare a feast for when we get back to Dragonsbond Academy to reward me for my bravery?*"

"*Gracious demons, no,*" Salanraja said. "*You are probably in trouble for running off from the Faerie Realm and into the Fifth Dimension like you did.*"

I growled. Esme had made me do it, in the name of fate and all that. But I realised there was no point arguing with Salanraja about it. "*So what's the news, then?*" I asked instead.

"*Well, as soon as she realised it was safe, the Oracle Fairy turned Max back into a normal dog again and sent him through a portal back to Dragonsbond Academy. He's waiting for us all to arrive.*"

Now that was good news, especially since I'd decided that as soon as I saw the Sussex spaniel I would ask him exactly what had happened to Capitut's Key, and why he hadn't told us that it was no longer on his person. It meant our whole quest to guard him had been pointless, as had Arran's and the warlocks' quests to remove it from his body in the first place. I'd wondered if Esme had known about it, but she swore she hadn't. Still, Bastet must have, and in a way it felt like we'd all been played with like pawns.

It seemed in fact that Bastet had known everything that had

happened was going to happen, though she hadn't chosen to warn us about everything. Yet what would I have done if I'd known Seramina would turn to the darkness like that? I doubt I'd have been able to stop it either way.

Nobody had warned me, either, that I would lose Ta'ra only to have her be replaced by a much less trustworthy *companion*. Esme had also become special to me in her own way, but I wasn't sure I'd ever come to trust her as I'd trusted Ta'ra. Now I wondered if I'd ever see the former Cat Sidhe again.

The rest of the journey was relatively uneventful. I appreciated the sunrise, and the clear sky we flew through once we had left the Wastelands. The warmth the sun cast down as it spun overhead helped abate the cold wind. Still, with my tummy rumbling and all the pain coursing through me, I could never get truly warm.

Eventually, the castle with its six towers came into view. Familiar dragons wheeled over the turrets, including Olan – the famous great white who belonged to none other than Aleam.

Aleam himself awaited us in the courtyard – looking in much better health than he had when we'd left Dragonsbond Academy. He stood there together with Driar Yila, Driar Lonamm, and Driar Brigel. No doubt our dragons had told their dragons we were coming. Somehow, the unicorns had managed to get ahead of us, giving Alliander an opportunity to talk to the four of them before we landed. As we drew closer, I saw that Esme was there too, and she was a part of the conversation.

Seramina and Asinda were also standing in front of them, but they didn't seem to be interacting with each other or those who were discussing their fate. Their dragons weren't there, so they must have already returned to their chambers in the towers.

Once Salanraja touched down, I scrambled the best I could down her tail. My muscles shook violently, but I made it down to the ground without falling off. Max barked then and rushed over to greet me. His wet slimy tongue slid over my nose and brow, which I didn't appreciate at all.

I cut straight to the point: so far neither Esme nor I had told anyone about Arran's revelation that Max no longer carried the Key to the Sixth Dimension. We wanted to get the information straight from the horse's mouth. I could already see Esme stalking over, and so I waited for her brush up beside me.

"Ben, it's so good to see you!" Max yipped excitedly. "Max is happy to see you! Max has never been happier!"

He didn't know cats well enough, it seemed, to realise that the way our tails were thrashing meant we weren't impressed. "What did you do with the Key to the Sixth Dimension?" I asked.

Max paused and studied us with wide eyes. He looked like a dog that had just stolen dinner off his owner's table. "It's inside me!" Max barked back. "I still carry the key."

"Arran seemed to think otherwise," Esme snapped back at him, and his excited bark was reduced to a whimper. "And so do we."

He turned his head twice between us, before he decided to whine out the truth. "It came out the other end, and I didn't want to swallow it again. So I took it out and buried it."

"And where exactly did you bury it?" I asked.

This time, Max displayed his teeth in a snarl. "That's Max's secret," he barked. "Bastet said – don't tell anyone!"

I hissed back at him, wanting to question him some more. But my chance was cut short when Initiate Yila bawled out at the top of her voice: "Initiate Ben! Initiate Esme! You are to come here at once."

47

CHANGES

Esme and I looked at each other, and we growled in unison. Then we stalked around Salanraja's hind leg towards where the four elders of Dragonsbond Academy stood talking to Captain Alliander, with Tanni standing not far away.

They were discussing what to do with us three dark mages – and especially Seramina. Though I wanted to listen in, I first wanted to check on my friends.

Seramina had now awoken, and she stood with her head tucked low as if in shame. Asinda was standing nearby, looking slightly angry. She turned her head towards a young man with dark hair, defined cheekbones, and yellow spaulders on his shoulders. It was her boyfriend, Lars.

Seeing him, Asinda's lips curled up into a smile. She beckoned him over, and he waved and ran forward. They embraced each other and kissed. Lars pulled back and swept Asinda's hair away from her face. He examined her, and grimaced when he saw that she had tears in her eyes.

"I love you, Asinda," Lars said, "and I missed you so much."

"I love you too," Asinda said.

"So what's the matter?"

"They're sending us away." Asinda gave Seramina an angry glare, as if she blamed us. "They wish to gentle our abilities by training us at the School of the White. But don't worry for now. How are you, High Prefect Lars, did you pass?"

"I did," he said. "I'm now Driar Lars, and so is Driar Calin. Aren't you also Driar Asinda, now? I heard the Council of Three gave you an automatic pass. Which means you're part of the Dragon Guard, right, and you don't need to go back to school?"

Asinda shook her head. "Alliander is the law, and she's made it so I need to spend another year as an Initiate. All of us are to go, including the cats ... and that one—" she pointed at Esme "—is to be our trainer."

I hadn't managed to get around to telling them what Bastet had said to Esme about us having to train at the School of the White. I hadn't even had a chance to think through all the implications yet. It meant that I'd be surrounded by unicorns, and horses were even worse than dogs.

Lars put a hand on his girlfriend's shoulder. "Don't worry," he said. "I'll apply for a post in Cimlean City, so that we can be close. We'll find a way to stay together.... Nothing will keep us apart."

Asinda took a deep breath. Wisely, she didn't mention what Esme had been telling her all this time – that she'd seen the future and these two weren't meant to be. "I hope so," she said.

"When do you leave?" Lars asked.

He was interrupted by Alliander banging the butt of her staff against the ground behind them. "They will leave within the hour," she said. "I am their appointed guard, and they must travel with me."

Seramina finally spoke, but she did so awfully meekly. The whole experience had broken her, and I wondered if she would ever be the same. "Can we at least take our dragons?" she asked. "I will need that, I think."

Alliander nodded. "Of course, it goes without saying that you will need them. You are bonded, and you cannot be kept apart."

That, I realised, was a huge relief. "What about Rine and Ange," I asked. "Can we bring them along too?"

"Of course not," Alliander snapped. "They are to continue their training here at Dragonsbond Academy. This is not meant to be easy, Dragoncat. Our goal is to train the three of you to handle the dark through use of the White. It will be gruelling, but it will keep you safe in the end."

I growled so quietly that I didn't intend for Captain Alliander to hear, but she seemed to notice anyway. "If it's any consolation for you," she continued. "The dog is to come too. My mission was to protect him, first and foremost, and that hasn't changed."

Whiskers, the Council of Three wouldn't be happy about that. None of the brand-new Initiates had gained their first abilities from their crystals yet, and they probably wouldn't be doing so any time soon. Alliander probably also didn't realise that Max didn't have the key inside him anymore. I decided not to tell her; I'd decided not to tell anyone, in fact. This would be Esme's, Max's, and my secret.

But that was that. I was finally leaving Dragonsbond Academy, and as the White Mage captain had said, we would leave within the hour. Without pause, I stalked off towards the kitchens to pester Matron Canda, because I knew one thing: I wasn't going on another journey without some roast duck in my tummy. I felt, after everything, I deserved that much at least.

On the way, I passed Rine and Ange. I didn't disturb them, and they didn't seem to notice me because they were currently engaged in a passionate kiss.

EPILOGUE

There was once a prince who believed himself so entitled that he thought he deserved to rule all the seven realms. But he was only a prince, and many stood between him and his uncle who sat on the throne. Later, that prince gained the ability to walk the dimensions, and brokered a pact with the demon overlord, Apopis, in the belief that he could hold such power alone.

They had once called that prince a fool, and I had finally come to realise how right they were. Because I was no longer Prince Arran, the idiot who not even his grandmother, Lasinta, respected. That prince had walked the dimensions, drinking up *Cana Dei,* thinking that he would be able to stop before it consumed him. He had thought he could become the most powerful warlock of them all.

He was naïve and a fool, and he had been wrong.

Now I still had Arran's body, but I was a servant of *Cana Dei,* and a much better man for it. I was calm, reserved, and humble. I had clarity of mind, and I knew how I could make all the worlds a better place. The dimensions didn't need a prince, nor did they need a king. They needed to learn of a better existence, of a better way to shape the worlds.

The universe needed *Cana Dei.*

I sat in a single chair at the top of a tower in the Crystal Mountains. The wind howled around me, but I didn't feel hot or cold. I had no need for human sensations anymore. Assisted by *Cana Dei,* I had used crystals from the Versta Caverns to build this place out of magic. In the end, it had only taken a couple of hours.

On one side of the turret, in front of the snowy peaks and fast-moving clouds, stood an open portal to the Seventh Dimension. Nothing needed to come out of it yet, but Apopis needed to enter. He had become injured, and he needed to heal so he could assist us once again.

Now *Cana Dei* finally had a warlock in the First Dimension, we had nothing to fear.

I heard the yips of the demon foxes coming over the mountains. They were still yipping the tune that the foolish prince had ordered them to sing, and they hadn't stopped since. But it wasn't very loud, which meant that there weren't many foxes left. They had given their life force to heal the snake. I had seen possible futures of what might happen when I started the chain of events that had pitted the young lady of chaos against the warlocks. Unfortunately, the least favourable of them had come to pass.

Cana Dei had shown me what had happened from a vision in the Ghost Realm. Apopis had thought he could win, but that dark mage – the Dragoncat – had summoned Apopis' nemesis, Bastet. The cat deity weakened the demon snake immensely and admittedly I was a little surprised there were any foxes left.

I couldn't see all futures in the Ghost Realm. Those who lived there learned quickly to hide from *Cana Dei.* But if I concentrated hard enough, I could learn from the Third Dimension what I needed to know.

I looked over the edge, to see that the power had already been sucked out of the demon dragons. As I'd thought, he'd consumed most of the power from the foxes too. He'd only just had enough strength to reach here.

Apopis slithered up the stairs I had built into the tower using magic alone. He looked at me as he passed. He sounded even weaker than he looked.

"So, you have become one of us, Warlock," he said.

"I have," I said. "I will find a way to bring an army of you from the Seventh Dimension into the others. But first, I will need to acquire Capitut's Key."

"And have you learned yet where to find it?"

"I have a plan," I said. "But I will need to exchange you for another."

Apopis looked back at the portal. "I will be glad to return there. It is, after all, my home."

He slithered through the portal. Four demon foxes followed him – there was no one else left. Before the portal winked shut, a three-headed hound leaped out to replace Apopis. It sat on the floor and looked up at me with yellow eyes, molten slaver dripping out of its droopy mouths.

There was no better tracker than this beast they called Cerberus, in all the dimensions. I smiled – the expression a vestige of the man who had once inhabited my body. Then, I leaned down to feed the beast a slab of steak.

After its three heads had wolfed it down, I decided it was time for us to start our quest. I slipped a lock of fur from my belt – acquired long ago from the tail of the Sussex spaniel that they called Max. I placed it to both the noses of the dog, and each head sniffed, understanding perfectly.

"If we find Capitut's Key first," I said, "then luck has favoured us. If we find the dog first, we will make him lead us to the key."

Three heads barked their approval. Together – the man known as Arran and the beast known as Cerberus – we descended the stairs onto a thick carpet of snow.

ACKNOWLEDGMENTS

With every novel I publish, I am incredibly grateful for the people who have helped in my journey.

Special thanks to Tarryn Thomas for her copyediting and proof-reading work, and to Carol Brandon for further proofreading. Both of you are invaluable for helping weed out those dratted typos. An additional thank you to Susan McConachie for catching some typos post-production. Also, I would be remiss not to give thanks to Wayne M. Scace, for all the support he has given for the Dragoncat series and my writing in general.

Thank you also to my family, especially my parents who continue to give me support throughout my writing career. Not to mention my dear wife, Ola, for reading the early draft of this novel and providing much needed feedback on how to make the story better.

I'd also like to express thanks to my ARC team for all the help that you've given me throughout my career. Finally, thank you to every single reader for everything that you do for the indie publishing community and the world of literature at large.

Thank you for reading "*A Cat's Guide to Travelling Through Portals*". I hope that you enjoyed it and that it added value for you in your every day life.

I have written a prequel novelette to this novel entitled "*A Cat's Guide to Serving a Warlock*", which you can download for free by signing up to my newsletter at https://chrisbehrsin.com/servingawarlock.

I send bi-monthly emails with promos, giveaways, information about new releases and news about what's going on in my life in general.

One key to save the worlds ...

Ben, the Bengal cat who has defeated warlocks, and his trusty dragon rider companions have a problem.

They've lost a magical key which the evil Warlock Prince can use to annihilate everything in all seven dimensions. Problem is, no one but he seems to know where it is.

Now the Warlock Prince plans to recover the key. Ultimately, his actions will thrust Ben and our dragon riding heroes into perilous battles against evil, demons, and themselves.

"A CAT'S GUIDE TO VANQUISHING EVIL" is the final book in the second Dragoncat trilogy – a series of fun and child-friendly dragon riding adventures where not only humans befriend dragons, but cats (and a dog) too.

AVAILABLE AT MAJOR RETAILERS

9 781915 886040